REVOLUTION 2020

Chetan Bhagat is the author of four bestselling novels – *Five Point Someone* (2004), *One Night @ the Call Center* (2005), *The 3 Mistakes of My Life* (2008) and *2 States: The Story of My Marriage* (2009).

Chetan's books have remained bestsellers since their release, and have been adapted into major Bollywood films. *The New York Times* called him the 'the biggest selling English language novelist in India's history.' *Time* magazine named him as one amongst the '100 Most Influential People in the world' and Fast Company, USA, listed him as one of the world's '100 most creative people in business.'

Chetan writes for leading English and Hindi newspapers, focusing on youth and national development issues. He is also a motivational speaker.

Chetan quit his international investment banking career in 2009, to devote his entire time to writing and make change happen in the country. He lives in Mumbai with his wife Anusha, an ex-classmate from IIM-A, and his twin sons Shyam and Ishaan.

To know more about Chetan visit www.chetanbhagat.com or email him at info@chetanbhagat.com.

D0483073

REVOLUTION 2020
Love. Corruption. Ambition

Chetan Bhagat

RUPA

Published by
Rupa Publications India Pvt. Ltd., 2011
7/16, Ansari Road, Daryaganj
New Delhi 110002

Sales centres:

Allahabad Bengaluru Chennai
Hyderabad Jaipur Kathmandu
Kolkata Mumbai

ISBN: 978-81-291-1880-6

30 29 28 27 26 25 24

The moral right of author has been asserted.

Disclaimer:
For authenticity, the author has used names of some real places,
people and institutions as they represent cultural icons of today and
aid storytelling. There is no intention to imply anything else.

Printed at Nutech Print Service, Faridabad

To my mother
To Varanasi
To the holy river
To the Indian student

Thanks to:

My readers, for their love and support.

God, who looks after me.

Shinie Antony, who remains the first reader and editor of my books.

Anubha Bang, for her suggestions at all stages in the writing of this book. Nutan Bendre, Niharika Khanna, Michelle Pereira, Prateek Dhawan, Zitin Dhawan and Anurag Anand, for their great comments on the manuscript.

Saurabh Rungta and Kishore Sharma, for their help in research.

The amazing, amazing people of Varanasi.

All the people I met during my travels and talks, who helped me understand my country better.

My mother Rekha, wife Anusha, brother Ketan, for being in my life. My sons Ishaan and Shyam, who tell me, 'It's OK, Daddy,' during my lows.

My extended family on Twitter and Facebook.

Rupa and Company, for publishing me.

The filmmakers who chose to make my stories into films.

And once again, you, dear reader, for wanting a revolution.

Prologue

'And I hope not just you but our whole country will keep that spark alive. There is something cool about saying – I come from the land of a billion sparks. Thank you,' I said, ending my motivational speech at Tilak Hall, Varanasi.

The claps and whistles were my cue to leave. Security volunteers formed a human barricade and soon I managed a neat exit from the hall.

'Thank you so much, sir,' someone said right behind me.

I turned around to face my host. 'Mr Mishra,' I said, 'I was looking for you.'

'Please call me Gopal,' he said. 'The car is over there.'

I walked out with the young director of GangaTech College, Gopal Mishra. His black Mercedes whisked us away from the crowded Vidyapath Road.

'So you saw the temples and the ghats?' Gopal asked. 'That's all Varanasi has, anyway.'

'Yeah, I went to the Vishwanath Temple and Dashashwamedh Ghat at five in the morning. I love this city,' I said.

'Oh, good. What did you like best about Varanasi?'

'Aarti,' I said.

'What?' Gopal looked surprised.

'The morning aarti at the ghats. I saw it for the first time, all those diyas floating at dawn. It was out of this world.'

Gopal frowned.

'What?' I said. 'Isn't Varanasi's aarti beautiful?'

'Yeah. Yeah, it is … it is not that,' he said, but did not elaborate.

'Will you drop me at Ramada Hotel?' I said.

'Your flight is only tomorrow morning,' Gopal said. 'Why don't you come home for dinner?'

'Don't be formal ...' I began.

'You have to come home. We must have a drink together. I have the finest whisky in the world,' he said.

I smiled as I shook my head. 'Thanks, Gopal, but I don't drink much.'

'Chetan sir, one drink? I can tell people I had a drink with "the" Chetan Bhagat.'

I laughed. 'That's nothing to brag about. Still, say it if you want. You don't actually have to drink with me.'

'Not like that, sir. I actually want to have a drink with you.'

I saw his intense eyes. He had sent me twenty invites in the last six months, until I finally agreed to come. I knew he could persist.

'Okay, one drink!' I said, hoping I wouldn't regret this later.

'Excellent,' Gopal said.

We drove ten kilometres outside the city on the Lucknow Highway to reach GangaTech. The guards saluted as the campus gates opened. The car came to a halt at a gray bungalow. It had a stone exterior that matched the main college and hostel buildings.

We sat in the living room on the ground floor. It opened out to a badminton court-sized lawn.

'Nice house,' I said as I sat on a cushy brown velvet sofa. I noticed the extra-high ceiling.

'Thanks. I designed it myself. The contractor built it, but I supervised everything,' Gopal said. He proceeded to the bar counter at the other end of the room. 'It's the bungalow of an engineering college director. You and your friends raided one, right?'

'How do you know?' I said.

'Everyone knows. We've read the book. Seen the movie.'

We laughed. He handed me a crystal glass filled with a generous amount of whisky.

'Thank you.'

'Single malt, twelve years old,' he said.

'It's the director's bungalow, but you don't have a daughter,' I said. 'You aren't even married. The youngest director I've ever seen.'

He smiled.

'How old are you?' I was curious.

'Twenty-six,' Gopal said, a hint of pride in his voice. 'Not just the youngest, but also the most uneducated director you've met.'

'Uneducated?'

'I never went to college.'

'What?' I said as I twirled the ice-cubes in my glass and wondered how potent this drink was.

'Well, I did do a joke of a correspondence degree.'

'Wow!' I said. 'It isn't a joke to open such a big college.'

'Sixteen hundred students now, Chetan-ji, across all batches. Each paying one lakh a year. We already have a sixteen-crore turnover. And you inaugurated the MBA coaching today. That's another new business.'

I took a sip. The smooth whisky burnt my throat. 'Do you have beer? Or wine?' I coughed.

Gopal's face fell. Not only had I ignored his impressive business statistics, I had also rejected his whisky.

'Not good?' Gopal asked. 'It's Glenfiddich, four thousand a bottle. Should I open Blue Label? That's ten thousand a bottle.'

It is not a price issue, I wanted to tell him but didn't. 'I don't drink whisky. Too strong for me,' I said instead.

Gopal laughed. 'Live life. Start having fine whisky. You will develop a taste.'

I attempted another sip and winced. He smiled and poured more water in my drink to dilute it. It ruined the scotch, but saved my sanity.

'Life is to be enjoyed. Look at me, I will make four crores this year. What is the point if I don't enjoy it?'

In most parts of the world, speaking about your income is taboo. In India, you share the figures like your zodiac sign, especially if you have lots.

He seemed to have put the question more to himself than to me. His dark eyes continued to bore into me. They demanded attention. The rest of him – wheatish complexion, modest five-feet-seven-inch height, side-parted hair – was reassuringly normal.

'Yeah, of course. One should enjoy …' I said as he cut me.

'Next year I will make five crores.'

I realised he would keep forecasting his salary until I demonstrated suitable awe.

'Five crores!' I said, my voice loud and fake.

Gopal grinned. 'Baby, eat this, for I have made it,' is probably the T-shirt slogan he would choose.

'That's incredible,' I murmured, wondering how I could switch the topic. I noticed stairs winding up. 'What's upstairs?' I said.

'Bedrooms and a terrace. Come, I will show you.'

We climbed up the steps and walked past a room with a luxurious king-sized bed.

I took in the panoramic view from the terrace.

'This was a wasteland, all of it. My grandfather's old agricultural land,' Gopal said.

'Ten acres?' I made a guess.

'Fifteen. We had fifteen acres more,' Gopal said, 'but we sold it to fund the construction.'

He pointed to a small array of lights towards the eastern wall of the floodlit campus. 'Right there, see. There is a mall coming up.'

'Every Indian city is building malls now,' I said.

'India shining, Chetan-ji,' he said and clinked his glass with mine.

Gopal drank more than four times my pace. I hadn't finished my first when he poured his fifth. 'You big-city types. Drinking for style,' he teased when I refused a refill.

'I don't drink much. Really,' I said. I checked the time; 10:00 p.m.

'At what time do you eat dinner?' he asked.

'Up to you,' I said, though I wished he'd decide to eat right away.

'What is the big hurry? Two men, one educated, one uneducated. Having a good time,' Gopal said and raised his glass in the air.

I nodded out of courtesy. My stomach rumbled for food. We came downstairs to sit down in the living room again.

'Did you really go to the professor's daughter's house?' Gopal asked.

I smiled. 'Love makes us do stupid things.'

Gopal laughed out loud. He gulped his drink bottoms-up, then grabbed the half-empty bottle to make his sixth tipple.

'Love? Forget stupid things. Love fucks you,' Gopal said.

'That's harsh,' I said. 'Is that why there is no Mrs Director yet?'

Gopal's hand trembled as he continued to pour his drink. I wondered if I should stop him from drinking more.

'Mrs Director!' Gopal smirked. He gripped the whisky bottle tight.

'Easy, Gopal, you are drinking too fast. It's dangerous.'

Gopal plonked the bottle on the coffee table. 'Why dangerous? Who is going to fucking cry for me? If I live, I want to enjoy. If I die, who cares?'

'Your parents?'

Gopal shook his head.

'Friends?'

'Successful people don't have friends,' Gopal averred. 'It's true, no?'

His lavish house felt cold and isolated. I took the whisky bottle and placed it back in the bar.

'Pessimist, eh?' I said. 'Surprising, given you are doing so well.'

'What well, Chetan-ji?' Gopal said, now completely drunk and, presumably, completely honest.

He pointed to the huge TV, stereo system and the silk carpet under our feet in quick succession.

'What does all this mean? I've lived with nothing ...'

Our conversation had become serious. I patted his back to cheer him up. 'So you read about my girlfriend in the book. How about you? You ever had one?'

Gopal didn't respond, but looked distraught. He placed his glass on the coffee table.

Touchy topic, I figured too late.

He retched.

'Are you okay?' I said.

He ran to the restroom. I heard him throw up. I browsed the display shelves to pass time. I saw framed news stories about GangaTech, trophies, *pictures of Gopal with guests who had visited the college. I wondered if my picture would also be there soon.*

When he hadn't returned in twenty minutes I called for the maid. She took me to the bathroom. I knocked at the door. No answer. I banged my fists on the door. Nothing.

'Looks like we will have to break the door,' the maid said.

I wondered how I, who had come as a chief guest for a college orientation programme, became involved with forcing open random toilets in Varanasi.

♦

The rustle of sheets on the hospital bed woke me from my nap. The bedside clock showed 3:00 a.m. I had brought a passed-out Gopal to the Heritage Hospital, in the Lanka area of Varanasi.

Gopal sat up on the bed now, massaging his temples.

His hangover reminded me of my college days. However, here the director had binged on alcohol, not a student.

'You were here all night?' He looked surprised.

'I could not let my host die on me,' I said.

'I am sorry. I had a bit too much.' Gopal gave a sheepish grin.

'Are you alright?'

'Yeah, I am good.'

'Not right now. Are you okay generally?'

He turned his head to stare at the opposite wall.

'How's life, Gopal?' I asked softly.

He didn't answer.

I stood up after a minute. 'I should leave, catch some sleep before my flight.' I walked to the door.

'Do you think I am a good person, Chetan-ji?' he said.

I turned around.

'Am I?' he asked again.

I shrugged my shoulders. 'I don't know you, Gopal. You organised the talk well. Treated me good. You seem fine,' I said.

'You think so?'

'You've achieved a lot. Take it easy. Even expensive whiskies can be harmful.'

He smiled and gave a brief nod. 'I will drink less,' he said. 'Anything else?'

'You are young. Don't give up on love yet,' I said, checking my watch. 'I really should go. It is almost time for the morning aarti.'

'That's her name,' he said.

I didn't want to stay any longer, but I was hooked. 'What name? Whose name?' I asked even as I reminded myself that this was not my business and I should leave soon.

'Aarti,' he said.

'Aarti who? Someone you like?' I hazarded a guess.

'Like is not the word, Chetan-ji.'

'You loved her?' I smiled.

'Imagine every sadhu and priest in Varanasi. More than all their devotion put together, that's how much I loved her.'

I absorbed the analogy. Curiosity had taken over my need for sleep. I allowed myself to ask one more question. 'She loved you too?'

He mulled over the question for a while. 'She didn't just love me, she owned me.'

I shifted from one foot to the other. I had a long day ahead. A sleepless night would be a bad idea. But I heard myself asking him, 'So what happened? Between you and Aarti.'

Gopal smiled. 'This is not an interview, Chetan-ji. Either you sit down and listen to this stupid man's whole story or you leave. Up to you.' His charcoal eyes met mine. Something about the young director intrigued me. His unusual achievements, his cockiness, his tortured voice or maybe this strange holy city made me want to know more about him.

I let out a huge sigh. He pointed to the chair next to him.

'Okay, tell me your story,' I said and sat down.

'Do you want another drink?' Gopal said.

I glared at him. He laughed. 'I meant tea,' he said.

We ordered a pot of extra-hot masala tea and glucose biscuits; nothing complements a conversation better.

'Where do I start?' Gopal said.

'Let's begin with Aarti. The girl who did this to you.'

'Aarti? She got me into trouble the first day we met,' Gopal said.

I dipped a biscuit in my tea and listened.

1

'Lazy parents, bread-butter again,' I grumbled, shutting a blue plastic tiffin in the second row. Raghav and I moved to the next desk.

'Forget it, Gopal. The class will be back any time,' Raghav said.

'Shh …'

'I've brought puri-aloo, we can share that. It's wrong to steal from others.'

I battled a small, round steel tiffin box. 'How does one open this?'

Neither of us had the sharp nails required to open the thin steel lid of the stubborn box. We had skipped the morning assembly for our weekly tiffin raid. We had ten more minutes till the national anthem began outside. After that class 5 C would be back. We had to find, eat and keep the tiffins back within that time.

'Its pickle and parathas,' Raghav said, having opened the lid. 'You want it?'

'Forget it,' I said as I returned the steel box to the student's bag. My eyes darted from one bag to another. 'This one,' I said, pointing to a pink imported rucksack in the first row. 'That bag looks expensive. She must be getting good food. Come.'

We rushed to the target's seat. I grabbed the Barbie bag, unzipped the front flap and found a red, shiny, rectangular tiffin. The cover had a spoon compartment. 'Fancy box!' I said, clicking the lid open.

Idlis, a little box of chutney and a large piece of chocolate cake. We'd hit the jackpot.

'I only want the cake,' I said as I lifted the huge slice.

'Don't take the whole thing. It's not fair,' Raghav said.

'If I eat only a bit, she will get to know,' I scowled.

'Cut it into two. Take one, leave the other,' Raghav said.

'Cut with what?'

'Use a ruler,' he suggested.

I ran to my desk. I brought back a ruler and made a clean cut. 'Fine?' I said. 'Happy now?'

'It's her cake.' Raghav shrugged.

'But you are my friend,' I said.

I offered a bite. He refused. I had not had any breakfast at home. I gorged on the cake, my fingers smeared with icing.

'Why don't you get your own tiffin?' Raghav said.

I spoke with my mouth stuffed. 'It will mean extra work for Baba. He makes lunch and dinner anyway.'

'So?'

'I tell him I don't feel hungry.' My father taught in a government school. He left home at six, even earlier than me. I licked the chocolate cream off my fingers. We could hear the national anthem.

'I can bring tiffin for you,' Raghav said and made me stand up along with him for the anthem.

'Forget it, your mom cooks boring stuff. Puri everyday,' I said.

We heard students chatter on their way back to class. I stuffed the remaining cake into my mouth.

'Hurry, hurry,' Raghav said.

I shut the red tiffin box and placed it back in the Barbie bag.

'Who sits here anyway?' Raghav asked.

I fumbled through the pink rucksack and found a brown-paper-covered notebook. I read out the label on the cover, 'Aarti Pratap Pradhan, Subject: Maths, Class 5, Section C, Age 10, Roll number 1, Sunbeam School.'

'Whatever. Are we done?' Raghav said.

I hung the bag back on Aarti's chair, in its original place.

'Let's go,' I said. We ran to our back-row seats, sat and put our heads down on the desk. We closed our eyes and pretended to be sick, the reason for skipping the morning assembly.

The entire 5 C entered the room, filling the class with the simultaneous cacophony of four dozen ten-year-olds.

Simran Gill madam, our class teacher, arrived a minute later and the noise died down. 'Multiplication,' she wrote on the board, even as the children were still settling down.

I sat up straight and craned my neck to see Aarti Pratap Pradhan, roll number one. She wore a white skirt, white shirt, red cardigan and had ribbons in her plaits, and she faced the teacher most seriously as she sat down.

'Eww,' Aarti screamed and jumped up. She picked up a chocolate-stained ruler from her seat. The back of her skirt had chocolate stains. 'Oh my God!' Aarti's shrill voice made the entire class take notice.

'Aarti, sit down!' Gill madam screamed in a voice loud enough to make the back rows shiver. Gill madam didn't like noise, even if it came from girls with cute plaits.

Raghav and I exchanged a worried glance. We had left behind evidence.

'Madam, someone has put a dirty ruler on my seat. My new school dress is spoiled,' Aarti wailed.

The whole class laughed and Aarti broke into tears.

'What?' the teacher said. She placed the chalk down, dusted her hands and took the ruler from Aarti.

Aarti continued to sniffle. The teacher walked along the aisles. Students shrank in their seats as she passed them. 'Who brought chocolate cake today?' she launched into an investigation.

'I did,' Aarti said. She opened her tiffin and realised how her own cake had been used to ruin her dress. Her howls reached new decibel levels. 'Someone ate my cake,' Aarti cried so loud, the adjacent class 5 B could hear us.

Half your cake, I wanted to tell her.

Raghav stared at me. 'Confess?' he whispered.

'Are you mad?' I whispered back.

When Gill madam walked by, I stared at the floor. She wore golden slippers with fake crystals on the strap. I clenched my fists. My fingers were greasy.

The teacher walked back to the front of the class. She took out a tissue from her purse and wiped the ruler clean. 'Admit it, else the punishment will be worse,' she warned.

I pretended not to hear and opened my maths notebook.

'Who is GM?' the teacher asked. She had read my initials. I had scraped them with a compass on my ruler. Damn!

We had two GMs in the class. One, Girish Mathur, sat in the first row. He stood up without provocation.

'I didn't do it, ma'am,' he said and pinched his neck. 'God promise, ma'am.'

The teacher squinted at him, still suspicious.

'I swear upon Ganga, ma'am,' Girish said as he broke down.

The Ganga reference worked. Everyone believed him.

'Who's the other GM? Gopal Mishra!' the teacher shouted my name.

All eyes turned to me. The teacher walked up to my desk. I stood up.

I didn't say a word. Neither did the teacher. Slap, Slap! Both my cheeks were stinging.

'Stealing food? Are you a thief?' the teacher said. She looked at me as if I had stolen the Kohinoor diamond from the British queen's museum, something the social studies teacher had told us about two days ago.

I hung my head low. She smacked the back of my neck. 'Get out of my class!'

I dragged my feet out of the class, even as the entire 5 C stared at me.

'Aarti, go clean up in the bathroom,' Gill madam said.

◆

I leaned against the wall outside the class. Aarti wiped her eyes and walked past me towards the toilet.

'Drama queen! It was only half a slice of chocolate cake!' I thought.

Anyway, that's how I, Gopal Mishra, met the great Aarti Pratap Pradhan. I must tell you, even though this is my story, you won't like me very much. After all, a ten-year-old thief isn't exactly a likeable person to begin with.

I come from Varanasi, which my social studies teacher says is one of the oldest cities on earth. People came to live here in 1200 BC. The city gets its name from two rivers, Varuna and Asi, which pass through the city and meet the Ganga. People call my city several names – Kashi, Benares or Banaras – depending on where they come from. Some call it the City of Temples, for we have thousands of them, and some the City of Learning, as Varanasi apparently has great places to study. I simply call Varanasi my home. I stay near Gadholia, a place so noisy, you need to put cotton balls in your ears if you want to sleep. Gadholia is near the ghats, along the river Ganga. So if the crowds of Gadholia become too much to take, you can always run to the ghats and sit by the Ganga and watch the temples. Some call my city beautiful, holy and spiritual – especially when we have to introduce it to foreign tourists. Many call it filthy and a dump. I don't think my city is dirty. It is the people who make it dirty.

Anyway, they say you must come to Varanasi once in a lifetime. Well, some of us spend a lifetime here.

I had a pencil in my pocket. I used it to scribble '5 C' on the wall. It helped me pass the time, and would make our class easier to find too.

She came out of the toilet – face wet, drama-queen expression intact and gaze firmly fixed on me – and walked back to the class.

She continued to stare at me as she came closer. 'You are scribbling on the walls!' she said.

'Go complain,' I said. 'Go.'

'How can you steal my tiffin?' she said.

'I didn't steal your tiffin,' I said. 'I had three bites of your chocolate cake. You wouldn't even have noticed.'

'You are a really bad boy,' Aarti said.

2

Dubey uncle, our lawyer, pushed a small box of four laddoos towards us.

'Sweets? What for?' my father said.

Dubey uncle had come home. Baba and I faced him across our ancient dining table.

'You've got a hearing date,' Dubey uncle said. 'This itself took so long, I thought we should celebrate.'

I wondered if I could give some laddoos to drama queen Aarti as compensation for the cake. I wanted to buy a chocolate cake and slam it on her desk. However, I didn't have money for that. My father didn't give me any pocket money, and he didn't have much money in his own pocket.

My mother's illness had wiped out all his savings. She died two weeks after I turned four. I don't remember much of her or her death. Baba did say he had to wear her dupatta and sleep next to me for a month. After her death the land dispute started. Dubey uncle had become a frequent visitor to our house for this reason.

'You brought sweets only because we have a hearing?' Baba coughed. The case had not given his land back to him, but it did worsen his respiratory ailment.

'Well, Ghanshyam wants to settle the case out of court,' Dubey uncle said.

Ghanshyam taya-ji, my father's respected elder brother, had screwed us. My grandfather had left his two sons thirty acres of agricultural land on the Lucknow Highway, to be divided equally. Soon after my grandfather's death, Ghanshyam uncle took a loan from the bank and mortgaged Baba's half of the property, forging the papers with wrong plot numbers and bribing the bank officer.

Ghanshyam taya-ji made bad business decisions and lost the money. The bank sent a foreclosure notice to us. Baba protested, and the bank slapped cases on both my father and uncle. The two brothers slapped cases on each other. All these cases moved through our legal system slower than a bullock cart on the national highway.

'Settle?' My father leaned forward.

I picked up a laddoo and put it in my pocket.

'Ghanshyam will give you some cash. He will take your share of the land and handle the bank and legal cases,' Dubey uncle said.

'How much?' Baba asked.

'Ten lakhs,' Dubey uncle replied.

My father kept quiet. I snuck away another laddoo. She should be happy with two, I thought.

'I admit the offer is ridiculously low for fifteen acres,' Dubey uncle continued. 'But there's a loan of a crore on your property.'

'It's not my loan!' Baba said in an uncharacteristically loud voice.

'He submitted your documents to the bank. Why did you give him your property papers?'

'He is my elder brother,' Baba said, fighting tears. The loss of a brother hurt him more than the loss of land.

'If you want more money, I can ask him. Why drag this forever?' Dubey uncle said.

'I am a farmer's son. I am not giving up my land,' Baba said, his eyes red. 'Not until I die. Tell him to kill me if he wants the land.'

Baba then stared at me as my hand reached for the third laddoo.

'It's okay, take all of them,' Dubey uncle told me.

I looked at both of them, picked up the box and ran out of the room.

✦

I placed the box on her desk with a thump.

'What is this?' She looked at me primly.

'I ate your cake. I'm sorry,' I said, my last word faint.

'I don't like laddoos,' she announced.

'Why? You firang or what?' I said.

'No, laddoos make you fat. I don't want to be fat,' she said.

'Chocolate cake doesn't make you fat?'

'I don't want it,' she said. She gently pushed the box towards me.

'Fine,' I said and took the box.

'Did you say sorry?' Aarti said.

'Yes, I did.' I noticed her loopy plaits, tied up with red ribbons. She looked like a cartoon character.

'Apology accepted,' she said.

'Thank you,' I said. 'Sure you don't want the laddoos?'

'No, fat girls can't become air hostesses,' she said.

'You want to be an air hostess?' I said.

'Yes.'

'Why?'

'They fly everywhere. I want to see different places.'

'Okay.'

'What do you want to be?' Aarti said.

I shrugged my shoulders. 'A rich man,' I said.

She nodded, as if my choice was reasonable. 'Are you poor right now?'

'Yes,' I said.

She said, 'I am rich. We have a car.'

'We don't have a car. Okay, bye.' I turned to leave when Aarti spoke again.

'Why doesn't your mother give you a tiffin?'

'I don't have a mother,' I said.

'Dead?' she asked.

'Yes,' I said.

'Okay, bye.'

I came back to my seat. I opened the box of laddoos and took one out.

Aarti walked up to me.

'What?' I asked.

'You can eat my tiffin sometimes. Don't take a lot though. And don't take any cake or nice treats.'

'Thanks,' I said.

'And don't make a mess. If you want, we can eat together during lunch-break.'

'You won't have enough food for yourself,' I said.

'It's okay. I am dieting. I don't want to be fat,' Aarti said.

Seven Years Later

3

'Walk me home first. Then go to the cricket ground,' Aarti said.

We were coming back after an afternoon of boating on the Ganga. Aarti and I had been doing this every week for the last five years. Phoolchand bhai, a boatman at Assi Ghat, let me borrow his boat. We walked down a bylane narrow enough to jam a fat cow, and came out on the main road adjacent to the ghats.

'I'm already late, Aarti. Raghav will scream at me.'

'So let me come with you. I don't want to be bored at home,' she said.

'No.'

'Why?' she blinked.

'Too many boys. Remember the whistles last time?'

'I can handle it,' Aarti said. She brushed some strands of hair away from her forehead.

I looked at her beautiful face. 'You have no idea what you do to them,' I said. You have no idea what you do to me, was what I actually wanted to tell her.

Aarti's looks had always drawn appreciative comments from the school teachers. However, two years ago when she turned fifteen, the whole school started talking about her. Statements such as 'the most beautiful girl in Sunbeam School', 'she should be an actress', or 'she can apply for Miss India' became increasingly common. Some of it came from people trying to please her. After all, a senior IAS officer father and a prominent ex-politician grandfather meant people wanted to be in her good books.

But yes, Aarti did make Varanasi skip a heartbeat.

Her entry into the Sigra Stadium cricket ground would definitely disrupt the game. Batsmen would miss the ball, fielders would miss catches and jobless morons would whistle in the way they do to give UP a bad name.

'I've not met Raghav for so long,' Aarti said. 'Let's go. I will watch you play.'

'You will meet him at tuitions tomorrow,' I said curtly. 'Go home now.'

'You want me to walk home alone?'

'Take a rickshaw,' I said.

She grabbed my wrist. 'You are coming with me right now.' She held my hand and swung it back and forth as I walked her home.

I wanted to tell her not to hold my hand anymore. It is fine at twelve, not at seventeen. Even though I liked it more at seventeen than at twelve.

'What?' she said. 'Why are you staring? I am only holding your hand so that you don't run away.'

I smiled. We walked past the noisy shopping streets to the calmer Cantonment area. We reached the bungalow of District Magistrate Pratap Brij Pradhan, Aarti's father.

The evening sky had turned a deep orange. Raghav was sure to sulk, as it would be too late to play. However, I could not refuse Aarti.

'Thank you,' Aarti said in a child-like voice. 'Coming in?'

'No, I am already late,' I said.

Our eyes met. I broke eye contact quickly. Best friends, that's all we were, I told myself.

Her hair blew in the breeze and wisps of black gently stroked her face.

'I should cut my hair, so hard to maintain,' Aarti said.

'Don't,' I said firmly.

'I'm keeping it long only for you. Bye!' she said. I wondered if she had also started to feel differently about me. But I didn't know how to ask.

'See you at tuitions,' I said, walking away.

◆

'Raghav Kashyap,' the teacher called out and held up an answer-sheet. Raghav, Aarti and I had joined JSR coaching classes in Durgakund to prepare for the engineering entrance exams. JSR, named after its three founders – Mr Jha, Mr Singh and Mr Rai – conducted frequent mock-tests for AIEEE (All India Engineering Entrance Exam) and the IIT JEE (Indian Institute of Technology Joint Entrance Exam). The AIEEE attracted ten lakh students annually for thirty thousand seats in the National Institutes of Technology (NITs) across the country. Every engineering aspirant took these exams. I didn't particularly want to become an engineer. Baba wished to see me as one, and that was why I went to JSR.

Raghav walked past the forty students in the crammed classroom to collect his answer-sheet.

'Sixty-six out of eighty. Well done, Raghav,' the teacher said.

'IIT material,' a boy whispered as Raghav walked past. 'He is a topper from Sunbeam.'

I could totally see Raghav follow in the footsteps of his IITian father, an engineer in BHEL. I scored fifty out of eighty, a borderline performance, good enough to become the twelfth man on a cricket team, but not quite player material.

'Focus, Gopal,' the teacher said. 'You need sixty-plus to be safe.'

I nodded. I wanted to get into a good engineering college. My father hadn't heard any good news in years.

'Aarti Pradhan!' the teacher called out. The entire class turned to look at the girl in the white salwar-kameez, who made the otherwise drab coaching classes worthwhile.

Aarti took her answer-sheet and giggled.

'Twenty out of eighty is funny?' the teacher frowned.

Aarti covered her mouth with her palm and walked back. She had no intention of becoming an engineer. She had joined JSR because a) attending coaching classes could supplement her class XII CBSE studies, b) I had also enrolled so she would have company and c) the tuition centre never charged her, given her father was about to become the District Magistrate, or DM of the city.

Aarti's father had a relatively honest reputation. However, free tuitions came under the ambit of acceptable favours.

'I have not even filled the AIEEE form,' Aarti whispered to me.

◆

'My AIEEE rank is going to be horrible,' I said to Raghav as I stirred my lemonade.

We had come to the German Bakery near Narad Ghat, a touristy firang joint where white people felt safe from germs and the touts roaming around Varanasi. People sat on beds with wooden trays to eat firang food like sandwiches and pancakes. Two malnourished, old men played the sitar in one corner to give the Varanasi effect, as white people found it a cultural experience.

I never thought much of the place. However, Aarti liked it.

'I like how she has used a scarf to tie her hair,' Aarti said, pointing at a female tourist. She had obviously ignored my AIEEE concerns.

'Ten more marks and you will be fine. Relax,' Raghav said.

'One lakh students stand between me and those ten marks,' I said.

'Don't think about the others. Focus on yourself,' he said.

I nodded slowly. Easy to give advice when you are the topper. I imagined myself in a sea, along with lakhs of other low-rankers, kicking and screaming to breathe. The waters closed over us, making us irrelevant to the Indian education system. Three weeks and the AIEEE tsunami would arrive.

Aarti snapped her fingers in front of my face. 'Wake up, dreamer, you will be fine,' she said.

'You are skipping it?' Raghav turned to Aarti.

'Yeah,' she giggled. '*Main Hoon Na* is releasing that week. How can I miss a Shah Rukh film? They should postpone AIEEE.'

'Very funny.' I grimaced.

'So you aren't becoming an engineer. What will you do in life?' Raghav asked Aarti.

'Do I have to *do* something? I am an Indian woman. Can't I get married, stay home and cook? Or ask the servants to cook?'

She laughed and Raghav joined her.

I didn't find this funny. I could not think beyond the teeming millions of wannabe engineers who would wrestle me down in three weeks.

'Why so serious, Gopal-ji? I'm joking. You know I can't sit at home.' Aarti tapped my shoulder.

'Shut up, Aarti,' I said. 'Yeah, I know you want to be an air hostess.'

'Air hostess? Wow!' Raghav said.

'That's not fair, Gopal!' Aarti screamed. 'You are telling the world my secret.'

'It's only me,' Raghav said.

Aarti gave me a dirty look.

'Sorry,' I said.

Aarti and I had a deeper relationship. We saw Raghav as a friend, but not a close one.

'You will make a great air hostess,' Raghav said, his tone flirtatious.

'Yeah, whatever,' Aarti said. 'Like dad is going to let me leave Varanasi. There are no airlines here. Only temples. Maybe I can be a temple hostess. Sir, please take a seat on the floor. Prayers will begin soon. Prasad will be served in your seats.'

Raghav laughed again, holding his muscular abdomen. I hate people who are naturally gifted with a flat stomach. *Why couldn't god make six-packs a default standard in all males? Did we have to store fat in the silliest places?*

Raghav high-fived Aarti. My ears went hot. The sitar players started an energetic tune.

'Aarti, what nonsense you talk,' I said, my voice loud. The foreigners around us, here in a worldwide quest for peace, became alert.

I didn't like the we-find-each-other's-lame-jokes-funny vibe between Raghav and Aarti.

Raghav sucked the straw in his lemonade too hard. The drink came out through his nose.

'Gross!' Aarti said as both of them started a laugh-fest again.

I stood up.

'What happened?' Raghav said.

'I have to go. Baba is waiting,' I said.

✦

The sound of Baba's coughing drowned out the sound of the doorbell the first couple of times.

'Sorry, I couldn't hear,' he said, opening the door.

'You okay?' I asked.

'Yes, it is the usual. I've made dal and roti.'

'That's the usual too.'

My father had turned sixty last year. His non-stop coughing bouts made him look like an eighty-year-old. The doctors had given up. We had no money for surgery either. His school had fired him long ago. You can't conduct a fifty-minute class with ten respiratory breaks. He had a pension that lasted us three weeks in a good month.

I ate in silence at the wobbly dining table.

'Entrance exam …' my father started and paused to cough five times. I understood his drift.

'I have finished the AIEEE preparation,' I said.

'JEE?' Baba said. It is harder to manage family expectations than prepare for exams.

'Don't have IIT hopes for me, Baba,' I said. My father's face fell. 'I will take the JEE. But, three thousand out of four lakhs … Imagine the odds.'

'You can do it. You are bright,' Baba said, paternal love obviously overestimating progeny's abilities.

I nodded. I had a shot at AIEEE, none at JEE. That was how I looked at it. I wondered if Baba realised that a rank would mean me leaving home. What if I had to go to NIT Agartala? Or somewhere far south?

'Engineering is not everything, Baba,' I said.

'It secures your life. Don't fight now, right before the exams.'

'I'm not fighting. I'm not.'

Post-dinner, Baba lay down on his bed. I sat next to him and pressed his forehead. He erupted into a coughing fit.

'We should consider the surgery,' I said.

'For two lakhs?' Baba said, lying back and shutting his eyes. I resumed the massage.

I kept quiet. I didn't want to bring up the touchy topic. We could have settled the land issue ages ago. Court hearings still haunted us, the land lay barren, and we had no money.

'From where will we get the money, tell?' my father said. 'You become an engineer. Get a good job. Then we will do the surgery.'

I could not stay quiet anymore. 'Taya-ji offered ten lakhs. The money would have doubled in the bank by now.'

Baba opened his eyes. 'What about the land?' he said.

'What use is the stupid land?'

'Don't talk like that,' he said, pushing my hand away. 'A farmer doesn't insult his land. He doesn't sell it either.'

I placed my hand back on his forehead. 'We are not farmers anymore, Baba. We can't use the land. Because your own brother …'

'Go. Go and study, you have your exams coming up.' Baba pointed to my room.

◆

The landline rang at midnight. I picked it up.

'I'm sleepy, Aarti,' I said.

'You don't sleep till one. Stop fibbing.'

'What's up?'

'Nothing. Just felt like chatting.'

'Chat with someone else,' I said.

'Aha,' she said. 'I know what's bothering you.'

'Bye, Aarti,' I said.

'Hey, wait. I found some of Raghav's jokes funny. That's all. You are still my best friend.'

'They weren't funny. And what's this best friend business?' I said.

'We've been best friends for eight years, though you still haven't bought me a chocolate cake.'

'And Raghav?'

'Raghav is only a friend. I talk to him because you are close to him,' Aarti said.

I kept silent.

'Chill now, Gopal. How're things at home?' she said.

'Screwed up as always. How are you?'

'I'm fine. Dad insists I finish college before I try any of this air hostess business. But you can even become one straight after class XII.'

'Go to college. He's right,' I said.

'Which college can I join with my marks? I am not smart like Raghav and you.'

'Raghav is smart, not me,' I corrected her.

'Why? Because of the mock-test? You are so stupid,' Aarti said.

'You are stupid.'

'We are both stupid, fine? Did you have dinner?'

She had asked me this question every night for the last five years. I wanted to stay mad at her, but could not. 'I did, thanks.'

'What thanks? Stupid. Go to bed now, sleep and don't think about the entrance exams.'

'Aarti,' I said and paused.

'What?'

'You are very nice,' I said. I couldn't come up with a better line.

'Nice and stupid? Or nicely stupid?' Aarti laughed.

'What would I do without you?'

'Shut up. I am here only,' she said.

'We are not young anymore, Aarti,' I said.

'Okay, okay. Not that again. Go to bed, Mr Grown-up Man.'

'Aarti, come on. You always avoid …'

'We'll talk, but not now. After your entrance exams.'

I kept quiet.

'Don't complicate life, Gopal. Aren't you happy with our friendship?'

'Yes, I am but …'

'But-but what? Good night, sweet dreams, sleep tight.'

'Good night.'

◆

'It's no use now,' I said, closing the maths textbook.

Raghav had come to my house on the eve of the exam. He had offered a last-minute trigonometry revision, my weak spot. Raghav picked up the textbook.

'You sleep, okay? Rest before the exam is a must. And take lots of sharpened pencils,' he said.

Baba came out of the kitchen when he saw Raghav leave. 'Stay for dinner,' Baba told him.

'Not today, Baba,' Raghav said. 'I will take a proper treat once Gopal gets a rank.'

4

I did get a rank. A fucked-up rank, that is.

'52,043,' I read out from the screen. I had come to Raghav's house in Shivpur. We had logged on to the AIEEE website.

Sure, I hadn't scored too badly. Out of ten lakh test-takers, I had beaten nine lakh fifty thousand. However, the NITs had only thirty thousand seats. Sometimes, life played cruel jokes on you. I'd be one of those unfortunate cases who had done well, but not well enough.

'5,820,' Raghav said, reading from the computer monitor.

Raghav's father had come into the room to stand behind us.

'What's that?' I said.

'My rank,' Raghav said.

'Excellent!' Raghav's father said delightedly.

Raghav smiled. He could not react more than that.

'This should give you lots of choices,' Raghav's proud father said. 'You can get Electronics in Delhi.'

'There's NIT Lucknow too, right?' Raghav said. 'Closer home.'

'Forget AIEEE, let us wait for JEE,' Raghav's father said, his voice elated.

Father and son took a while to remember my presence in the room. They saw my crestfallen face and fell silent. 'I have to go home,' I mumbled.

'Fifty thousand should get you something, no?' Raghav's father said, fully aware it would not. He didn't mean to hurt me, but it felt bad. Never in my life had I felt so small. I felt like a beggar hanging out with kings.

'I'll see you later, Raghav,' I said and scurried out of their house. I didn't want anyone to see my tears.

Raghav came running after me in the lane outside his house. 'You okay?' he asked.

I swallowed hard and wiped my eyes before turning to him. 'I'm fine, buddy,' I lied. 'And congrats! You owe us a treat. But your dad is right. We will take the real party after JEE.'

I continued to ramble until Raghav interrupted me. 'Will Baba be fine?' he asked.

I shrugged my shoulders and fought the lump in my throat.

'Should I come with you?' he offered.

Yeah right, take a top-ranker to meet your parent when you've flunked, I thought.

'Don't worry. He's faced worse things in life,' I said.

◆

'Aren't the AIEEE results due today? They are not in the papers,' Baba said as soon as I entered the house. Four different newspapers lay open on the floor.

'No, they don't publish results in the newspaper anymore. Baba, what is this mess?' I said.

I bent down to collect the papers. I did not mention that the results were available online.

'So how do we find out the results? Isn't today the date?' he said.

I kept quiet as I stacked the newspapers. I wanted to tell him the results won't be out for a while. Peace for a few more days would be nice, even if temporary. I saw his aged face, the wrinkles around his eyes. Eyes that were extra bright today.

'Should we go to NIT Lucknow?' Baba said, happy to make the five-hour journey to find out his son was a loser.

'Baba!' I protested.

'What?'

'Let's make lunch.' I moved to the kitchen. The antique gas stove took six tries to start. I placed a bowl of water on a burner to boil dal.

My father stood behind me. 'We *have* to get the results. Let's go,' he said. When old people get stuck on something, they don't let go.

'Let me make the meal,' I said. 'I will call you when it is ready.'

Telling your parents you've failed at something is harder than the actual failure. I cooked lunch for the next hour. I wondered if life would ever be the same again. One stupid exam, half a dozen mistakes in multiple-choice problems had changed my life forever.

My father and I ate in silence, his hopeful eyes pinned on me. My hiding the news did not help anyone.

I went to him after dinner. 'I know the results, Baba,' I said softly.

'And?' he said, eyes wide.

'My rank is 52,043.'

'Is that good?'

I shook my head.

'You won't get a good branch?'

'I won't get into NIT,' I said.

My father's expression changed. He had the look every child dreads. The look that says, *'I brought you up, now see what you have done!'*

A bullet in the head is preferable to that look.

Baba got up agitatedly and started to circle the dining table. 'How can you not get a good rank?'

Well, not everyone does, Baba. Nine lakh fifty thousand of us didn't. But I did not air my thought.

'Now what?' he said.

I wondered if I should suggest some options – suicide, penance in the Himalayas or a life of drudgery as a labourer?

'I am sorry, Baba,' I said.

'I told you to study more,' he said.

Which parent doesn't?

He went to his room. I gathered the courage to enter his bedroom after half an hour. He had kept a hot-water bottle on his head.

'I could do a BSc, Baba,' I said.

'What good will that do, huh?' he said, his voice too loud for a sick man.

'I'll finish my graduation. Look for a job. There should be plenty of opportunities,' I said, making up words as I spoke.

'Who gives a good job to a simple graduate?' Baba said.

Correct, a 'simple' graduate meant nothing.

'We don't have money for a donation college, Baba,' I reminded him.

He nodded. He spoke after some thought. 'Try again?'

Baba had not made an unreasonable suggestion. However, he had horrible timing.

The entrance exam had given me so much pain. The mere thought of repeating it caused physical agony. 'Stop it, Baba,' I screamed. 'If you had settled on the land, we would have money for a private college. You didn't, so I have to keep suffering.'

My father pressed the hot-water bottle harder against his forehead. He looked pained, by the headache and me. 'Go away,' he said.

'I am sorry,' I said automatically.

'Fail exams, scream at your father. You are going in the right direction, son,' he said, eyes closed.

'I'll do something. I won't let you down. I will become rich one day,' I said.

'It is not easy to become rich. You have to work hard. You don't,' he said.

I wanted to tell him that I did work hard. You don't get a fifty-thousand rank, however useless that may be, without working hard. I wanted to say I felt fucked up inside. I wished he would figure out I wanted to cry, and that it would be great if he hugged me.

'Go away. Let me have some peace in my final days,' he said.

I went to my room and sat in silence. I had never really missed my mother all these years. However, on the day of the AIEEE results, I wished she was around. I kicked myself for not getting those six extra problems right. I kept rewinding to the day of the exam. As if my brain could go back in time, recreate the same scenario, and I wouldn't make the same mistakes again. Regret – this feeling has to be one of the biggest manufacturing defects in humans. We keep regretting, even though there is no point to it. I stayed in my bed, dazed.

I came to the living room at midnight. I called Aarti.

'Hey, you okay?' Her voice was calm.

She knew my results. Yet she hadn't called. She knew I'd call her when I was good and ready. Aarti and I were in sync.

'We will talk on the boat,' I said.

'Four-thirty tomorrow morning at Assi Ghat,' she said.

I went back to bed after the call. I lay down but couldn't sleep. I tossed and turned for ages. There would be no sleep till I sorted things out with Baba.

I went to his room. He was asleep, the hot-water bottle still by his head.

I kept the bottle aside. My father woke up.

'I am sorry, Baba,' I said.

He didn't say anything.

'I'll do whatever you tell me. I will try again if that's what you want. I'll become an engineer, Baba,' I said.

He placed a hand on my head as if in blessing. It acted as a tipping point for my emotions. I broke down.

'I'll work extra hard,' I said as tears rolled down my cheeks.

'God bless you, go to sleep,' he said.

♦

I reached Assi Ghat at four-thirty in the morning. Phoolchand, my boatman friend, smiled as he handed me the oars. He had never charged me in all these years. I would take his boat for an hour, and buy him tea and biscuits in return. Firangs would pay five hundred bucks for the same.

Sometimes I'd help him negotiate with foreigners in English, and he'd give me a ten per cent commission. Yes, I could make money like this too. Maybe not a lot, but enough to survive. If only Baba would understand this.

'Come back by five-thirty,' Phoolchand said. 'I have a booking. Japanese tourists.'

'I won't take more than half an hour,' I promised.

He smirked. 'You are going with a girl. You may forget the time.'

'I won't.'

'You have a setting with her?' Phoolchand said as he untied the anchor rope. In small towns, everyone is interested in every male and female interaction.

'Phoolchand bhai, I will be back in half an hour,' I said and got into the boat.

Phoolchand frowned at my curt reply.

'She is a classmate from school. Have known her for eight years,' I said.

He smiled. His paan-stained teeth shone in the semi-darkness of dawn.

'I'll help you with the Japanese, we will rip them off together,' I said, holding the oars.

Aarti was waiting twenty metres ahead of the ghat pier, away from the stare of boatmen and sadhus. She stepped into the boat, one foot at a time. I whisked the boat away from the shore.

'Let's go that way,' she said, pointing in the quieter western direction. On the east, the morning aarti had commenced at the crowded Dashashwamedh Ghat. Dashashwamedh, believed to be the place where Brahma performed ten ashwamedha yajnas (horse sacrifice), is the hub of all holy activities on the banks of Ganga in Varanasi.

The sound of bells and chants faded as I rowed further away. Soon, the only sounds came from the periodic slapping of the oars on the water.

'It happens,' said Aarti.

Her face had an amber hue from the morning sun. It matched her saffron and red dupatta.

My arms and shoulders felt tired. I stopped rowing and put the oars down. The boat stood still somewhere in the middle of the Ganga. Aarti stood up to come and sit beside me. Her movement shook the boat a little. As per ritual, she took my tired palms and pressed them. She held my chin and made me face her.

'I'm scared, Aarti,' I said in a small voice.

'Why?'

'I'll get nowhere in life,' I said.

'Nonsense,' she said. 'So people who don't have a top AIEEE rank get nowhere in life?'

'I don't know. I feel so ... so defeated. I let Baba down.'

'Is he okay?'

'He wants me to try again. He is obsessed with making me an engineer.'

'Do you want to be an engineer?' Aarti said.

'My dad is not in the IAS. My grandfather was not a minister. We are from a simple Indian family. We don't ask these questions. We want to make a living. Engineering gives us that,' I answered.

'How old-fashioned!'

'Filling your stomach never goes out of fashion, Aarti,' I said.

She smiled and placed a hand on my arm. I hugged her. As I held her, I brought my mouth close to hers.

'What are you doing?' Aarti said, pushing me away.

'I ... I just ...'

'Don't,' Aarti said sternly. 'You will spoil our friendship.'

'I really like you,' I said. I wanted to say 'love', but did not have the courage.

'I like you too,' she said.

'Then why won't you kiss me?' I said.

'I don't want to.' She faced me squarely. 'Don't get me wrong. You have been my best friend for years. But I've told you earlier ...' She went silent.

'What?'

'I don't see you that way,' she finished.

I turned away from her.

'Gopal, please understand. You are disturbed so I don't want to ...'

'You don't want to what, Aarti? Hurt my feelings? Well, you have.'

I checked the time. My watch said 4:50 a.m. I had to return the boat. I picked up the oars again. 'Go back to your place,' I said. She complied. We remained silent till we reached the ghats. Phoolchand gave us a smile, which evaporated fast when I glowered at him.

We stepped off the boat.

'You want to come home later today?' Aarti said.

'Don't talk to me,' I said.

'You are being an idiot.'

'I *am* an idiot, don't you know? That's why I couldn't clear the AIEEE,' I said and walked away without looking at her.

5

Like AIEEE, I did not make it in the JEE either. Raghav did, with an all-India rank of 1123. It turned him into a mini-celebrity in Varanasi. Local papers carried big stories the next day. Four students from Varanasi had cracked the JEE. Among those four, only Raghav had cleared the exam as a resident of Varanasi. The other three had appeared from Kota.

'Why did they go to Kota?' Baba mused, looking up from the newspaper.

Baba had resigned himself to my being a loser. He did not react to my not obtaining a JEE rank at all.

'Kota is the capital of IIT coaching classes. Tens of thousands go there,' I explained.

Every year, the tiny western Indian town of Kota accounted for a thousand, or a third of the total IIT selections.

'What?' Baba said. 'How is that possible?'

I shrugged my shoulders. I didn't want to discuss entrance exams any more. I had secured seventy-nine per cent in class XII. I could do BSc at the Allahabad University. The 120-kilometre commute would be difficult, but I could move there and visit Baba on weekends.

'Which IIT is Raghav joining?'

'I don't know,' I said. 'Baba, can you give me two hundred rupees. I need to buy college admission forms.'

Baba looked like I had stabbed him. 'Aren't you repeating AIEEE?' he said.

'I will join the Allahabad University and repeat from there,' I said.

'How will you prepare while doing another course?'

'I can't waste a year,' I said and left the house.

◆

I had to meet Raghav. I had not even congratulated him. True, I did not feel any happiness about his JEE selection. I should have, but did not. After all, we had been friends for ten years. One should be happy for pals. However, he would be an IIT student and I'd be a fucking nobody. Somehow, I could not feel thrilled about that. I practised fake smiles while pressing his doorbell. Raghav opened the door and hugged me straight off.

'Hey, nice to see you,' he said.

'Congrats, boss,' I said, my lips streched into a smile and teeth sufficiently visible.

'Now I can say I know a celeb.'

I came inside his house, a modest three-bedroom, BHEL-provided apartment. Newspapers with articles about his selection lay on the dining table. Raghav's father sat on a sofa with visiting relatives. They had come to congratulate the Kashyaps. An IIT rank is a huge event – akin to climbing the Mount Everest or being on a space mission. Mr Kashyap smiled at me from a distance. Call it my over-imagination, but his greeting seemed like the one you give to people well beneath your stature. I am sure if I had had a rank, he would have stood up and shook hands with me. Anyway, it didn't matter. Raghav and I went to his room. I sat on a chair and he on the bed.

'So, how are you feeling?' I said. I wanted to know how it felt to get one of those stupid ranks that turned you from coal to diamond in a day.

'Unbelievable,' Raghav said. 'I had thought AIEEE maybe, but JEE, wow.'

'Which IIT?' I said.

'I will join IT-BHU. I will get a good branch and be in Varanasi too,' Raghav said.

IT-BHU, the Institute of Technology at the Banaras Hindu University, was the most prestigious college in Varanasi. It conducted its admission process through the JEE. However, it didn't have the same brand equity as an IIT.

'Why BHU?' I said.

'I want to do journalism part-time. I have contacts in newspapers here,' Raghav said.

When people are offered something on a platter, they don't value it. Sure, Raghav had a thing for writing. He had published some letters to the editor and a couple of articles in some papers. However, this sounded insane.

'You will give up an IIT for a hobby?' I said.

'It is not a hobby. Journalism is my passion.'

'Why are you doing engineering then?'

'Dad. Why else? Oh, I have told him I am taking BHU because I will get a better branch like Computer Science. Don't tell him anything else.'

'Raghav, you still …'

'Raghav!' Mr Kashyap shouted from outside.

'My relatives, sorry. I have to go,' Raghav said. 'Let's catch up later. Call Aarti also. I owe you guys a treat.'

He got up to leave.

When people achieve something, they become self-obsessed.

'Want to know what I am going to do?' I said casually.

Raghav stopped. 'Oh, sorry. Sure, tell me,' he said. I don't know if he cared, or if he felt obligated.

'Allahabad University. I will take a second attempt from there,' I said.

'Sounds good,' Raghav said. 'I am sure you will crack something. At least AIEEE.'

When people clear JEE, they start using phrases like 'at least AIEEE'.

I smiled. 'Baba wants me to drop a year to attempt again.'

'You could do that too,' Raghav said. His father shouted out for him again.

'Go, it's okay,' I said. 'I'll also leave.'

'See you, buddy.' Raghav patted my shoulder.

◆

'No, Baba,' I said. 'I am not going to Kota.'

Without my knowledge, my father had spent one whole week researching on Kota. 'Bansal and Resonance are the best,' he said.

'How do you know?'

'I am a retired teacher. I can find out.'

'Great,' I said.

'I am ready to send you. Tuition is thirty thousand a year. Living expenses around three thousand a month. How much is that for twelve months? Thirty plus thirty-six thousand ...' Baba mumbled to himself.

'Sixty-six thousand!' I said. 'And a wasted year. Baba, who are we? Kings?'

'I have a forty-thousand fixed deposit I haven't told you about,' Baba said. 'I saved whatever I could in the past three years. Enough to get you started. We'll figure out the rest.'

'So blow up whatever little money we have on tuitions? In some faraway place? Where is Kota, anyway?'

'In Rajasthan. It's far, but there is a direct train. Takes twenty-two hours.'

'Baba, but ... why can't I join college? Give me the money for that. At least I will have a degree.'

'What's the point of a useless degree? And how will you do a repeat attempt without better coaching? You just missed a good rank because of a few marks. Maybe Kota will help you get those extra marks.'

I was confused. I had never thought of a second attempt, let alone going so far for a year.

'You have to give it your best. Look at Raghav. He's set for life,' Baba said.

'Look-at-Raghav', yes, the new medicine being shoved down every Varanasi kid's throat right now. 'We can't afford it,' I said, collecting my thoughts. 'Besides, who will take care of you here? Allahabad is nearby. I can come every week. You can visit ...'

'I can manage. Don't I do most of the housework?' Baba said.

I thought of Aarti. Sure, she had said no to me in the boat, but I knew how much she cared for me. Not a day went by without us talking. It was she who suggested I go to a college here, and I'd already found out the best course I could get with my percentage. How could I tell her I am going to Kota?

Of course, I couldn't give Baba this reason to stay in Varanasi. 'I promise I will work harder next time,' I said.

We finished dinner and I began to clear the table.

'You will keep doing domestic chores here,' Baba shouted suddenly. 'You are going.'

'You have forty thousand. What about the rest? What about expenses such as travel, books, entrance exam fees?' I said.

My father showed me his shrivelled index finger. It had a thick gold band around it. 'I don't need this useless ring,' he said. 'We also have some of your mother's jewellery.'

'You want to sell Ma's jewellery for coaching classes?'

'I had kept all that for your wife, but after you become an engineer, you can buy them for her yourself.'

'What if you fall ill, Baba? Better to preserve all this for medical emergencies.'

'You join an engineering college and my age will reduce by ten years,' Baba laughed, trying to soften the situation. I saw his face, one front tooth missing. His laughter meant everything to me. I thought about Kota. They did seem good at making students clear entrance exams. I thought about the downside – the money required, the uncertainty and, of course, staying away from Aarti.

'Do it for your old man,' he said. 'I'd move with you to Kota, but it's hard for me to travel so far. We have to maintain this little house too.'

'It's fine, Baba. If I go, I'll go by myself,' I said.

'Your mother too wanted you to become an engineer.'

I looked at my mother's picture on the wall. She looked happy, beautiful and young.

'Take care of your father,' she seemed to tell me.

'Will you go?' Baba said.

'If it makes you happy, I will.'

'My son!' Baba hugged me – the first time since the AIEEE results.

♦

'Show us the black ones,' Aarti said to the shopkeeper. She pointed to a set of twelve clothes hangers.

We had come to a household items shop in Nadeshar Road to buy things I'd need in Kota.

'Just because I am helping you shop doesn't mean I am happy about you leaving Varanasi,' Aarti said.

'I won't. Say the word and I will cancel my ticket.'

She placed a palm on my cheek. 'I hate it that my best friend is leaving. However, it is the right thing for you to do.'

She approved of the hangers. They cost fifty bucks a set. 'Uncle, I am buying towels, soap dishes and so many other things. You better give a good discount.'

The shopkeeper grimaced, but she ignored him.

'Thank you for coming. I would not have known what to buy,' I told her.

'Have you taken cooking vessels? Forgot, no?'

'I am not going to cook. They have a tiffin system.'

Aarti ignored me. She went to the utensils section and picked up a large steel bowl and held it up.

'For emergencies,' Aarti said. 'If I came to Kota with you, I'd cook for you everyday.'

Her fair hands held up the shiny vessel. The picture of her cooking in my kitchen flashed in my head. *Why does Aarti make statements like these? What am I supposed to say?* 'I'll manage fine,' I said.

The shopkeeper made the bill. Aarti looked at me. She hypnotised me every time. She was turning prettier every week.

A small girl who had come to the shop with her mother came up to Aarti. 'Do you come on TV?'

Aarti shook her head and smiled. She turned to the shopkeeper. 'Uncle, twenty per cent discount.' Aarti wasn't too conscious of her looks. She never checked herself out in mirrors, never had make-up on, and even her hair often flopped all over her face. It made her even more attractive.

'Should we leave?' she said.

'Whatever.'

'What happened?'

'At the last minute you say random things like "if I came to Kota".'

'I could. I will tell dad I also want to repeat a year. You never know.' She winked.

I stared at her, seeking a hint of seriousness in her comment. Would that be possible?

'Really?' I said, almost believing her.

'I'm joking, stupid. I told you. I've enrolled for Psychology honours at the Agrasen College.'

'I thought you …'

'Why are you so gullible?' She burst into peals of laughter.

'Gulli … what?' I said. She pulled my cheek. 'Oh,' I said and composed myself.

Of course, no way she could come to Kota. I am not a gulli-whatever person. I understand things. Still, Aarti could defeat my logical faculties. I stopped thinking when I was with her.

I collected the purchased items and noticed her paying the shopkeeper.

'Wait,' I said. 'I will pay.'

'Forget it. Let's go,' she said. She tugged at my elbow and dragged me out of the shop.

'How much?' I said as I fumbled with my wallet.

She took my wallet and placed it back in my shirt pocket. She placed a finger on my lips.

Why do girls send confusing signals? She had rebuffed me on the boat the other day. Yet she comes to shop with me for boring clothes hangers and doesn't let me pay. She calls me three times a day to check if I've had my meals. Does she care for me or not?

◆

'You want to try the new Domino's at Sigra?' she said.

'Can we go to the ghats?' I said.

'Ghats?' she said, surprised.

'I want to soak in as much Varanasi as possible before I leave.'

We walked to the steps of the Lalita Ghat, quieter than the busy Dashashwamedh on our right. We sat next to each other and watched the Ganga change colours with the evening sun. On our left, flames flickered from the never-ending funeral pyres in the Manikarnika Ghat. The ghat, named after Shiva's earring that he dropped here during a dance, is considered the holiest place for cremation.

She held my elbow lightly. I looked around. Apart from some tourists and sadhus, I spotted a few locals. I shook my elbow free.

'What?' she said.

'Don't. It's not good. Especially for you.'

'Why?'

'Because you are a girl.'

She smacked my elbow. 'So what?'

'People talk. They don't say good things about girls who sit on the ghats holding elbows.'

'We are just really good friends,' she said.

I hated that term. I wanted to talk about my place in her life, even though I did not want to make things unpleasant. 'But now I am leaving,' I said.

'So? We will be in touch. We will call. We can chat on the net. There are cyber cafés in Kota, right?'

I nodded.

'Don't look so glum,' she said. We heard the temple bells ring in the distance. The evening aarti was about to begin.

'What is your problem?' I said.

'About what?' she said.

'About us. Us being more than friends.'

'Please, Gopal, not again.'

I became quiet. We saw the evening aarti from a distance. A dozen priests, holding giant lamps the size of flaming torches, prayed in synchronised moves as singers chanted in the background. Hundreds of tourists gathered around the priests. No matter how many times you see it, the aarti on Varanasi ghats manages to mesmerise each time. Much like the Aarti next to me. She wore a peacock blue salwar-kameez and fish-shaped silver earrings.

'I don't feel that way, Gopal,' she said.

'About me?'

'About anyone. And I like what you and I share. Don't you?'

'I do. But I am leaving now. If we had a commitment, wouldn't it be better?'

'Commitment? Gopal, we are so young!' She laughed. She stood up. 'Come, let's float diyas. For your trip.'

Girls are the best topic switchers in the world.

We walked down to the waters. She purchased a set of six lit diyas for five rupees. She passed one to me. She set one diya afloat. Holding my hand, she said, 'Let's pray together, for success.'

'May you get what you want in Kota,' she said, eyes shut.

I looked at her. *What I really want is not in Kota, I am leaving it behind in Varanasi ...*

Kota

6

It took me twenty-three hours in the hot and stuffy Dwarka Express to reach Kota.

I had emailed Vineet, a Varanasi boy who'd spent the last year in Kota. I learnt about the coaching classes; Bansal and Resonance had the best reputation. However, they screened students with their own tests. If I did not get into Bansal or Resonance, Kota had other, less selective coaching classes that catered to losers like me.

However, before I joined a coaching ghetto I had to find a place to live in. Vineet had told me about some paying guest accommodations. I hailed an auto from the railway station. 'Gayatri Society Building,' I said, 'in Mahavir Nagar, near Bansal classes.'

The auto drove down the dusty streets of Kota. It looked like any other small town in India, with too much traffic and pollution and too many telecom, underwear and coaching-class hoardings. I wondered what was so special about this place. How could it make thousands of students clear the most competitive exam in the world?

'IIT or Medical?' asked the auto driver, who had gray hair and matching teeth.

I figured out what made Kota different. Every one was clued into the entrance exams.

'IIT,' I said.

'Bansal is the best. But their entrance exam is scheduled for next week.'

'You know all this?' I said, baffled by the driver's knowledge.

He laughed and turned around. 'My whole family is into education. My wife runs a tiffin business. You want food delivered?'

I nodded.

'Shankar, originally from Alwar,' he said. He extended his grease-stained hand.

I shook it as little as possible. 'Gopal from Varanasi.'

He gave me a business card for the tiffin service. Two meals a day for a monthly cost of fifteen hundred bucks.

'Let us take care of the food. You boys study, it is such a tough exam.'

'Which exam?' I said.

'For IIT it is JEE. Come on, Gopal bhai. We are not that uneducated.'

◆

We reached the Gayatri Society compound. A rusty iron gate protected a crumbling block of apartments. A sweeper with a giant broom produced dust clouds in the air in an attempt to clean the place. I went to the small guard post at the entrance of the building. A watchman sat inside.

'Who do you want to meet?' the watchman said.

'I want to rent a room,' I said.

The watchman looked me over. He saw my two over-stuffed, over-aged and over-repaired suitcases. One held clothes, the other carried the books that had failed to get me anywhere so far. My rucksack carried the stuff Aarti had bought me. I missed her. I wondered if I should find an STD booth and call her.

'IIT or Medical?' the watchman asked, crushing tobacco in his hand. Kota locals find it hard to place outsiders until they know what they are there for.

'IIT,' I said. I wished he would give me more attention than his nicotine fix.

'First-timer or repeater?' the watchman asked next, still without looking up.

'Does it matter?' I said, somewhat irritated.

'Yes,' he said and popped the tobacco into his mouth. 'If you are a first-timer, you will join a school also. You will be out of the house more. Repeaters only go for coaching classes. Many sleep all day. Some landlords don't like that. So, tell me and I can show you the right place.'

'Repeater,' I said. I don't know why I looked down as I said that. I guess when you fail an entrance exam, even a tobacco-chewing watchman can make you feel small.

'Oh God, another repeater,' the watchman said. 'Anyway, I will try. Fix my fee first.'

'What?' I said.

'I take half a month's rent. What's your budget?'

'Two thousand a month.'

'That's it?' the watchman said. 'Make it four thousand. I will get you a nice, shared air-conditioned room.'

'I can't afford to pay so much,' I said.

The watchman sneered, as if someone had asked for country liquor in a five-star bar.

'What?' I said, wondering if I'd be spending my first night in Kota on the streets.

'Come,' he beckoned. He opened the gate and kept my suitcases in his cabin. We climbed up the steps of the first apartment block.

'Will you share with other boys? Three to a room,' the watchman said.

'I could,' I said, 'but how will I study? I want a private one, however small.'

Studies or not, I wanted to be left alone.

'Okay, fifth floor,' the watchman said.

We climbed up three floors. I panted due to the exertion. The extreme heat did not help. 'Kota is hot, get used to the weather,' the watchman said. 'It is horrible outside. That is why it is a good place to stay inside and study.'

We reached the fourth floor. I struggled to catch my breath. He couldn't stop talking. 'So you will study for real or you are just ...' he paused mid-sentence.

'Just what?' I said.

'Time-pass. Many students come here because their parents push them. They know they won't get in. At least the parents stop harassing them for a year,' he said.

'I want to get in. I will get in,' I said, more to myself than him.

'Good. But if you need stuff like beer or cigarettes, tell me. This housing society doesn't allow it.'

'So?'

'When Birju is your friend, you don't have to worry.' He winked at me.

We rang the bell of the fifth-floor flat. An elderly lady opened the door.

'Student,' the watchman said.

The lady let us in. Her place smelt of medicines and damp. The watchman showed me the room on rent. The lady had converted a storeroom into a study and bedroom. The lady, watchman and I could barely stand in the tiny room together.

'It's perfect for studying,' said the watchman, who probably hadn't studied even one day in his whole life. 'Take it, it is within your budget.'

I shook my head. The room had no windows. The old lady seemed arrogant or deaf or both. She kept a grumpy face throughout. I did not want to live here. Why couldn't I study in my Varanasi? What was so special about this godforsaken place? I wanted to get out of Kota ASAP.

I walked out of the flat. The watchman came running after me.

'If you fuss so much, you won't get anything.'

'I'll go back to Varanasi then,' I said.

I thought about how different my life would have been if I had answered six more multiple-choice questions. I thought of Raghav, who would, at this moment, be attending his orientation at the BHU campus. I thought of Aarti and our heart-to-heart conversations. I thought of Baba's ill health and his determination to kick me into this dump. I fought back tears. I started to walk down the stairs.

'Or increase your budget,' the watchman said as he came up behind me.

'I can't. I have to pay for food and the coaching classes,' I said.

We walked down the steps and reached the ground floor. 'It happens the first time,' the watchman said, 'missing your mother?'

'She's dead,' I said.

'Recently?' the watchman said. Some people find it perfectly normal to cross-examine strangers.

'She died fourteen years ago,' I said.

I came to the guard post and picked up my bags. 'Thank you, Birju,' I said.

'Where are you going? Take a shared room,' he pleaded.

'I'll find a cheap hotel for now. I am used to being alone. I'll figure things out.'

Birju took the suitcases from me and placed them down. 'I have a proper room,' he said, 'double the size of what you saw. It has windows, a big fan. A retired couple stays there. Within your budget ...'

'Then why didn't you show it to me earlier?'

'There's a catch.'

'What?'

'Someone died in the house.'

'Who?' I said. Big deal, I could take death. I'm from Varanasi, where the world comes to die.

'The student who rented it. He didn't get through, so he killed himself. Two years ago. It has been empty since.'

I did not respond.

'Now you see why I didn't show it to you,' Birju said.

'I'll take it,' I said.

'Sure?'

'I've seen dead bodies burning and floating all my life. I don't care if some loser hanged himself.'

The watchman picked up my suitcases. We went to the third floor in the next flat. A couple in their sixties stayed there. They kept the place immaculately clean. The spartan to-let room had a bed, table, cupboard and fan.

'Fifteen hundred,' I said to the couple. The watchman gave me a dirty look.

The couple looked at each other.

'I know what happened here,' I said, 'and it's fine by me.'

The old gentleman nodded. 'I am RL Soni, I used to work in the PWD.' He extended his hand.

I gave him a firm handshake. 'I'm Gopal, an IIT repeater. I plan to get in this time,' I said.

7

I dumped the brochures on the bed, and took off my shoes and socks. I had spent the day visiting various coaching schools. At three in the afternoon, my room felt at ignition point.

Mr Soni gently knocked on the door of my room. 'Your lunch,' he said and kept the tiffin on my study table.

I nodded in gratitude. It felt too hot to exchange pleasantries. I had arranged for my meals and a place to stay. However, my main challenge in Kota, apart from constantly fighting off thoughts about Aarti, was to enrol in a good study programme. I had spent the last three days doing the rounds of every coaching school. I took in their tall claims about zapping any primate into an IITian. I went through their super-flexible (not to mention super-expensive) fee structures. Bansal, Resonance and Career Path seemed to be everyone's top choices. Each of them had their own, rather difficult, entrance exams. In fact, Kota now had small coaching shops to coach you to get into the top coaching classes. From there, you would be coached to get into an engineering college. Once there, you study to become an engineer. Of course, most engineers want to do an MBA. Hence, the same coaching-class cycle would begin again. This complex vortex of tests, classes, selections and preparations is something every insignificant Indian student like me has to go through to have a shot at a decent life. Else, I could always take the job of Birju the watchman or, if I wanted it simpler, hang myself like my erstwhile room-resident Manoj Dutta.

I switched on the same fan that helped Manoj check out of the entrance exam called life. The moving blades re-circulated the hot air in the room.

'Called home?' Mr Soni said.

'I did,' I said. Mr Soni asked me this question at least twice a day. I guess Manoj Dutta didn't call home often enough, leading to his loneliness and early demise.

'Keep them informed, okay? Nobody loves you more than your parents,' Mr Soni said as he left the room.

I shut the door and removed my shirt. I hadn't rowed in ten days. My arms felt flabby. I wanted to exercise, but I had to figure out the ten million brochures first.

I had indeed called Baba, twice. He seemed fine. I told him I had started preparing for next year, even though I couldn't bear to open any textbook. I didn't care. Whichever coaching class I joined would make me slog soon.

I wanted to talk to Aarti first. I'd called her four times but could not speak to her even once. Her mother had picked up the phone the first two times. She told me politely that Aarti had gone out – with friends once, and another time to submit her college admission form. I called twice the next day and Aarti's mother picked up again. I hung up without saying anything. I did not want Aarti's mother going 'why is this boy calling you so many times from so far?' It did not create a good impression. Aarti had mentioned she would get a cellphone soon. I wished she would. Everyone seemed to be getting one nowadays, at least the rich types.

Aarti did not have a number to reach me. I would have to try again tomorrow.

I picked up a green-coloured brochure. The cover had photographs of some of the ugliest people on earth. The pictures belonged to the IIT toppers from that institute. They had grins wider than models in toothpaste ads but not the same kind of teeth.

Since my favourite hobby was wasting time, I spent the afternoon comparing the brochures. No, I didn't compare the course material, success rates or the fee structures. In any case, everyone claimed to be the best in those areas. I compared the pictures of their successful candidates; who had the ugliest boy, who had the cutest girl, if at all. There was no point to this exercise, but there was no point to me being in Kota.

I saw the Bansal brochure, the holy grail of Kota-land. Bansal students had a chip on their shoulder, even though they weren't technically even in a college. The Bansalites were Kota's cool. I had to crack their exam. However, I had little time to prepare for the test scheduled in three days. In fact, many of the coaching classes had their exams within a week. The next set of exams was a month away. I had to join something now. Staying idle would make me go mad faster than the earlier occupant of this room.

Each institute asked for a thousand bucks for an application form. Whether they selected you or not, whether you joined or not, the fee had to be paid. I had fifty thousand rupees with me, and Baba had promised me more after six months. I had limited money, I could only apply selectively.

I shortlisted five coaching institutes – Bansal, Career Path, Resonance, and two new, cheaper ones called AimIIT and CareerIgnite.

The brochure of AimIIT said: 'We believe in the democratic right of every student to be coached, hence we don't conduct our own entrance tests.' It meant they weren't in the same league as the top ones to be choosy.' They might as well have written: 'If you have the cash, you are welcome.'

I spent the rest of the afternoon filling the tiresome and repetitive forms. I kept myself motivated by saying I would call Aarti once more before dinner.

✦

I went out for an evening walk at 7:00 p.m. The streets were filled with nerdy students out for their daily dose of fresh air.

I found an STD booth.

'Hello?' Mr Pradhan said in a firm voice. I cut the phone on reflex.

The meter at the STD booth whirred.

'You still have to pay,' the shopkeeper said sourly. I nodded.

I needed to speak to someone. I had already called Baba in the morning. I called Raghav.

'Raghav, it's me. Gopal. From Kota,' I said, my last word soft.

'Gopal! Oh, wow, we were just talking about you,' Raghav said.

'Me? Really? With who?' I said.

'Aarti's here. How are you, man? How's Kota? We miss you.'

'Aarti is at your place?' I asked, puzzled.

'Yeah, she wanted me to help her choose her course. She is not sure about Psychology.'

Aarti snatched the phone from Raghav mid-sentence.

'Gopal! Where are you?'

'In Kota, of course. I called you,' I said. I wanted to ask her why she had come to Raghav's place. However, it didn't seem the best way to start a conversation.

'Why didn't you call back? I don't even have a number to call you,' she said.

'Will ask my landlord if I can receive calls. Tell me when you will be home. I will call you. I want to talk.'

'Talk now. What's up?'

'How can I talk now?'

'Why?'

'You are with Raghav,' I said.

'So?'

'What are you doing at Raghav's place?'

'Nothing. Generally.'

When girls use vague terms like 'generally', it is cause for specific concern. Or maybe not. It could be my overactive mind.

'I have to choose a course. Should I do Psychology or BSc Home Science?' she said.

'What do you want to do?' I said.

'I have to finish my graduation before becoming an air hostess. That's the only reason I am doing it. I want an easy course.'

'Oh, so your air hostess plans are not dead,' I said.

'Well, Raghav says one should not give up one's dream so easily. Maybe BSc Home Science is better, no? Sort of related to hospitality industry. Or should I leave Agrasen and join hotel management?'

I kept quiet. *Raghav's advising her? Who is he? A career counsellor? Or does he have the license to preach now because he has a fucking JEE rank?*

'Tell me no, Gopi,' Aarti said. 'I am so confused.' Then I heard her titter.

'What's so funny?' I said.

'Raghav is pretending to be an air hostess. He has a tray and everything,' she said, greatly amused.

'I'll talk to you later,' I said.

'Okay, but tell me which course to take,' she said, her tone finally serious.

'Ask Raghav, he is the better student,' I said.

'C'mon, Gopi. Nonsense you talk.'

'Let us talk when you are alone,' I said.

'Call me this time tomorrow.'

'Okay, bye.'

'Bye,' Aarti said.

'I miss you,' I said, a second too late. I only got a click in response.

I returned to my room where my dinner tiffin and the brochures awaited me. I imagined Aarti at Raghav's place, in peals of laughter. My insides burnt.

I picked up a brochure in disgust. I took a blade from my shaving kit, cut out the cover pictures of the IIT-selected students, and ripped them to shreds.

◆

Bansal classes did not look like the small tuition centres run out of tiny apartments in Varanasi. It resembled an institute or a large corporate office. I stood in the gigantic lobby, wondering what to do next. Students and teachers strode about in a purposeful manner, as if they were going to launch satellites in space. Like in many other coaching classes in Kota, the students had uniforms to eliminate social inequality. You had rich kids from Delhi, whose parents gave them more pocket money than my father earned in an entire year. On the other hand, you had losers like me from Varanasi, who had neither the cash nor the brains required to be here.

Equality in clothes didn't mean Bansal believed all students were equal. A class system existed, based on your chances of cracking the entrance exam.

The person at the admissions office took my form. 'High performer?' he quizzed.

I wondered how anyone could respond to such a question. 'Excuse me?'

'If you have more than 85 per cent aggregate in class XII, or if you have an AIEEE rank up to 40,000, you get a thirty per cent discount,' the bespectacled gentleman at the counter explained to me.

'I have 79 per cent. AIEEE rank 52,043,' I said.

'Oh. In that case you apply for full-rate programme,' the admission officer said. I didn't realise my AIEEE rank could directly translate into money.

'Can I get a discount?' I said, wondering if one could bargain here.

'Depends on how you do in our entrance exam,' the officer said and stamped my form. He handed me a receipt-cum-admit card for the entrance exam.

'Do I have to study for your entrance exam?' I said.

'What will you study in two days? Anyway, you don't look like such a bright student going by your marks. My suggestion is to apply to other institutes,' he replied.

'Thanks, I will,' I said.

The officer looked around to ensure nobody could hear us. 'My cousin has just started an institute. I can get you a fifty per cent discount there,' he whispered.

I kept quiet. He slipped me a visiting card: 'Dream IIT'.

'Why waste money? Course material is the same. My cousin is an ex-Bansal faculty.'

I examined the card.

'Don't tell anyone, okay?' he said.

I had similar experiences at other institutes. Walls covered with stamp-sized pictures of successful JEE candidates, resembling wanted terrorists, greeted me everywhere. I also realised that the reputed institutes kicked up a bigger fuss about 'repeaters'. After all, we had failed once, and institutes didn't want to spoil their statistics. Top institutes claimed to send up to five hundred students a year to IIT. Of course, the institutes never reveal that they enrol ten thousand students, out of which only five hundred make it. This meant a low selection ratio of five per cent. However, the JEE had an overall selection ratio of less than two per cent, and Kota institutes claimed to beat it. The pre-screening of candidates could be the sole reason for the higher-than-average selection. However, students like me flocked from around the country anyway, and queued up to submit the admission forms.

AimIIT and CareerIgnite had less people lining up. In fact, they gave me spot offers. The latter even offered a twenty per cent discount.

'The discount is applicable only if you sign up right now, not if you come again,' the aggressive salesman-cum-admissions in-charge told me.

'But I have not decided yet,' I protested.

'You are appearing for Bansal, aren't you?' he said and gave me an all-knowing look.

I kept quiet.

'I am an ex-Bansalite,' he said.

'Is there anyone in Kota who is not?' I said and left the institute.

8

'Gopal! So nice to hear your voice,' Aarti said. She recognised me in a second. It felt good.

'Go to hell, you don't care,' I said.

'Huh? How stupid. I do care. Firstly, do you have a number I can call?'

'Yes,' I said and gave her my landlord's number. 'But don't call a lot. He said no more than twice a week.'

'So what? I will be the only one calling you, no?' Aarti said.

'Yeah. Anyway, how's life? I hate it here.'

'Is it that bad? Have you started studying?' she asked.

'No, I can't. It is hard to pick up the same books again. Maybe I will get motivated after I join a coaching class.'

'I should have been there, I would have motivated you.' She laughed.

'Don't make such jokes.'

'You will be fine, Gopi. One more attempt. If you get through, your career will be made.'

'I miss you,' I said, less interested in useless things like my career.

'Oh,' she said, somewhat surprised by my shifting gears. 'I miss you too.'

'I have no one, Aarti,' I said.

'Don't say that. Baba is there. Raghav, me … We talk about you a lot.' Her voice trailed off.

'Why don't we become a couple?'

'Don't. Please don't start that again. We have discussed it enough,' she said.

'Why not? You say you miss me. You care for me. Then?'

'I care for you a lot. But not in that way. Anyway, we have to focus on our respective careers. You are there, I am here.'

'If I had a girlfriend, at least I could talk to her. I feel so lonely, Aarti,' I said.

'Aww Gopal, you are homesick. Talk to me whenever you want. Or we can chat.'

'On the Internet?' I had seen some cyber cafes around my house.

'Yeah, make a Gmail ID. Mine is flyingaarti@gmail.com. Invite me.'

'Flying Aarti.' I laughed.

'Shut up.'

I laughed harder.

'At least it cheered you up,' she said.

'Think about my proposal,' I said.

'There is no proposal. And now don't waste your money on calls. We can chat in the evenings. I'll tell you about my life, and you about yours. Okay?'

'Okay. Hey, listen. Should I join a reputed but expensive institute or the upcoming but cheaper ones?'

'The best you can get, always,' Aarti said promptly. 'And now, bye. They are calling me for dinner.'

◆

One week in Kota, and I had a few decisions made for me. One, I didn't clear the Bansal exam. I could join their separate correspondence programme, which kind of defeated the purpose of being in Kota. Resonance hiked its fees at the last minute. It became unaffordable for me, so I didn't even write their entrance exam. I made it to the waitlist of the Career Path programme.

'Your chances are good. Many will join Bansal and Resonance, anyway,' the Career Path guy said.

Even the Career Path waitlist had value. AimIIT and CareerIgnite offered me a thirty per cent discount.

'You have calibre,' the AimIIT person told me. 'You have cleared Career Path, which shows your potential. Now study with us at a much cheaper price and clear the exam.'

'You will be lost amongst the thousands at Career Path. At Ignite, you will be special,' said the ex-Bansalite running down another ex-Bansalite's institute.

However, five days later Career Path told me I had made it. I handed the accountant at Career Path a twenty-thousand-rupee draft with trembling hands.

'This is the best investment you will make in your life,' the accountant said.

I picked up the items required for the first term – course material, ID card, timetable, circulars and various worksheets required in the next three months. I also collected three sets of the Career Path uniform. Wearing it made me look like a budget hotel receptionist.

I walked out of the institute with the uniform in my hands.

'Congratulations!' A man in a black coat stopped me.

'Hello,' I said, not sure what else to say.

'I am Sanjeev sir. They call me Mr Pulley here. I teach physics.'

I shook his hand. Apparently, nobody could solve pulley problems in Kota quite like Sanjeev sir. I soon realised there were subject experts across institutes in Kota. Career Path had its own wizards. Mr Verma, who taught maths, had the moniker of Trignometry-swamy. Mr Jadeja taught chemistry. Students affectionately addressed him as Balance-ji. He had a unique method of balancing chemical equations. According to rumours, he had tried to patent it.

'I am Gopal, from Varanasi.'

'AIEEE programme?' Mr Pulley said.

'JEE also, sir.'

'Good. High potential?' He referred to Career Path's internal classification of students.

'No, sir,' I said and trained my gaze down. Once you get low marks, you learn to lower your eyes rather quickly.

'It's okay. Many non-high potential students make it. It all depends on hard work.'

'I'll do my best, sir,' I said.

'Good,' Mr Pulley said and smacked my back.

◆

I could call myself a true Kota-ite a month into moving there. Like thousands of other students, my life now had a rhythm. Career Path resembled a school, but without the fun bits. Nobody made noise in class, played pranks on one another or thought of bunking classes. After all, everyone had come here by choice and had paid a big price to be here.

We had three to four classes a day, which started in the afternoon. In theory, this allowed the current class XII students to attend school in the morning. In reality, the class XII students never went to school. Career Path had an agreement with a cooperative CBSE school, which had a flexible attendance policy. It was rumoured that the CBSE school received a handsome kickback from Career Path for the cooperation extended.

I hated the brutal Career Path schedule at first. Lectures started at two in the afternoon and went on until nine in the evening. After that students rushed home to eat dinner, and do the 'daily practice sheets', a set of ten problems based on the current lesson. I usually finished by midnight. After a few hours of sleep I would wake up and prepare for the next day's classes. In between, I did household chores, such as washing clothes and shopping for essentials. I went along with the madness, not so much because of the zeal to prepare, but more because I wanted to keep myself busy. I didn't want Kota's loneliness to kill me.

One night our classes ended late. I reached the cyber café at nine-thirty, later than my usual chat time with Aarti. To my surprise she was still online.

I typed in a message from my usual handle.

GopalKotaFactory: Hi!
FlyingAarti: Hey!! Guess what!

If girls got to set grammar rules in this world, there would only be exclamation marks.

GopalKotaFactory: What?

FlyingAarti: I'm at the BHU campus. At their computer centre!!

GopalKotaFactory: How come?

FlyingAarti: Raghav joined college. He brought me here. He said I can come and use the computer centre anytime.

GopalKotaFactory: Isn't it too late to be in his college? How will you get back?

FlyingAarti: I have dad's red-light car. Who will dare to mess with me?

GopalKotaFactory: How often do you visit Raghav?

I waited for her to type a message.

FlyingAarti: What sort of a question is that? Do you keep tabs on meeting friends?

GopalKotaFactory: Just a friend, right?

FlyingAarti: Yes, dear. You should become a detective, not an engineer.

GopalKotaFactory: Hmmm.

FlyingAarti: I only came to see his campus. So, what's up with you?

GopalKotaFactory: I completed one month in Kota.

FlyingAarti: At least you don't refer to it as a godforsaken place anymore!

GopalKotaFactory: True. I am quite busy though. Mugging away. We even had class tests.

FlyingAarti: You did okay?

GopalKotaFactory: In top fifty per cent. Not bad for such a competitive class.

FlyingAarti: I am sure you will crack JEE this time.

GopalKotaFactory: Who knows? If I do, will you go out with me?

FlyingAarti: HERE WE GO AGAIN!!!!

GopalKotaFactory: ?

FlyingAarti: I like us how we are. And how is it linked to JEE? You are my favourite!!!

GopalKotaFactory: Stop using so many exclamation marks.

FlyingAarti: Huh??!!!
GopalKotaFactory: Nothing. Anyway, I better go. Have to do my
daily worksheet.
FlyingAarti: Okay.

I expected her to ask me to chat for a few more minutes. Not just give me
a bland okay. She didn't even ask me if I had had my dinner ...

FlyingAarti: Did you eat dinner?
GopalKotaFactory: Not yet. Will do so when I get home.
FlyingAarti: Cool!

When girls are hiding something, they start speaking like boys and use
expressions like 'cool'.

GopalKotaFactory: How about you?
FlyingAarti: Raghav's treating me. Only at his canteen though.
Cheapo!
GopalKotaFactory: You still seem excited.

She did not respond. If someone stalls you on a chat, every minute seems
like an hour. She finally typed after five long minutes.

FlyingAarti: What?

I tried the waiting game on her. However, I could not last more than ten
seconds.

GopalKotaFactory: Nothing.
FlyingAarti: Okay, anyway, Raghav's here. He says hi. I have to
quickly eat and head back home. Chat later then. Xoxo ...

I didn't know what 'xoxo' implied. The x's were supposed to be hugs, and
the o's kisses. I don't think Aarti meant them.

She logged out. I had twenty minutes of Internet time left. I spent
them doing what most guys who came here did – surf the official IIT
website or watch porn. I guess these are the two things boys wanted most
in Kota. At least the coaching centres could help you get one of them.

9

On the eve of Aarti's birthday I had finished three months in Kota. For the first time I managed to reach the top twenty-five percentile in a class test. Balance-ji congratulated me. My chemistry score had improved by twenty points. Mr Pulley didn't like my average physics performance. Shishir sir, also known as Permutation guru, paused a few extra seconds by my seat as my maths score had improved by ten per cent.

I kept my answer-sheet in my bag as I sat for the physics class. I looked around the three-hundred-seat lecture room. Mr Pulley was speaking into a handheld mike, tapping it every time he felt the class was not paying enough attention.

I still had a long way to go. One needed to reach at least the top-five percentile in the Career Path class to feel confident about an IIT seat.

'An IIT seat is not a joke,' Mr Pulley said, even though nobody ever claimed it was.

Increasing your percentile in a hyper-competitive class is not easy. You have to live, breathe and sleep IIT.

The top twenty students in every class test received royal treatment. They were called Gems, a title still elusive to me. Gems stood for 'Group of Extra Meritorious Students'. Gems comprised of ultra-geeks who'd prefer solving physics problems to having sex, and for whom fun meant memorising the periodic table. Career Path handled Gems with care, as they had the potential to crack the top hundred ranks of JEE, and thus adorn future advertisements. Gems were treated preciously, similar to how one would imagine Lux soap officials treat their brand ambassador Katrina Kaif.

I had not come close to being one of the Gems. However, the top twenty-five percentile felt good. I wanted to share this with Aarti. Also, I had told her I'd be the first one to wish her on her birthday.

I reached the STD booth close to midnight. I picked up the phone at 11:58 p.m. and dialled her number. I got a busy signal. I tried again but couldn't get through. I made five attempts but the line was still engaged.

'Let other customers call,' the shopkeeper said.

Fortunately, only one other person stood in line – a student waiting to call his mother in Guwahati to wish her a happy birthday. I waited patiently as he ended his call at 12:05 a.m.

I rushed into the booth and called Aarti again. The line came busy. After several attempts the shopkeeper gave me looks of sympathy. He told me he had to shut his shop by 12:30 a.m. I tried calling many more times, at two-minute intervals, but to no avail.

I don't know why, but I decided to call Raghav's house. It being a Friday night I knew Raghav would be home for the weekend. I hesitated for a second before I dialled his number. Of course, if the phone rang so late the whole house would be startled. However, my suspicions were right. The line was busy.

I tried Raghav's and Aarti's numbers in quick succession. I could not get through to either.

My good wishes for Aarti vanished as my excitement gave way to anger.

Why did Raghav have to wish her at midnight? And do birthday wishes take so long?

The shopkeeper tapped my booth window. 'The police will harass me if I stay open any longer.'

'Do you know where I can find an STD booth open?' I said.

'Railway station,' the shopkeeper said. He switched off the lit sign.

No auto-rickshaw agreed to go to the railway station at a reasonable price at that hour. If I ran I could cover the five-kilometre distance in half an hour.

I reached platform 1 of Kota station at 1:00 a.m., panting after my five-kilometre jog. Even at this hour the station was bustling. A train arrived and the general-quota passengers ran for seats.

I found an STD booth and called Aarti. This time the phone rang. I took a deep breath. My temper was not something I was proud of. I wanted to keep it under check as the birthday girl picked up the phone.

'Hello?' DM Pradhan spoke instead.

'Hello, uncle? Uncle, Gopal,' I blurted out, even though I should have probably hung up. After so many attempts I *had* to talk to her.

'Oh, yes. Hold on,' he said and screamed for Aarti.

Aarti came close to the phone. I could hear her conversation with her father.

'How much will you talk on the phone? Your friends keep calling,' her father grumbled.

'It's my birthday, dad,' Aarti said and picked up the phone.

'Happy birthday, Aarti,' I said, trying to sound excited.

'Hey, Gopal! Thanks. That's so sweet of you. You stayed up so late to wish me?' she said.

I also ran five kilometres and will walk back five more, I wanted to say but didn't. 'I've been trying to reach you for an hour.'

'Really?' Aarti said.

'Yeah, the line was busy. Who were you talking to? I wanted to be the first,' I said.

'Oh, my cousins, you know in the US? I have my aunt there, no?'

Her voice sounded overtly casual. Aarti forgot I had known her for eight years. I could sense it when she lied.

'They spoke long-distance for an hour?'

'What one hour? I spoke to them for two minutes. Maybe I didn't place the phone back properly. Leave it, no. How are you? Wish you were here.'

'Do you?'

'Yeah. Of course! I miss you,' Aarti said, her tone so genuine that it was hard to believe she had lied to me ten seconds ago.

'If you had placed the phone incorrectly, who placed it back correctly now?'

'Gopal! Stop interrogating me. I hate this. It is my birthday.'

'And you lie on your birthday?'

'What?'

'Swear on our friendship that Raghav didn't call?' I said.

'What?' Aarti said, her voice loud. 'Swear? How old are we, ten?'

'He called, no? You were speaking to him. What's going on between you guys?'

'It's my birthday. Can you not make it so stressful?'

'You haven't answered my question.'

'It's late. Dad is hovering around. Chat tomorrow on the net? After my college?'

'I have classes,' I said.

'Sunday. Let's chat on Sunday, around noon, okay?'

'Aarti, just be honest with me. I value honesty a lot,' I said.

'Of course. Okay, bye now. Dad's giving me dirty looks. Honestly!'

'Bye,' I said.

I walked back, trying not to cry.

Wait till Sunday, I consoled myself.

◆

She never came online on Sunday. I spent two hours at the cyber café. Noon became one, and one became two. There's only so much porn one can watch. I downloaded enough x-rated clips to open a video library. I couldn't bear it anymore.

How hard was it to deliver on a simple promise? I had done nothing but wait for Sunday to talk things out with her. She had suggested the time, not I. I wanted to vent my anger, but had no outlet.

I kicked the CPU of the computer in frustration. The power went off.

'What are you doing?' The owner of the cyber café came running.

'Sorry, I have a temper problem. I am working on it,' I said and rushed out.

I went to the STD booth. I called her home. Her mother picked up.

'Good afternoon, aunty. Gopal here.'

'Hello, Gopal,' Aarti's mother said curtly. Her husband might be the DM, but she had more attitude than him.

'Aunty, is Aarti around?'

'She left early morning with Raghav for Kanpur.'

'Kanpur?' I said, shocked. She had gone three hundred kilometres away from Varanasi with Raghav.

'Yes, some festival at IIT Kanpur. Raghav is in the debating team. She's also participating. Singing, I think.'

'Okay,' I said, wondering what question to ask next to get more information.

'Anything important?' Aarti's mother said.

Hell, it is important, aunty. I want to know if your daughter is having a scene.

'Nothing urgent. They'll come back tonight, right? The roads are not safe,' I said.

'Of course. She's gone in the government car. With a security guard.'

I wanted to post my own security guards next to Aarti.

'Thanks, Aunty,' I said.

'Okay. You study. Then you can also be in a proper college and have fun like Raghav.'

'Yes, Aunty,' I said, reaffirming my commitment to join a proper college before I hung up.

I checked my wallet. I had only hundred bucks left of my self-assigned monthly allowance of a thousand bucks. The month of November still had ten days left. I scolded myself for spending too much on calls.

One moment I told myself not to chase her. *Let her call or mail back.* However, the next moment I could think of nothing but her. I had crazy mental conversations with myself.

She couldn't be dating him. She said she is not ready for a relationship. If she is, she will go out with me, Mr Optimist Gopal said.

However, Mr Pessimist Gopal did not buy it.

Okay, so Raghav has better looks. But Aarti is not so shallow. I have known her for a decade, Mr Optimist-me argued.

Raghav also has better future prospects, Mr Pessimist-me said.

But would she choose a guy just on the basis of his JEE rank? She is a girl, not a damn institute, said Mr Optimist-me.

She finds him funny, Mr Pessimist said.

She will even find jokers in the circus funny, Mr Optimist said.

My head hurt as the two morons inside would not stop arguing. Girls have no idea what effect their wavering has on boys. I had to talk to Aarti. I wanted to shake her and make her talk.

My temper flared again. I wanted to run to the Kota station and travel unreserved to Varanasi. I couldn't think about Balance-ji or my percentile or the stupid Career Path.

If Raghav did anything with Aarti, I would fucking kill him.

I pressed the doorbell six times when I reached home.

'Everything okay?' uncle said.

'I'm not going to fucking kill myself, okay?' Shouting helped release tension.

'What?' he said, shocked by my language.

'Sorry,' I said. You don't use f-words with your landlord.

I didn't sleep the whole night. I kicked myself for thinking about her so much.

She is a liar, ditcher and heartless person, I told myself fifty times.

She also happened to be someone I couldn't stop thinking about. Love, officially, is nothing but a bitch.

10

We had a surprise test in class the next day – which went badly. In the chemistry class Balance-ji scolded me as I could not answer even a simple question. I didn't give a fuck. I wanted to get hold of this girl.

I ran to a cyber café after class. She wasn't online. I did not know what to do. It would be way too desperate to call her again.

I had a horrible week at Career Path. My results slipped to the eightieth percentile. Four-fifths of the class had done better than me. Career Path had a software that picked out students with the maximum improvement or deterioration. I featured in the latter.

'This is not acceptable,' Shishir sir, Permutation guru and partner in Career Path, said.

'I'm sorry, sir,' I said.

'You are not in bad company, I hope.'

'I have no friends. There is no company,' I said truthfully.

'Get some then,' Shishir sir said. 'You need some friends in Kota to cope.'

I looked at Shishir sir. He seemed young and genuine. 'I know how hard it is. I am a Kota product myself.'

On Sunday I went to the cyber café again. As usual, no email. However, she came online in five minutes.

A part of me resisted. I initiated the chat anyway.

GopalKotaFactory: Hi.

She didn't respond for two minutes. I sent another hi.

FlyingAarti: Hi Gopal.

She had not called me Gopi. It did not seem normal.

> GopalKotaFactory: Are you upset?
> FlyingAarti: I'm Fine.

A girl's 'I'm Fine', especially with capital F, is like an 'icebergs ahead' sign for a ship.

> GopalKotaFactory: Can we chat?
> FlyingAarti: Only if you don't yell at me.
> GopalKotaFactory: I'm sorry I did that day.

I also wanted to add that she ditched me last Sunday on chat. I wanted to ask why she went to IIT Kanpur with Raghav. However, if I came on too strongly she would give me the silent treatment that could kill me. First and foremost, I had to get information out of her.

> GopalKotaFactory: You know my temper problem. I am working on it.
> FlyingAarti: It's fine. Apology accepted.

I found it strange that I ended up saying sorry when she owed *me* an apology. *Is it ever the girl's fault?* The good thing about chatting on the internet is that you can control your impulses. I took a couple of deep breaths and typed something neutral.

> GopalKotaFactory: So, what's up?

When in doubt, stick to open-ended questions.

> FlyingAarti: Not much. College is busy. Made some friends. Not many.
> GopalKotaFactory: Any special friends? ☺

I had placed a strategic smiley after the question. It hid my intense curiosity and anger.

> FlyingAarti: C'mon, Gopi.

There, my nickname was back. Her mood had lightened.

GopalKotaFactory: It's okay. Tell me. You won't tell me? Your best friend.
FlyingAarti: I don't know. You get so upset.

My heart started to beat fast. I typed one character at a time.

GopalKotaFactory: Tell, tell. Let's hear it ☺☺☺

I overdid the smileys just to make her feel comfortable enough to talk.

FlyingAarti: Well, there is someone special.

A rusted iron knife jabbed my chest. I fought the pain and typed.

GopalKotaFactory: ☺
FlyingAarti: You know him.
GopalKotaFactory: ☺
FlyingAarti: Very well, in fact.
GopalKotaFactory: Say who ☺
FlyingAarti: Mr BHU, who else?

The knife was now slicing through my heart. I clenched my teeth hard.

GopalKotaFactory: Really? ☺

Keep breathing, keep up the smileys.

FlyingAarti: Yeah. He's mad. Mad stupid Raghav!!! He trapped me.
GopalKotaFactory: So … you guys close?
FlyingAarti: Kinda.

I couldn't keep up the smileys anymore.

GopalKotaFactory: Kinda?
FlyingAarti: Shush. Don't ask all that.
GopalKotaFactory: You've done it?
FlyingAarti: How cheap, Gopi. No, not yet.
GopalKotaFactory: Meaning?
FlyingAarti: Meaning almost … Oh, don't embarrass me.

GopalKotaFactory: What the fuck?

FlyingAarti: Excuse me???

GopalKotaFactory: I thought you are not interested in that stuff.

FlyingAarti: What stuff?

GopalKotaFactory: You said friendship is all you wanted. With me. With anyone.

FlyingAarti: Did I? I don't know. It just kinda happened.

GopalKotaFactory: How did it kinda happen? You just kinda removed your clothes?

My temper had returned and taken over my remote control.

FlyingAarti: Watch your language.

GopalKotaFactory: Why? You someone pure or what? Behaving like a slut.

She didn't respond. I continued.

GopalKotaFactory: Can you tell me why? Because he has a JEE rank?

FlyingAarti: Shut up, Gopal. It's a very special bond between him and me.

GopalKotaFactory: Really? What makes it special? Did you give him a blow job? Where? In his hostel or in Kanpur?

She didn't respond. I realised I had said too much. However, you cannot undo a line sent on chat. And I did not want to fucking apologise again.

I kept waiting for an answer.

After three minutes a message flashed on my screen: FlyingAarti is offline.

I refreshed my screen. I had another notification: FlyingAarti is no longer a contact.

She had removed me from her list.

'You need to extend your time?' the café owner asked me.

'No, that won't be necessary, not for a long time,' I said.

◆

The day Aarti cut off contact with me was the day I stopped doing my daily practice sheets. I no longer went to the cyber café either. Instead, I hung out every night at the roadside Chaman chai shop near my house. Students, teacups in one hand and worksheets in another, occupied the one dozen wooden benches. I didn't bring any reading material to the shop. I sat there, killing hours, watching the crowd and nursing cups of tea.

One day I ran out of money to pay for my order.

'I am sorry,' I said to Chaman, the shop-owner, 'I will bring the cash tomorrow.'

Someone I didn't know stepped forward and handed the shopkeeper ten bucks. 'Chill,' the newcomer said to me.

'Oh, thanks,' I said.

'Bansal?' he said, as he collected the change.

'Career Path,' I said. 'I'll pay you tomorrow. I forgot my wallet at home.'

'Relax,' he said and extended his hand. 'I'm Prateek. From Raipur.'

His stubbled face made him look more like an artist than an IIT aspirant. 'Repeater?' Prateek said.

I nodded.

'Quitter,' he said.

'What's that?'

'Tried Kota. Didn't work. Still hanging around here to get some peace.'

I laughed. 'I had AIEEE 50,000. I think I may have a chance if I try again.'

'Do you want to?' Prateek said.

I kept quiet. We sat down on the wooden stools outside the shop.

'You look like you are on the verge of becoming a quitter,' he said.

'I'm fine. A little low. The next installment at Career Path is due. My father doesn't have much cash on him.'

'Go back,' Prateek said. He lit a cigarette and offered it to me. I declined.

'I can't. All his hopes are pinned on me. He'll borrow money and send it.'

Prateek dropped his head back and blew smoke towards the sky.

'I had reached the top twenty-five percentile,' I said, to justify my existence in this place.

'*Had* reached? You are still doing the course, right?'

'I slipped in the past few weeks.'

'Why?'

'Nothing.' I sipped my tea.

Prateek drained his cup and ordered another. 'Is it a girl?' he said.

'I don't even know you. I'll pay you your ten bucks. Stop probing,' I said.

'Chill, man, I am only making conversation.' He laughed and patted my shoulder.

I kept quiet. Images of countless boat rides with Aarti passed through my mind. How I rowed with my bare hands. How she used to massage my palms afterwards … I flexed my hands, remembering.

I hate her. But I miss her.

Prateek smoked two cigarettes without uttering a word.

'It *is* a girl,' I said grudgingly.

'Left you?' He grinned.

'Never came to me.'

'Happens. We are losers. We don't get things easily. Marks, ranks, girls – nothing is easy for us.'

'Yeah, everyone takes us for a ride. From Kota classes to the bitch back home,' I said.

'Bitch, eh? You seem like a fun guy.' Prateek high-fived me.

'I better go home.'

'We don't have a home. We are like people stuck in outer space. No home, no school, no college, no job. Only Kota.' He winked at me.

Prateek studied at Resonance, as a second-time repeater. He had become a quitter the first time, and even now he had almost given up. We became friends, meeting at Chaman's every night.

One day the tea didn't seem enough. Mr Pulley had thrown me out of his class.

'So what if he asked you to leave. It's not like a real college,' Prateek said.

'I fell asleep. Such a boring lecture,' I said.

He laughed.

'I gave them their bloody second installment today. Still they do this to me,' I said.

'Chill, we need more than tea today.' Prateek stood up. We walked out of the teashop.

'Where are we going?'

'My place,' he said.

◆

Prateek's room didn't look like that of a hardworking repeater in Kota. Beer bottles outnumbered books, cigarette butts exceeded pens. The walls had posters of scantily-clad women instead of Resonance circulars.

'You've really settled down here,' I said.

'I would if I could. My parents won't fund me here after this year,' he said. He took out a bottle of Old Monk from his cupboard. He poured the rum neat for me. It tasted terrible.

'What happens after this year?' I said.

'Nothing. Reality check for my parents. Both of them are teachers. Hopefully, the passing of two years and half their life savings will make them realise that their son can't crack any entrance exam.'

'You can if you work hard,' I said and kept my drink aside.

'No, I can't,' Prateek said, his voice firm. 'The selection rate is less than three per cent. Most of us can't crack these tests, basic probability. But who will drill it into our parents' heads? Anyway, finish your drink in one shot.'

The rum tasted like some hot and bitter medicine. I forced it down my throat. I had to get over Aarti. Sometimes the only way to get rid of an unpleasant feeling is to replace it with another unpleasant feeling.

I asked for another drink, and then another. Soon, Aarti didn't seem so painful.

'You loved her?' Prateek said.

'What is love?'

'Love is what your parents give you if you clear the IIT exam,' he said.

We high-fived. 'I did I guess,' I said after a while.

'How long?' He lit a cigarette.

'Eight years.'

'Holy shit! Did you guys meet at birth in the hospital?' Prateek said.

I shook my head. Over the next three hours I told him my entire one-sided love story. From the day I had stolen her tiffin to the day she massaged my hand for the last time, and until she finally logged out and removed me as a contact.

Prateek listened in silence.

'So, what do you think? Say something,' I said. To my surprise he was still awake.

'You can talk a lot, man!' He poured out the remaining rum for me.

'Sorry,' I said sheepishly. 'Did I bore you?'

'It's okay. Try to forget her. Wish her happiness with her JEE boy.'

'I *can't* forget her. I haven't studied a day since she stopped talking to me.'

'Don't worry. You will get another girl. Everybody gets a girl. Even the last rankers. How do you think India has such a large population?'

'I'll never marry,' I said.

'Then what? Marry your hand?' Prateek burst out laughing.

Men are useless. They hide their inability to discuss relationships behind lame jokes.

'I better go,' I said.

He didn't stop me. He lay on the floor, too tired to go to his bed. 'Don't lose your grip, man,' he shouted after me as I left his house.

Grip. Yes, that's the word. The trick to these entrance exams is that you have to get a grip on them. You need a game plan. What are your strong subjects, which are your weak ones? Are you working with the teachers on the weak areas? Are you tracking your progress on the mock-tests? Are you thinking about nothing but the exam all day? Do you eat your meals and take your bath as fast as possible so that you have more time to study? If your answer is 'yes' to all these questions, that's when you can say you have a grip. That's the only way to have a shot at a seat. Of course, you could be one of those naturally talented students who never have to study much. But most of us are not, courtesy our parents' mediocre genes. Ironically, these same parents who donated these dumb genes take the longest time to understand that their child is not Einstein's clone.

I had lost my grip. At least for the three months after Aarti cut me off. The spaced-out Prateek became my new and only friend. I attended classes, though my hangover made it difficult to understand Benzene structures or radioactive isotopes. I tried to do my practice sheets, but could not focus. The teachers started to see me as a quitter and stopped paying attention to me. I became a sucker-student, one of the no-hope kids who are only kept around because they paid the coaching centre.

I had another problem to deal with. My expenses had increased, for I had to pay for rum. Prateek treated me a few times, but after a while he asked me to pay my share. I knew Baba had borrowed to pay the last installment and had no money. However, I had little choice.

I dialled home from the STD booth one night.

'Sorry, I didn't call last week, Baba,' I said.

'It's okay. You are studying hard,' Baba said, his voice very weak.

'Baba, there is a little problem,' I said.

'What?'

'I need some new books. They are supposed to be the best for maths.'

'Can't you borrow them from someone?'

'Hard to,' I said. 'Everyone wants to keep theirs.'

Baba paused. I kept quiet, trying to recuperate from uttering so many lies at once.

'How much?'

'Two thousand. They are imported.'

'Okay.'

'Do you have the money, Baba?'

'Can I send it in a week?'

'How much loan did you take, Baba?' I said.

'Fifty thousand,' he said. 'I sent you thirty, but needed some extra to repair the roof.'

'What about your medical bills?'

'I owe twenty thousand to the hospital.'

'You will anyway borrow more, right?'

'Probably.'

'Send whatever you can. I will go now, it is an expensive call,' I said, wanting to end the ordeal as soon as possible.

'You will get selected, no, Gopi?'

'Yes, yes, I will.'

I kept the receiver down. I felt terrible. I resolved to study harder. *I will get back into the twenty-five percentile, and then the top five percentile.* I decided to study the entire night. However, I had a craving for rum first. My resolve weakened. I went to Prateek's house and spent most of the night there. Nothing could motivate me to study. Then came my birthday.

11

My birthday came five months after my arrival in Kota. I did not think of it as a special day and planned to attend classes as usual. However, late night on my birthday eve, Mr Soni knocked on my door.

'Someone on the phone, asking for you.' He sounded drowsy.

'Who is it?' I said, surprised. 'Baba?'

'A girl,' Mr Soni said. 'And happy birthday, by the way.'

'Thanks,' I said and picked up the phone. Who could it be? I thought. A teacher from Career Path? Did I do something wrong?

'Happy birthday, Gopal.' Aarti's wonderful words fell like raindrops on a hot Kota afternoon. Emotions surged within me. I felt overwhelmed.

'Aarti?' I said. Uncontrollable tears ran down my cheeks.

'So you still recognise my voice? I thought I'll play a guessing game. Can we talk? Or am I disturbing you?'

I had played out this scene – of speaking with Aarti – a million times in my head. I thought I would be curt with her if she ever called me. Like I didn't care who she was. Or I would pretend to be busy. Of course, all those mental dress rehearsals flew out of the window. 'No, no, Aarti,' I said. 'You are not disturbing me at all.'

I had not felt better in months. Why did birthdays come only once a year?

'So, doing anything special on your birthday?' Aarti said.

'Not really. Will go out for dinner with a friend.'

'Friend? Date, eh?' she said in her trademark naughty voice.

'Prateek. It's a guy,' I said.

'Oh, okay,' Aarti said. 'That's nice.'

'I am sorry about the chat the last time.'

She kept quiet.

'I shouldn't have said those things. But you cut off contact …'

'Nobody has ever spoken to me like that.'

'I'm sorry.'

'It's okay. Anyway, it's your birthday. I don't want you to feel horrible.'

'How's Raghav?' I said, unable to control myself. More than anything, I wanted to know their relationship status.

'He's great. Finished his first semester at BHU.'

'Must be mugging away.'

'No, not that much. In fact, he edits the campus magazine now. Keeps talking about that.'

'That's great,' I said. She still hadn't told me about both of them. I did not want to pry too much like the last time.

'He's a great guy, Gopal. You should see him, how much he wants to do for the world.'

I did not mind Raghav doing whatever he wanted for the world, as long as he left one person in the world alone. 'I never said he is a bad person,' I said.

'Good. And I am happy with him. If you care for me as a friend, you should accept that.'

'Are we friends?' I asked.

'I wouldn't be talking to you otherwise, right?' she said.

I wanted to tell her she hadn't spoken to me for three months. However, girls get extremely upset if you give them evidence contrary to their belief.

'Yes, I guess,' I said, and paused before I spoke again. 'So we can talk?'

'Yeah, as long as you don't make me feel uncomfortable. And …'

'And what?'

'Accept Raghav and me.'

'Do I have a choice?' I said.

'That's the point. I want you to accept it happily. I will be happy for you if you find the girl of your dreams.'

So that's it, Raghav is the man of her dreams.

The rusty knife returned to my gut. I wondered what to say. 'I do accept,' I said after a while. More than anything, I didn't want to lose touch with her again. My life in Kota had become hell after she disappeared.

'Cool. Because I miss you,' she said, 'as a friend.' She emphasised the last qualifier.

Girls always leave subtle phrases as qualifiers, so you can't put them in a spot later. Like if I told her, 'but you said you missed me', she would jump and say, 'but I also said as a friend!' as if we were in a court of justice. It is so hard to figure girls out. I could bet even the Career Path Gems could not do it.

'You there?' she said, interrupting my chain of thought.

'Yeah,' I said.

'Okay, I have to go. Happy birthday again!'

'Thank you, bye. Will speak to you or chat …' I said and paused.

'I will add you back on chat,' she laughed.

'Sorry again,' I said.

'Don't be stupid, birthday boy. If you were here I'd pull your cheeks,' she said.

That's it. She had done it again – confuse me with a throwaway affectionate line. Did she like me or not? Oh well, Raghav is her man, I reminded myself.

'Chat soon,' she said and hung up.

I felt so good that even the physics solutions guide on my desk looked kissable. I wanted to study. I wanted to live.

◆

Career Path would never know why I made it to the most-improved list once again. Aarti had me go back to studies in a big way. Maybe it was her simple 'how was your day?' in our chats. I also liked to be accountable to her, and report back to her on how productive the day had been. I told her about the equations taught in class, the feedback the teacher gave me (especially the praise), and how I planned to study late into the night.

Deep down, I still wanted to impress her. I never gave up the idea of her having a change of heart. Mr Optimist-me never gave up.

Maybe she will tell me on chat today how things aren't working out with Raghav, or how she connects with me so much better than with her boyfriend.

However, she never said such things, even though sometimes she came close. Once she told me Raghav was a stubborn pest. She said it after Raghav had ditched her for a movie date twice, because of a publication deadline for his college magazine. I couldn't imagine any man skipping a chance to be with Aarti. I could skip my Career Path mock-test, let alone a stupid deadline for a stupid magazine. However, I didn't tell her this. I knew my place; I, who could never compare myself to Raghav.

I chatted with her one evening and talked about my class performance.

GopalKotaFactory: So I reached 20th.

FlyingAarti: 20th what?

GopalKotaFactory: My percentile in class. This means 80% of the class did worse than me. My best performance ever!

FlyingAarti: Wow! Cool!

GopalKotaFactory: Long way to go still.

FlyingAarti: You will get there, there's time.

GopalKotaFactory: Hardly. JEE and AIEEE are less than two months away.

FlyingAarti: You'll be fine.

GopalKotaFactory: I hope so. I had slipped in the middle of the course.

FlyingAarti: How come?

GopalKotaFactory: No reason as such. Lack of focus. Anyway, can't wait to get out of Kota.

FlyingAarti: I know … it's been so long since I saw you. Miss you.

GopalKotaFactory: You do?

FlyingAarti: Of course. See, Raghav has ditched me for *Chak de India* all week. If you were here, I could have seen it with you.

GopalKotaFactory: You will come for movies with me?

She didn't respond. I waited for five minutes.

GopalKotaFactory: ??
GopalKotaFactory: You there?

She didn't answer. I wondered if I had asked something inappropriate. My heart began to beat fast. I wrote after five minutes.

GopalKotaFactory: Hey, you upset? I am sorry if I said something wrong … You don't have to …
FlyingAarti: Hey, sorry …
FlyingAarti: Boyfriend called to apologise. He's finished his work. We are going for the movie!!
GopalKotaFactory: Oh, that's great.
FlyingAarti: What were you saying … wait. Of course, we can see movies when you are back. Why are you sorry?
GopalKotaFactory: Nothing, I just felt ...
FlyingAarti: Relax. Okay, I have to go get ready.
GopalKotaFactory: Fine.
FlyingAarti: I better look smashing to get his attention. Else, he'll be proof-reading his articles on our date.
GopalKotaFactory: Okay. I better study too.
FlyingAarti: Two more months. Then we can all have lots of fun.
GopalKotaFactory: Yeah. Thanks.
FlyingAarti: Bye. Xoxoxo.

And FlyingAarti logged out.

I walked back home as slowly as possible. After all, I had nothing to look forward to but books. I tried not to imagine both of them in a theatre, hand in hand. I debated if I should be in touch with Aarti at all. However, I remembered the abyss I had fallen into the last time. A few jabs at the heart are better than a complete nervous breakdown.

◆

The Career Path instructors told us to go to sleep at 8:00 p.m. the night before the JEE exam. In our last class we had motivational speeches. Balance-ji gave examples of people ranging from Mahatma Gandhi to Muhammad Ali, people who never gave up and won against all odds. I pumped my fist like Ali, and charged out of the institute like Gandhi, to crack one of the toughest entrance exams in the world. On my way home, I called the two people who I thought may want to wish me luck.

'My best wishes are always with you, my Gopi. Tomorrow is your chance to make your family name famous,' Baba said.

'Thank you, Baba,' I said, keeping the call short.

I dialled Aarti's number next.

'Hello?' a male voice surprised me. It did not sound like her father.

'May I speak to Aarti, please,' I said.

'Sure, who's this?' the voice asked.

'Gopal.'

'Hi, Gopal. It's Raghav,' the voice said.

I almost dropped the phone. 'Raghav?' I said. I had not spoken to him in almost a year.

'You don't keep in touch, Gopal. Though it's my fault too,' Raghav said.

I didn't know how much Raghav knew about Aarti and me, in particular about our showdown and the subsequent resumption of communication. I kept to a neutral tone and topic. 'How's BHU?'

'So far so good. It's like any other college. Just better facilities. How are you?'

'JEE tomorrow. You can guess.'

'I know. My college is a centre too. You didn't come here to take it?'

'I have classes until the last minute. Plus, my AIEEE final refresher starts tomorrow.'

'Glad I am done with all that, man,' Raghav laughed. Not unkindly, but I winced. When someone refers to your weak spot even indirectly, it hurts.

'Me too, hopefully soon,' I said.

'You'll crack it. Aarti tells me you are doing well.'

So they do talk about me, I thought. 'Who knows? Depends on the paper. So much of it is luck.'

'True,' Raghav said.

We had an awkward nothing-to-say moment. It was his fault, as he forgot I had called for Aarti.

'So, is Aarti around?'

'Oh yes, hold on a second.'

I heard her giggle. I wondered if Raghav had joked about me.

'Hey! Best of luck, JEE boy,' Aarti said.

'Thank you. Need it.'

'I went to the Vishwanath Temple,' Aarti said, 'to pray for you.'

'You did?'

'Yes. I dragged this lazy Raghav to take a bath and come along too,' she said and laughed again. 'We just came back ... Hey, Raghav stop ... stop ... Hold on, Gopal.'

I paid long-distance to hear their private banter. I heard Aarti tell Raghav to stop imitating her. But Raghav didn't seem to have anything better to do.

'Hello?' I said after sixty seconds.

'Hey, sorry,' Aarti said as she composed herself. 'Okay, now I have managed to turn away from him. Gopi, you will go into the exam centre super-confident, promise?'

'Yes,' I said, like an obedient child. I liked her maternal instinct with me.

'I want you to feel that you can get whatever you want in life. Because I know you can,' Aarti said.

I cannot get you, I wanted to tell her. Still, I appreciated her boosting me up for the big test. 'AIEEE ends, and I am on a train in the next four hours.'

'Yes, we are waiting too. Come back soon. When the results come out, we will celebrate your victory together.'

'Only if I get in,' I said.

'Do not think like that. Believe you have already made it,' Aarti said, 'for my sake.'

Her last phrase meant the world to me. Yes, I wanted to make it – for her sake.

◆

The city had changed, but the JEE exam centre in Kota gave me the same feeling as last year. Parents came by taxi-loads and auto-loads. Some rich kids came in air-conditioned cars. Mothers performed little pujas and rituals for their children, ironically, right before they went in to show their mastery of science. I did not have anyone from my family fussing over me. I didn't care. Tilaks on the heads and curd in the mouth didn't matter. Once you went inside, you had to beat the hell out of the ninety-nine per cent of the half a million students sitting for the exam across the country.

I had a good start. I solved the first few problems with relative ease. The middle became tough. Some questions belonged to chapters taught during my drunken and depressed phase in Kota. I got stuck on one problem. I thought I could solve it, became possessed, and wasted ten minutes. I suppose I have a problem letting go. Ten minutes are crucial in the JEE. I mentally kicked myself and moved on to the next problem. I went on solving as many problems as I could before the dreaded bell rang.

The examiner snatched my paper away even as I begged him to let me write one last answer. Leaving that one question could cost me five hundred ranks, but … the JEE had ended!

'How did it go?' Baba asked me in the evening.

I tried to be as honest as possible. 'Better than last time.'

'Good. But don't relax. Give your full attention to AIEEE.'

'I will,' I said.

Aarti and I chatted briefly. She, predictably, reassured me about things. She had term break in her college. Her parents had planned a family trip to the USA, to visit her aunt.

'Even if I cannot call or chat, I will email you from Chicago,' she said. She did send me a couple of mails wishing me luck for the AIEEE exam.

Aarti also wrote to me that Raghav had his vacation, and was interning at a local newspaper.

'So Raghav's dad is not too happy about his engineer-to-be son at the newspaper. I say what is wrong with it?' Aarti wrote in one of her emails.

As people took international holidays and indulged their passions, I took the AIEEE. It went off smoothly, much better than the previous time. However, it is a speed-based test. You can't really tell if you did well as compared to others. One is lucky to be able to attempt seventy per cent of the questions. I felt I had a much better shot than last time. In any case, I submitted my answer-sheet and ran home to pack. I had a train to catch. I had served my Kota sentence.

Prateek came to drop me at the station. He helped me place my heavy bags in the compartment.

'When are you going back to Raipur?' I said.

'Whenever they come fetch me,' Prateek said cheekily and waved goodbye.

Varanasi

12

Only the sights and smells of Varanasi came to receive me at the station. I hadn't told anyone about my arrival, hadn't wanted Baba to waste money on an auto-rickshaw to the station. He'd told me that the loans and interest we owed totalled one and a half lakhs. Loan sharks continued to charge interest at three per cent a month.

'You join a good college, and the State Bank of India will give us a cheaper loan,' Baba had told me.

Even the filthy and crowded streets of Gadholia seemed beautiful to me. No place like your hometown. More than anything, I wanted to meet Aarti. Every inch of Varanasi reminded me of her. People come to my city to feel the presence of god, but I could feel her presence everywhere. However, I had to go to Baba first.

I rang the doorbell at home.

'Gopal!' Baba exclaimed, hugging me with his weak arms.

'I missed Varanasi, Baba. I missed home. I missed you.'

The house appeared messier than before. I suppose Baba could only clean it so much. I picked up a broom to sweep the floor.

'Stop it, you have come after a year. What are you doing?' Baba snatched the broom from me.

We ate runny yellow dal and dry chapatis for lunch. Home-cooked food felt delicious. My father had not spoken to anyone in a long time, so he talked with his mouth full.

'The case is going nowhere. Ghanshyam won't even show up for the hearing. I think he feels I will die soon. It will be easier to resolve afterwards, anyway,' he said.

'What are you talking about, Baba?'

'He's right. How much can my lungs take?' He had a coughing fit even as he said this.

'Nothing will happen to you. Let me speak to the lawyer.'

'No use. I have no money to pay him. He doesn't take my calls anymore. Forget about all this. When is your entrance result?'

'In one month,' I said absent-mindedly, trying to decide if I should call Aarti first or wash my hands.

I dialled her number with dal-smeared fingers.

'Hello?' she said.

'Boat ride this evening, madam?' I said.

'Gopal! You are back? When did you come?'

'An hour ago. When do we meet?' I said. 'This evening at the ghats?'

'Yes, sure, oh wait. No, I have to go to Raghav's college. You are welcome to come along.'

'No, thanks.'

'Why not? He is your friend too.'

'I want to catch up with you first.'

'We will catch up on the way. I'll send dad's car. Come, okay?'

I had little choice. I didn't want to wait another day to see her.

'Raghav won't mind?'

'He will be thrilled. It's his big event.'

'Event?'

'I will tell you when we meet. Wow, almost a year, right?'

'Three hundred and five days,' I said.

'Someone's returned a geek. See you.'

✦

There's a sense of power when you sit in a white government Ambassador car with a red light on top. Traffic eases, policemen salute you for no reason, and you start to wonder if civil services are where you should be.

The car took me to the DM's bungalow. Located in the posh Cantonment area, the two-acre property had a serpentine driveway.

'Tell Aarti madam I am waiting in the car,' I told the driver.

I did not want to discuss Kota and the upcoming entrance exam results with her parents.

Her pink salwar-kameez became visible at a distance. As she came closer, I saw her face – no make-up apart from the lip-gloss. I had not seen anything more beautiful in three hundred and five days. I controlled my excitement as she opened the car door.

'Hi, Aarti,' I said.

'Why so formal? Come here,' Aarti said and hugged me. Her sequined dupatta poked me in the chest while her scent went to my head. 'Raghav's college,' she said to the driver, and he understood.

'So, how's life? Aren't you glad to be back?' she said.

'It's my happiest day ever. I hope I never leave Varanasi again,' I said fervently.

'Unless it is for IIT,' she said and winked at me.

I couldn't respond.

'What? You will leave for an IIT, right?'

I collected myself. 'It's not like I have anything in hand. Anyway, what's Raghav's event?'

'He's revamped the college magazine. Today is the launch of the new issue.'

'Is he even doing his BTech? I only hear about his magazine.'

Aarti laughed. God, I had missed that laugh. I wanted to record it and play it on a loop.

'He is,' she said and grinned again. 'Though I also call him the fake engineer.'

'How did his newspaper internship go?'

'Not bad. They didn't let him write much though. They found his articles …' she searched for the right words, 'too radical and different.'

We drove into the sprawling BHU campus. Manicured lawns and well-kept buildings made it look like another country compared to the rest of Varanasi.

'G-14 hall,' Aarti instructed her driver.

We entered the five-hundred-seater auditorium, packed to capacity. A huge banner of the new magazine cover flapped across the stage.

Raghav had changed everything; layout, look, content and even the title. The cover read *BHUkamp*, or earthquake. I noticed the smart utilisation of the university acronym. The magazine's tagline said: 'Shake the world'.

Aarti and I sat in the second row. The lights dimmed and music filled the hall. The crowd roared in anticipation.

'Raghav's backstage,' Aarti told me. 'Too many loose threads to tie up. He'll meet us later.'

A group of ten students took the stage. They were covered head to toe in black tights with skeletons painted on them. Ultra-violet lights came on and the skeletons glowed.

Michael Jackson's *Man in the Mirror* filled the auditorium.

I'm gonna make a change
For once in my life

The crowd roared in excitement as the skeletons performed an acrobatic dance. The song continued.

If you wanna make the world a better place
Take a look at yourself and then make a change

'Is this a magazine launch or a dance show?' I sniggered.

'Entertain them first, grab their attention and then say what you want to say,' Aarti said.

'Huh?' I looked at her. Her face was bathed in the ultra-violet light.

'That's what Raghav says – entertain and change.'

I shrugged my shoulders. I turned around to look at the crowd. I wondered how many of them had spent time in Kota. Statistically speaking, a third of them had come from the city I'd just left behind.

I couldn't help thinking: *of all these seats in the hall, could I not get just one?*

The skeletons finished their act. The crowd broke into applause. A tall man in a black suit came on stage. 'Good evening, BHU,' his familiar voice filled the hall.

'It's Raghav,' I said, stunned by the transformation. I had never seen him in a suit. He looked like a rockstar. His toned body meant he made good use of the college sports facilities. In comparison, I felt fat and old after a year in Kota.

Raghav began his speech.

'This is not an ordinary college. You are not ordinary students. We cannot have an ordinary magazine. Ladies and gentlemen, I present *BHUkamp!*'

The spotlight fell on the magazine cover. The crowd cheered. Aarti clapped loudly, her eyes fixed unblinkingly on the stage.

'The world has changed. Our college, our city, our country need to change too,' Raghav continued. 'Who is going to change them? We are. It starts here. We will shake the world.'

The crowd cheered again, more at the enthusiasm in Raghav's voice than his words.

Raghav's editorial team of students started to chant 'Bhukamp, Bhukamp' on the stage. The crowd picked up the chant.

'We will print what nobody has the guts to print. Issues that affect us. No bullshit,' Raghav said.

The editorial team stepped off the stage and started distributing copies of the magazine.

Raghav continued his speech. 'Our first cover story is about the state of our hostel kitchens. Our secret team went and took pictures. Have a look at how your food is prepared.'

I flipped the pages of *BHUkamp*. There were pictures of cockroaches on the kitchen floor, flies feasting on mithai and mess workers kneading dough with their feet. A collective wave of disgust ran through the crowd.

'Eww,' Aarti said as she saw the pictures. 'I am never eating in BHU again.'

'*BHUkamp* will change our college for the better. These pictures have been sent to the director,' Raghav said. 'But don't think *BHUkamp* is only serious stuff. We have loads of jokes, stories and poetry. We even have tips from dating to making of resumes. Happy reading. Long live BHU!'

The crowd's applause continued for a minute after he left the stage.

◆

Raghav pushed a stainless steel plate with two slices of bread towards Aarti. 'Butter toast. It is clean, I promise,' he said to her.

We had come to the BHU college canteen post-event. Aarti held the sandwich gingerly.

'Canteen is fine. It's the hostel kitchens that had a problem,' Raghav said. 'And they will clean it up after the issue. Eat, Gopal.'

I had ordered a plain paratha. I nibbled at it. Raghav picked up Aarti's sandwich and fed her. She smiled. I burned.

'What did you think of Kota?' Raghav asked me. 'We have tons of people from there.'

'If I get into a good college, Kota is great. If not, the worst place in the world.'

'You will be fine. You almost made it last year.' Raghav tore his masala dosa with his right hand. In his left hand was a copy of *BHUkamp*.

'You've changed, Raghav,' I said.

'How?' He looked up.

'This magazine and stuff. Why?'

'Why? I like it, that's why,' he said.

Aarti didn't speak. She merely watched us talk. I wondered what went through her head. *Did she compare us? Well, I did not match up to Raghav. Except in the amount I loved her. No man could love her like I did.*

'You don't come to a professional engineering college to edit magazines. People work their ass off here to get a good job,' I said.

'That's such a narrow-minded view. And what about the things around us? The food being cooked in an unhygienic manner. Labs with outdated machines. Look at our city. Why is Varanasi so dirty? Who is going to clean our rivers?' Raghav's black eyes were feverish.

'Not us,' I retorted. 'Sorting out our own life is hard enough.'

Raghav picked up his spoon and pointed it at me. 'That's the attitude,' he said, 'that I'm here to change.'

'Oh, fuck off,' I said. 'Nobody can change anything. Hostel workers are not going to cook like your mother. And Varanasi has been the world's dumping ground for thousands of years. Everyone comes here to dump their sins. Does anyone give a fuck about us residents, the people who deal with all the crap left behind?'

'Boys, can we not be so serious? I'm bored,' said Aarti.

'I am just …' I said.

'He won't listen. He is Mr Stubborn,' Aarti said and tweaked Raghav's nose. A shiver ran through me.

Raghav extended his hand and Aarti held it. She stood up and went to sit on his lap.

Raghav became self-conscious as heads turned towards us. Engineering colleges don't witness public displays of affection. People in love sometimes don't realise how stupid they look to the world.

'Stop it, Aarti,' Raghav said, shifting her off his lap. 'What are you doing?'

Pouting, she went back to her seat. 'Mr Editor, don't edit me out of your life, okay?' she said.

I felt like a voyeur sitting there. This was not how I wanted to meet Aarti. I wanted to run away. 'Should we leave?' I said to Aarti.

'Sure, I have to be home before ten.'

We finished our dinner and Raghav settled the bill.

'How's Baba?' Raghav asked me.

'Sick,' I said. 'Worse since I left. I suspect he's hiding something.'

'What?' Aarti said.

'He needs an operation, but will not admit it. He's trying to avoid more expense.'

'That's ridiculous,' Raghav said.

'Yes, we had an offer to sell the disputed land years ago. Even at the throwaway price we would have covered expenses.'

'It's your land. Why should you sell it cheap?' Raghav said.

'Baba will be happy to hear you,' I said.

The driver started the car as he saw us approach. The headlights lit up the parking lot.

'Get into the car, Gopal. I'll be back in a second,' Aarti said.

I waited in the car. Though I vowed not to look out, I couldn't help but take a peek. Through the tinted glass I saw both of them walk behind a tree. They embraced. Raghav lowered his head as he brought his face close to hers. I thought I would vomit.

She was back in five minutes. 'Did I take too long?' she asked gaily.

I kept quiet. I didn't make eye contact. She signalled the driver to leave.

'Nice evening, no?' Aarti said.

I nodded.

'Isn't the campus beautiful?' she said as we left the BHU gates.

We sat in silence. The car stereo played music. A Kailash Kher song about a bird with broken wings that would never fly again played in the car. The song talked about dreams being broken to pieces, and yet urged the listener to smile in god's name.

I glanced at her face sideways a couple of times. Her lip-gloss had vanished. Despite my best efforts not to, I couldn't but imagine them in more intimate situations.

'You okay?' Aarti said.

'Huh? Yeah, why?' I said.

'Why so quiet?'

'Thinking about Baba.'

She gave me an understanding nod. But she could never understand that losers, even if they do not have a brain, have a heart.

13

Weeks passed, and the day of the results came closer. Baba seemed even more anxious than me. One night when I went to give him his medicines, he asked, 'When are the results?'

'Next week,' I said.

'IIT?'

'A week after that,' I said.

'If IIT happens it will be amazing, no?' Baba said, his eyes bright.

I covered him with a blanket. 'Baba, did the doctor say you need an operation?'

'Doctors want more business these days, what else?' he said.

'Should we ask Ghanshyam taya-ji to give us whatever he wants for the land?' I said.

'No use. He won't listen. Anyway, what will I do with an operation at this age?

'You never listen, Baba.' I shook my head and switched off the light.

◆

'It isn't the end of the world, Gopal. It isn't.' She reached out for my hand. 'Say something.'

Aarti had invited me home on the day of the AIEEE results. She had an Internet connection and, despite my insisting otherwise, didn't want me to see the results all on my own.

I remember everything about that moment. The red and black embroidered tablecloth on the computer table, the noisy fan above, the various government trophies that belonged to her father, the black colour of the laptop, and the screen that showed my rank.

'44,342,' it said irrevocably next to my roll number.

After one whole year of cramming courses that I hated, staying in a dusty city all alone, and putting my father irretrievably in debt, I had only reconfirmed – *I am a failure*.

I didn't react. I didn't cry, I didn't feel anger, fear, frustration, anything. I remember Aarti hovering around, talking to me. However, I couldn't really comprehend her words.

I stood up like a zombie.

'Are you okay?' Aarti shook me. She, me, the PC, the world, everything seemed to be in slow motion. 'What about JEE?' she was saying.

'Will be worse. My paper did not go well.'

She fell silent. What could she have said, anyway?

'I have to go,' I said.

'Where will you go?' she said, asking me the most important question. Yes, where could I go? Home? And tell Baba he had wasted all his borrowed money on me.

'I'll come home with you. I can talk to Baba.'

I shook my head.

'Are you sure?' she said.

I didn't respond. I couldn't. I hurried out of her house.

✦

'Where had you gone?' Baba said as he opened the door.

I went straight to my room. Baba followed me.

'You don't want to see your AIEEE result?' he said.

I kept quiet.

'You said it comes out today.'

I didn't respond.

'Why aren't you speaking?'

I looked into Baba's anxious eyes.

'I have bad news,' I said.

Baba spoke in a hushed voice. 'What?'

'The worst has happened.'

'What?'

I shrugged my shoulders.

'When are the AIEEE results out?'

'They are out,' I said and walked into the living room.

'And?' Baba followed me and stood right in front of me.

I turned my gaze down. Baba waited for a few seconds.

Slap! I felt my right cheek sting. For his age and strength, my father could strike quite a blow. He had hit me for the first time in more than ten years. I deserved it.

'How?' Baba said. 'You did nothing in Kota, right? Nothing.'

Tears filled my eyes and my ears buzzed. I wanted to tell him that I spent nights doing assignments, sat through classes all day, improved my percentile. I had had a decent chance to make it. A few marks are all it takes to fall behind ten thousand ranks.

I didn't say anything. I cried like a child, as if my remorse would make him feel better.

'How do we return the money?' Baba said, turning to practical matters faster than I thought.

I had improved my rank, I wanted to tell him. The teachers at Career Path had told me I had potential. Yes, I did get distracted for a little while, and maybe that was why I hadn't made it. Anyway, not everyone in Kota had made it. Most students of Career Path had not made it. In fact, Vineet, the boy from Varanasi who went before me to Kota, hadn't made it either. But all I showed Baba was my sullen face.

'What are you thinking? Do you have any shame?' he said and went into a coughing fit. His body shook, he found it hard to balance.

'Sit down, Baba,' I said as I moved forward to hold him. His body felt warm.

'Don't come near me.' He pushed me away.

'You have fever,' I said.

'Guess who gave it?' he said.

I didn't know what to say or do. I didn't even find myself worthy enough to fetch his medicines from the other room. I had to let him be. When you screw up someone's life, the least you can do is leave the person alone.

◆

'I have gone through it all. You must be so fucked,' Vineet said to me.

We sat on the steps of Assi Ghat, close to the pier. I had arranged a secret meeting with Vineet. I did not know him too well. I had only exchanged some emails with him before I left for Kota. But he seemed an ideal companion right now. Yes, Aarti kept in touch, asking me about my well-being and even going on boat rides with me. Yet, I had nothing to say to her. I thought about jumping into the Ganga and ending my life. Raghav was someone I avoided automatically now. I did not want reassurance from an IT-BHU guy, especially someone who did not even seem to care about his degree.

Vineet, an ordinary guy like me, was someone I felt comfortable with. He had joined a private engineering college. 'So I can tell people I am doing BTech,' Vineet said and laughed. 'Just avoid the college name. Anyway, it is unknown to most people.'

I collected a few pebbles from the ghat steps and sent them skipping on the holy river.

'You will be fine, dude,' Vineet said. 'Never completely fine, but at least better than right now.'

'How did you choose among the private colleges?' I said. There were dozens of them, with new ones opening every week.

'I went to a career fair. I asked around. RSTC seemed slightly better than others. I don't think there's much difference.'

'What's RSTC?' I said.

'Riddhi Siddhi Technical College. The owners have a sari business with the same name.'

'Oh,' I said, trying to make a connection between saris and education.

'Quite a backward name, no? So we say RSTC, sounds cooler.' Vineet grinned.

'Do you get a job afterwards?'

'If you are lucky. Sixty per cent placements. Not bad.'

'Forty per cent students don't get placed?' I said, shocked. This could be worse than Kota, to finish your degree and get nothing at the end of it.

'The stats are improving every year. Plus, you can manage some job. There are call centres, credit card sales. Be open-minded and things work out.'

'Finish engineering and join a call centre?'

'Dude, don't be so shocked. We, like millions of other students, are the losers in the Great Indian Education Race. Be happy with whatever you get. Of course, if your parents are rich, do an MBA after BTech. Another shot at a job.'

'And if not?' I said.

Vineet said nothing. Exasperated, I threw all the pebbles into the Ganga. Like low-ranked students, the stones sank and disappeared without a trace.

'Hey, don't be mad at me. I didn't make the system.' Vineet patted my shoulder. 'The longer you sit idle, the worse you will feel. The dream is over. Join a college, any college, at least you will be with other students.'

'Other losers,' I said.

'Don't look down upon your own kind,' Vineet said.

He had a point. 'I am sorry,' I said. 'How much does your BTech cost?'

'One lakh a year for four years, including hostel.'

'Fuck,' I said. 'That's many years of salary a job would pay, if there is a job at the end of it.'

'I know. But your parents pay the fee. And they get to brag to everyone their son is becoming an engineer. You are free for the next four years. Think about it, not a bad trade.'

'We have no money,' I said flatly.

Vineet stood up. 'That, my friend, is going to be an issue.'

'Leaving?' I said.

'Yeah, campus is twenty kilometres out of Varanasi. Cheer up. You have seen life at its most fucked-up stage. It only gets better from here.'

I stood up and brushed the dust off my trousers. I dreaded going home. Baba had not spoken to me for three days.

We walked through the narrow Vishwanath Gali to reach the Gadholia main road.

'There's a career fair at Dr Sampooranand Sports Stadium in two weeks,' Vineet said. 'Go, maybe you will find cheaper colleges.'

'There is no money. We are neck-deep in debt,' I said.

'Well, no harm in paying a visit. You can get a discount, especially from the new ones, if you have a decent AIEEE rank.'

◆

I walked back home. The one-hour walk in the fresh air made me feel better temporarily. I should not talk to Baba about expensive private colleges, I thought. Maybe I should talk to him about me making money in a job rather than spending more. First, I would have to end his sulking though.

I went to his room. He was lying in bed.

'I want to get a job, Baba. Let me make some money before I decide about college.'

He didn't say a word. I continued, 'I understand you are upset. It is justified. There is a Café Coffee Day opening in Sigra. It is a high-class coffee chain. They want staff. Class XII-pass can apply.'

I only heard the slow whirr of the fan in response.

'I've applied. I won't be working in a coffee shop forever. But they pay five thousand a month. Not bad, right?'

Baba kept quiet.

'If you remain quiet, I will assume you are okay with it.'

Baba continued to mope silently despite my provocative comment. I wanted him to scold, yell, anything, and end this silence.

I leaned over him. 'Baba, don't punish me like this,' I said. I held his arm to shake him. It felt limp and cold. 'Baba?' I said again. His body felt stiff.

'Baba?' I said again. It finally dawned on me: I had become an orphan.

14

Ease of cremation is one solid advantage of being in Varanasi. The death industry drives the city. The electric crematorium at Harishchandra Ghat and the original, and still revered, Manikarnika Ghat burn nearly forty-five thousand bodies a year, or more than a hundred corpses a day. Only little children and people bitten by cobras are not cremated; their bodies are often dumped straight into the river. '*Kasyam maranam mukti*,' goes the Sanskrit saying, which means dying in Kashi leads to liberation. Hindus believe that if they die here, there is an automatic upgrade to heaven, no matter what the sin committed on earth. It is amazing how god provides this wild-card entry at death, which in turn allows my city to earn a living.

Specialist one-stop shops provide you everything from firewood to priests and urns to ensure that the dead person departs with dignity. Touts on Manikarnika Ghat lure foreigners to come watch the funeral pyres and take pictures for a fee, thereby creating an additional source of revenue. Varanasi is probably the only city on earth where Death is a tourist attraction.

But for all my city's expertise in death, I had personally never dealt with a dead body in my entire life, let alone that of my father. I did not know how to react to Baba's still body. I did not, or rather could not, cry. I don't know why. Perhaps because I was too stunned, and emotionally drained out. Perhaps I had few emotions left after mourning my second entrance-exam disaster. Perhaps I had too much work related to the funeral. Or perhaps it was because I thought I had killed him.

I had to organise a cremation, then a couple of pujas. I didn't know who to invite. My father had very few friends. I called some of his old students who had kept in touch. I informed Dubey uncle, our lawyer, more for practical reasons than anything else. The lawyer told Ghanshyam taya-ji. My uncle had sucked my father's blood all his life. However, his family now offered unlimited sympathy. I found his wife, Neeta tayi-ji, at my doorstep. She saw me, extended her arms and broke down.

'It's okay, tayi-ji,' I said, extracting myself from the bosom hug. 'You need not have come.'

'What are you saying? Husband's younger brother is like a son,' she said.

Of course, she did not mention the land she stole from her 'son'.

'When is the puja?' she asked me.

'I have no idea,' I said. 'I have to get the cremation done first.'

'Who is doing that?' she said.

I shrugged my shoulders.

'Do you have the money to do a cremation at Manikarnika?' she said.

I shook my head. 'The electric one at Harishchandra Ghat is cheaper,' I said.

'What electric? It is broken most of the time, anyway. We have to do a proper one. What are we here for?'

Soon, Ghanshyam taya-ji arrived with the rest of his brood. He had two sons and two daughters, all dressed in rich clothes. I didn't look like their relative at all. After my uncle arrived, they took over the cremation. They called more kith and kin. They arranged for a priest, who offered a ten-thousand-rupee package for the cremation. My uncle bargained him down to seven. It felt macabre to bargain for a funeral, but someone had to do it. My uncle paid the priest in crisp five-hundred-rupee notes.

Twenty-four hours later I lit my father's firewood-covered body at Manikarnika Ghat. Even though he had died, I felt the fire must hurt him. I remembered how he would dress me up for school when I was a child, comb my hair ... Smoke rose from the pyre and tears finally welled up in my eyes. I began to sob. Aarti and Raghav had come to the funeral. They stood with me, condoling in silence.

Half an hour later most of the relatives had left. I watched as the flames ate up the wood.

I felt a tap on my shoulder. I turned around. Two muscular men with paan-stained lips stood behind me. One of them had a thick moustache curved upwards.

'Yes?' I said.

The moustached man pointed his finger at the pyre. 'Are you his son?'

'I am.'

'Come aside,' he said.

'Why?' I said.

'He owed us two lakhs.'

◆

'Ghanshyam taya-ji wants to offer three lakhs?' I said to Dubey uncle, shocked.

He flipped through the document he had prepared for me. 'You sign here, you get three lakhs. Loan sharks are after you. They are dangerous. I am trying to help you.'

I examined the document. I didn't really understand it. 'Three lakhs is too low. They offered ten lakhs ages ago,' I said.

'That's right, ages ago. When your father didn't take it. Now they know you can't do anything. And you need the money.'

I kept quiet. Dubey uncle stood up. I wondered whose side my lawyer represented anyway.

'I realise it isn't an easy time for you. Think about it,' he said.

◆

I attended the career fair held in a giant tent put up in the Dr Sampooranand Sports Stadium.

Vineet had urged me to go. 'Meet my friend Sunil there. He is the event manager of the fair and knows all the participants.'

I entered the main tent. Hundreds of stalls made it resemble a trade expo. Private colleges around the country were trying to woo the students of Varanasi. Members of managing bodies of colleges stood with smiling faces. Banners inside the stalls displayed campus pictures like real estate projects. In cases where parts of the college building were under construction, the pictures were an artist's rendition.

'Once complete, this will be the best campus in Uttar Pradesh,' I heard one stall-owner tell a set of anxious parents. He skipped the part about how during construction students would have to study in makeshift classrooms surrounded by concrete mixers.

Loud posters proclaimed college names along with emblems. Names varied, but were often inspired by gods or grandfathers of rich promoters.

Select faculty and students from each college greeted us with glossy brochures of their institute in these stalls. Everyone wore suits and grinned like a well-trained flight crew. Hundreds of loser students like me moved restlessly from one stall to the next. Seventy per cent of the stalls comprised of engineering colleges. Medical, hotel management, aviation academies and a few other courses like BBA made up the rest.

I reached the Sri Ganesh Vinayak College, or SGVC, stall at noon – the designated place and time to meet Sunil.

I picked up the SGVC brochure, with its smiling students on the cover. The boys seemed happier and the girls prettier than the JEE toppers in the Kota brochures. The back cover of the brochure carried praise for the facilities and faculty of the institute, enough to make an IIT director blush. Inside the booklet I found a list of the programmes offered. From computer science to metallurgy, SGVC offered every engineering course.

I read through the entire brochure. I read the vision and mission statements of the founders. I read the college's philosophy on education, and how they were *different*. Other career fair veterans grinned as they walked past me. I seemed to be the only person actually reading the document.

Sunil found me at the stall for the Sri Ganesh Vinayak College, deep in study.

'Gopal?' he said tentatively.

'Huh?' I turned around. 'Sunil?'

Sunil gave me a firm handshake. Stubble and sunglasses covered most of his face. He wore a purple shirt and tight black jeans with a giant silver buckle. 'What the hell are you doing?' he asked straight off.

'Reading the brochure,' I said.

'Are you stupid? Go to the fees and placements page. See the average salary, check the fee. If two years' income pays the cost, shortlist it, else move on.'

'What about teaching methods? Learning …'

'Fuck learning,' Sunil said and snatched the brochure from my hand. I found his mannerisms and language rather rough. He borrowed a calculator from one of the students at the stall. 'See, tuition fifty thousand, hostel thirty thousand, let's say twenty thousand more for the useless things they will make you buy. So you pay a lakh a year for four years. Average placement is one and a half lakhs. Fuck it. Let's go.'

'But …' I was still doing the calculations.

'Move on. There are a hundred stalls here.'

We went to the next stall. The red and white banner said 'Shri Chintumal Group of Institutes, NH2, Allahabad'. A small map showed the college location, thirty kilometres from Allahabad city.

'I can't go to a college called Chintumal,' I said.

'Shut up. You never have to say your college's name, anyway.' Sunil picked up a brochure. Within seconds he found the relevant page. 'Okay, this is seventy thousand a year. Final placement one lakh forty thousand. See, this makes more sense.'

A fat man in his forties came to us.

'Our placement will be even better this year,' he said. 'I am Jyoti Verma, dean of students.'

I had never expected a dean to sell the college to me. He extended his hand. Sunil shook it purposefully.

'Yes, your fees are also lower than theirs,' I said and pointed to the Sri Ganesh stall.

'Their placement numbers are fake. Ours are real, ask any of our students,' Jyoti said.

He pointed to his students, three boys and two girls, who had worn suits for the first time in their life. They smiled timidly. I browsed through the campus pictures in the Chintumal stall.

A man from the Sri Ganesh stall came to me. He tapped my shoulder.

'Yes,' I said.

'Mahesh Verma from Sri Ganesh. Did Chintumal say anything negative about us?'

I looked at him. Mahesh, in his forties and fat, looked a lot like Jyoti Verma.

'Did they?' Mahesh said again.

I shook my head.

'You are considering Chintumal?' he said.

I nodded.

'Why not Sri Ganesh?'

'It's expensive,' I said.

'What's your budget? Maybe we can help you,' he said.

'What?' I said. I couldn't believe one could bargain down college fees.

'Tell me your budget. I will give you a ten per cent discount if you sign up right now.'

I turned to Sunil, unsure of what to say or do next. Sunil took charge of the situation.

'We want thirty per cent off. Chintumal is that much cheaper,' Sunil said.

'They don't even have a building,' Mahesh said.

'How do you know?' I said.

'He's my brother. He broke off and started his own college. But it has got bad reports,' Mahesh said.

Jyoti kept an eye on us from a distance. Yes, the brothers did resemble each other.

'We don't care. Tell us your maximum discount,' Sunil said.

'Come to my stall,' Mahesh signalled us to follow him.

'Stop,' Jyoti barred our way.

'What?' I said.

'Why are you going to Sri Ganesh?'

'He is giving me a discount,' I said.

'Did you ask me for a discount? Did I say no?' Jyoti said, his expression serious. I had never seen a businessman-cum-dean before. 'Mahesh bhai, please leave my stall,' Jyoti said in a threatening tone.

'He's my student. We have spoken,' Mahesh bhai said and held my wrist. 'Come, son, what's your name?'

'Gopal,' I said as Jyoti grabbed my other wrist. 'But please stop pulling me.'

The brothers ignored my reqest.

'I will give you the best discount. Don't go to Sri Ganesh and ruin your life. They don't even have labs. Those pictures in the brochure are of another college,' Jyoti said.

'Sir, I don't even know …' I said and looked at Sunil. He seemed as baffled as me.

'Shut up, Jyoti!' a hitherto soft-spoken Mahesh screamed.

'Don't shout at me in my own stall. Get out,' Jyoti said.

Mahesh gave all of us a dirty look. In one swift move he ripped off the Chintumal banner.

Jyoti's face went as red as his college emblem. He went to the Sri Ganesh stall and threw the box of brochures down.

I tried to run out of the stall. Jyoti held me by my collar.

'Wait, I will give you a seat for fifty thousand a year.'

'Let … me … go,' I panted.

Mahesh returned with three people who resembled Bollywood thugs. Apparently, they were faculty. They started to rip out all the hoardings of the Chintumal stall. Jyoti ordered his own security men to fight them.

As I tried to escape, one of Sri Ganesh's goons pushed me. I fell face-down and landed on a wooden table covered in a white sheet. It had a protruding nail that cut my cheek. Blood covered one side of my face. Sweat drops appeared on my forehead. I had finally given my blood and sweat to studies.

Sunil helped me up. I saw the blood on the white sheet and felt nauseous. A crowd had gathered around us. I did not say anything and ran out. I left the stadium and continued to sprint down the main road for two hundred metres.

I stopped to catch my breath and heard footsteps as Sunil jogged towards me.

Both of us held our sides and panted.

'Fuck,' Sunil said. 'Lucky escape.'

We went to a chemist's where I applied some dressing on my cheek.

'Come, I will take you to CCD. It opened last week,' Sunil said.

◆

We walked to Café Coffee Day at IP Mall, Sigra. Sunil bought us two cold coffees with a crisp new hundred-rupee note. I could live on that cash for a week.

'What was that? They own a college?' I said.

'It is the Verma family from Allahabad. They are into country liquor. Now they have opened a college.'

'Why?' I said.

'Money. There's huge money in private colleges. Plus, it enhances their name in society. Now they are noble people in education, not liquor barons.'

'They behaved like goons.'

'They *are* goons. Brothers had a fight, college split and now they try to bring each other down.'

'I can't do this,' I said.

'Don't worry, we will get you another college. We will bargain hard. They have seats to fill.'

'It scares me to even think of studying at these places. Liquor barons running colleges?'

'Yeah, politicians, builders, *beedi*-makers. Anybody with experience in a shady business does really well in education,' Sunil said. He picked his straw to lick the cream off.

'Really?' I said. 'Shouldn't academicians be opening colleges? Like ex-professors?'

'Are you crazy? Education is not for wusses. There's a food chain of people at every step,' Sunil said. He jiggled his leg as he spoke to me. He took out his mobile phone. Cellphones had started to become common, but they still counted as a status symbol.

Sunil called someone who seemed to be in a crisis. 'Calm down, Chowbey-ji. MLA Shukla-ji has blessed the fair. Yes, it is closing time. Give us two more hours ... Hold on.' Sunil turned to me. 'Events business, always on my toes,' he said to me in an undertone. 'Mind if I step out? I'll be back.'

'Sure,' I said.

I sat alone with my drink. I scanned the crowd. Rich kids bought overpriced doughnuts and cookies to go with their whipped-cream coffee.

Two men in leather jackets came inside CCD. I recognised them from the funeral. I shifted sideways on my seat to avoid them. However, they had already seen me. They walked up to my table.

'Celebrating your father's death?' said one. His muscular arm kept a cup of chai on the table.

'I don't have the money right now,' I said in a soft voice.

'Then we will take your balls,' said the person with the moustache. He gripped a can of Coke in his right hand.

'Except they are not worth a lakh each,' the teacup goon said. They laughed.

Sunil returned after his call. He was surprised to see the new guests.

'Your friends?' he said.

I shook my head.

'His father's,' said the teacup guy.

'I have seen you ...' Sunil said.

'This is our town. We are everywhere,' the Coke guy said.

'You work for MLA Shukla-ji, don't you?' Sunil said.

'None of your business,' the teacup guy said, his voice a tad nervous.

'I saw you at his house. Hi, I'm Sunil. I am a manager at Sunshine Events. We work with MLA Shukla-ji a lot.' Sunil extended his hand.

After a few seconds of hesitation, they shook Sunil's hand.

'Your friend owes us money. He'd better pay up soon. Or else.' The teacup guy paused after 'or else', partly for effect but mostly because he didn't know what to say next.

Sunil and I kept quiet. The moustache goon tapped the table three times with his bike key. After a few more glares they left.

I let out a huge sigh. Fear had flushed my face red. 'I don't need college. I'd be dead soon anyway,' I said.

'You okay?' Sunil said. 'Let me get some more coffee.'

I'd have preferred he gave the extra money to me instead of more coffee, but kept silent. Over my second cup, I gave Sunil a summary of the story so far – my childhood, Kota, my failure, Baba's death.

Sunil placed his empty cup on the table with a clink. 'So now you have loans. And no source to pay them?' he summarised.

'My home, maybe. But it is not worth much. And I won't have a place to live in after that.'

'And the property dispute?'

I had mentioned the property dispute to Sunil in brief. I had not given him specific details. 'That's an old dispute,' I said, surprised Sunil caught on to it.

'What property is this?'

'Agricultural land,' I said dully.

'Where?' he said.

'Ten kilometres outside the city.'

Sunil's eyes opened wide. 'That's quite close. How big is the land?'

'Thirty acres. Our share is fifteen acres.'

'And what does your uncle say?'

'Nothing. He wants the full thing. It is a mess. Many papers are forged. The case has been going on for twelve years.' I finished my beverage. 'So yes, I'm fucked. Maybe they can sell my house and recover the money. Thanks for the coffee.'

I stood up to leave.

'What will you do?' Sunil said, still in his seat and pensive.

'I will join a shady part-time college and take whatever job I can get.'

'Wait, sit down,' Sunil said.

'What?' I sat down.

'I'll suggest something to you. And I will help you with it as well. But I need a cut. A big cut.'

'Cut?' I said. *Cut of what, my fucked-up life?*

'So, ten per cent. Done?' Sunil said.

'Of what?'

'Of whatever you make. Ten per cent equity in your venture.'

'What venture?' I said, exasperated.

'You will open a college.'

'What?!'

'Relax,' Sunil said.

'Do you take bhang like the sadhus on the ghat?' I said. How else could I account for his hallucinations?

'See, you have the land. That's the most important part. Land close to the city,' he said.

'I don't *have* it. The case has been dragging with no end in sight.'

'We can fix that.'

'We? Who? And it is agricultural land. You can only grow crops there. It's the law,' I said.

'There are people in our country who are above the law,' Sunil said.

'Who?' I said.

'MLA Shukla-ji,' he said.

'Shukla who?'

'Our MLA, Raman Lal Shukla. You've never heard of him?' Sunil said.

'You mentioned him earlier on the phone,' I said.

'Yes. I have done twenty events with his blessings. How else could I get city authority approvals? I personally take his cut to him. I will take you too. For my own cut,' he said and winked at me.

'Cut?'

'Yes, cut. Ten per cent. Forgot already?'

'What exactly are you saying?'

'Let us meet Shukla-ji. Bring whatever property papers you have.'

'You serious?'

'Do I look like someone who is not serious?' Sunil said.

I saw his gelled hair and the flashy sunglasses perched on his head. I reserved my opinion.

'You want me to open a college? I haven't even been to college,' I said.

'Most people who own colleges in India haven't. Stupid people go to college. Smart people own them,' said Sunil. 'I'll set it up for next week. And remember.'

'What?'

He snapped his fingers. 'My ten per cent.'

15

Aarti and I went for a long boat ride. Her green dupatta flew backward in the early morning breeze. 'Decided what to do next?' she asked.

'I am exploring private engineering colleges.'

'And?'

'Too expensive and too shady,' I said.

I paused to rest. The boat stood still in the middle of the river. I wondered if Aarti would come and sit next to me to massage my palms. She didn't.

'So? What next?' Aarti said.

'A correspondence degree and a job.'

'What about the loans?'

'Manageable. Baba settled most of them,' I lied. I did not want to burden her with my woes and spoil my time with her.

'Good. Don't worry, it will work out.' She got up to sit next to me. She took my hand in hers and, as if thinking of something else, began to crack my knuckles.

'You are happy with Raghav, right?' I asked.

I hoped she wouldn't be, but was pretending like I wanted her to be.

'Oh yes.' She looked at me with shining eyes. 'Raghav is a good person.'

I withdrew my hand. She sensed my disappointment.

'I never said he's not.' I looked away.

'You cool?'

'Yeah,' I said and managed a fake smile. 'How is he, anyway?'

'Told his parents he won't take up engineering as a profession. They aren't too happy with that.'

'He's an idiot. What will he do?'

'Journalism,' she said. 'He loves it. That's what he is meant to do. He wants to change things. He's also joined university politics.'

'Totally stupid,' I said. I picked up the oars again. Aarti went back to her seat.

We kept silent on the ride back. The splash of oars in the water was the only sound breaking the silence. Aarti's hair had grown, and now reached her waist. I saw her eyelashes move every time she blinked. The dawn sun seemed to light up her skin from the inside. I avoided looking at her lips. If I looked at them I wanted to kiss them.

She belongs to someone else now, even your limited brain should know that. My head knew this, but my heart didn't.

'Why did we grow up, Gopal?' Aarti said. 'Things were so much simpler earlier.'

◆

I had never been to an MLA's house before. We reached Shukla-ji's sprawling bungalow in the Kachehri locality at three in the afternoon. Police jeeps were parked outside and security guards surrounded the entire property. Sunil introduced himself at the gate, and later we were let in.

Several villagers sat in the front lawn, awaiting their turn to meet the MLA. Sunil had said MLA Shukla stayed alone. His family mostly stayed abroad as his two sons went to college there. Filled with party workers, MLA Shukla's home resembled a party office more than a residence.

Sunil had brought along Girish Bedi, 'an experienced education consultant'. I had a rucksack full of property documents and court-related papers. Guards checked my bag three times before we reached the MLA's office.

A middle-aged man in a crisp white kurta-pyjama sat behind an ornate, polished wooden desk. Despite a slight potbelly, for a politician Shukla-ji could be considered handsome. He gestured at us to sit as he continued to speak on his cellphone.

'Tell the scientist that Shukla wants to see the report first. Yes, I have to see it. It's my Ganga too. Yes, okay, I have a meeting now, bye.'

The MLA sifted through the files on his desk as he spoke to us.

'Sunil, sir. Sunshine Events. W … we do career fairs,' Sunil said, the stammer in his voice in sharp contrast to his confidence in the outside world.

'Tell me the work,' Shukla-ji said.

'Land, sir,' Sunil said.

'Where? How much?' Shukla-ji said. His eyes stayed on his files as his ears tuned in. Politicians can multitask better than most people.

'Thirty acres, ten kilometres outside the city on the Lucknow Highway,' Sunil said.

The MLA stopped his pen midway. He looked up at us.

'Whose?' he said. He closed his files to give us his full attention.

'Mine, sir,' I said. No idea why I called him sir. 'I am Gopal Mishra.' I opened my rucksack and placed the property documents on the table.

'And you?' Shukla-ji said, turning to Bedi.

'Education consultant. He helps design and open new colleges. Our own person,' Sunil said.

'New college?' Shukla-ji said.

'It is agricultural land, sir,' Sunil said.

'You can obtain permission to convert agricultural land to educational use,' Bedi spoke for the first time.

'You look young,' Shukla-ji said to me. 'Who are your parents?'

'They died, sir,' I said.

'Hmmm. What's the problem?' Shukla-ji said. His finger traced the location of the land to the centre of the city.

'My uncle,' I said.

'This is right near the upcoming airport,' Shukla-ji said, as he made sense of the map.

'Is it?' I said.

Shukla-ji picked up his intercom. He told his staff not to disturb him until this meeting was over.

'Gopal, tell me everything about the land dispute,' Shukla-ji said.

Over the next hour I told him my entire story. 'And the fact is I even owe your men two lakhs,' I said as I ended my monologue.

'Would you like tea? Soft drink?' Shukla-ji said.

I shook my head.

'You owe money to my men?' Shukla-ji said.

'No sir, not your men,' Sunil said and stamped my foot. 'Bedi sir, tell him your view.'

I did not realise that the loan sharks operate with the MLA's blessings, but denied any overt links with him.

'Ideal engineering college site, sir,' Bedi said. 'His share of fifteen acres is enough.'

'Why fifteen? When there is thirty, why would we take fifteen?' Shukla-ji said.

I felt overwhelmed with emotion. For the first time in my life a powerful person had shown support for me. I missed out that he said 'we'.

Sunil gave me a smug smile. He had brought me to the right place.

'Fifteen is enough, sir,' I said, not sure how we would get even that.

'Thirty. Keep the remaining for later. It is close to the city … Once the college opens and the airport is built, we may even get residential or commercial zoning,' Shukla-ji said.

I didn't really understand what he said but I figured he knew more than me. Besides, he seemed to be on my side.

'But how will we get this?' I said. My uncle had been sitting on the property for years.

'You leave that to us,' Shukla-ji said. 'You tell me this, can you run a college?'

'Me?'

'Yes, because you will be the face and name of the college. I will be a silent partner,' he said.

'But how?' I said. 'I have no experience. I have no money.'

'Mr Bedi will give you the experience. I will give you the money for construction and everything else.'

I am missing something here. Why had the world suddenly decided to help me? What's the catch?

Sunil understood my dilemma.

'Shukla-ji sir, if you could tell him your terms. And of course, whatever you feel is good for me,' Sunil said and gave an obsequious grin.

'I don't want anything. Open a college, it is good for my city,' Shukla-ji said.

Nobody believed him. Yet, we had to indulge him. 'Sir, please,' Sunil said, 'that won't be fair.'

'I'll think about my terms. But tell me, boy, are you up to it?' Shukla-ji looked at me. I think I grew older by ten years under that gaze.

I hid my hesitation as much as possible. 'How about we get the land and just sell it?' I said.

'It is tough to sell the land with all the past cases,' Shukla-ji said. 'It is one thing to get possession for you, quite another to find a new buyer.'

'Exactly. The cases, how do we fix them?' I said.

Shukla-ji laughed. 'We don't fix cases. We fix the people in the cases.'

The MLA had laughed, but his eyes showed a firm resolve. He seemed like the kind of guy who could fix people. And more than acquiring the land, I wanted to teach my relatives a lesson.

'If you can fix them, you can take whatever share you want,' I said.

'Fifteen acres for me,' Shukla-ji said. 'I will keep it until the area gets re-zoned to commercial or residential. We will make the college in the other fifteen.'

'How much ownership in the college do you want?' I said.

'Whatever you want. College is a trust, no profit there,' Shukla-ji said with no particular expression.

'Really?' I said, surprised.

'It is true,' Bedi spoke after a long time. 'Every college must be incorporated as a non-profit trust. There are no shareholders, only trustees.'

'Why would a private player open a non-profit college?' I said.

Bedi took a deep breath before he proceeded to explain. 'Well, you take a profit. The trustees can take out cash from the trust, showing it as an expense. Or take some fee in cash, and not account for it. Or ask a contractor to pay you back a portion of what you pay them. There are many more ways …'

Bedi continued speaking till I interrupted him. 'Wait a minute, aren't these illegal methods?'

Everyone fell silent.

Shukla-ji spoke after a while. 'I don't think this boy can do it. You have wasted my time.'

Bedi and Sunil hung their heads in shame. I had let them down with my curiosity about propriety.

'I am sorry, I am only trying to understand,' I said.

'What?' Bedi said, his tone irritated.

'Are you telling me that the only way to make money from a college is through illegal methods? Sorry, I am not being moral, only questioning.'

'Well,' Bedi said, 'you are not actually supposed to make money.'

'So why would anybody open one?' I said.

'For the benefit of society, like us politicians,' Shukla-ji said.

Everyone but me broke into laughter. I guess the joke was on stupid, naïve me.

'Listen, Gopal,' Sunil said, 'that is how the rules are. They are stupid. Now you can either figure out a way around them, or remain clueless. There has to be a trust, you and Shukla-ji sir will be trustees. Bedi will explain everything.'

Bedi gave me a reassuring nod. Yes, the man knew the system, and how to bend it.

'Mr Bedi, also explain to the boy not to question legality much. Education is not the business for him then,' Shukla-ji said.

'Of course,' Bedi smiled. 'Shukla sir, taking money out of the trust is the least of the problems. What about all the permissions and approvals required? Every step requires special management.'

'So that's what the boy has to do. I am not visible in this. I am only the trustee, to benefit society,' Shukla-ji said.

'Do what?' I said.

'Don't worry, I will explain it,' Bedi said. 'You need Varanasi Nagar Nigam's approval for the building plans, AICTE approval for the college. There are inspections. Everyone has to be taken care of. It is standard.'

'Bribes?' I said.

'Shh!' Shukla-ji reprimanded. 'Don't mention all this here. You do your discussions outside. Leave now.'

We stood up to go.

'Stay for a minute, Gopal,' the MLA said.

'Yes?' I said after Sunil and Bedi had left the room.

'Will you do what it takes?' Shukla-ji said, 'I don't want to waste my time otherwise. Tell me now if you want to quit.'

I paused to think. 'It's not easy,' I admitted.

'It is never easy to become a big man in life,' Shukla-ji said.

I kept quiet.

'You want to be a big man, Gopal?'

I continued to look down. I examined the black and white patterns on the Italian marble floor.

'Or you want to remain an average kid while your friends race ahead of you.'

I swallowed the lump in my throat. I looked up to make eye contact with him.

'You have a girlfriend, Gopal?'

I shook my head.

'You know why? Because you are a nobody.'

I nodded. The memory of Aarti and Raghav kissing each other passionately in the BHU car park flashed through my mind. If I had made it to BHU and Raghav had gone to Kota, would her decision have been different? I saw Shukla-ji. Every inch of him felt wrong. But he offered me a chance. A job, an admission, a fucking chance, that is all one needs in life sometimes.

'I'll do it. It isn't like I am the only guy in India paying bribes,' I said. 'But I want to be big.'

Shukla-ji stood up. He came around his desk and patted my back. 'You are already a big man,' he said, 'because you have me behind you. Now go, and leave your harami uncle's details with my secretary outside.'

'What about the money I owe your people,' I said.

'Two lakhs? It's a joke for me, forget it,' Shukla-ji said. He went back to his desk and opened a drawer. He took out two bundles of ten-thousand rupees and tossed them at me. 'One for Sunil, the other for you,' he said.

'Why for me?' I asked.

'For running my college, Director sir.' He grinned.

16

I accepted Shukla-ji's ten thousand bucks, if only to pay for basic necessities. I allowed myself one indulgence – I took Aarti out for dinner to Taj Ganga, the most expensive restaurant in town.

'Are you sure?' Aarti asked again, as we entered the coffee shop at the Taj. 'We could always eat chaat at the ghats.'

She wore a new full length, dark blue dress her relatives had sent from the US. She had matched it with fake, understated gold jewellery purchased from Vishwanath Gali.

'My treat,' I said.

The waiter pulled out a chair for Aarti. She thanked him as we sat down. Aarti wanted to watch her weight but eat chocolate cake too. We decided to have soup and salad for dinner so we could save calories for dessert.

She stirred the hot soup with a spoon. 'Sorry, but how did you get the money for this? Baba left you a huge will?'

I laughed. 'No, he left me loans.'

'Then?'

'I am starting a new business.'

'Smuggling?' Aarti inclined her head to one side.

'Shut up. I am opening a college.'

'What?' Aarti said, loud enough for the entire place to hear.

'Sorry,' she whispered. 'Did you say you are opening a college?'

'Yeah, on my disputed land.'

'How? Isn't the land stuck? And how will you make the college?'

'I have partners. Good partners.'

'Who?' Aarti said.

'I'll tell you. We are finalising plans.'

'Really?' Aarti said. 'Oh, so you are serious?'

'Yeah, it is fifteen acres right outside the city. If we settle the dispute and get re-zoning done, it is ideal for a college,' I repeated Bedi's words.

'Wow,' Aarti said and chuckled. 'You are hitting the big time, Gopal.'

She meant it as a joke, but it hurt a little. 'Why? You didn't think I could?'

'No, I didn't mean that,' Aarti said. 'I am just … surprised.'

'I have to do *something* in life.'

'Sure. You will do more than something. What about your uncle?'

'We are trying to reach an amicable settlement with him,' I said.

Shukla's men, who handled the loan-shark business, had initiated the settlement process with Ghanshyam taya-ji. Amicable is not the word one could use to describe their methods.

They had visited my uncle's house thrice. The first time they emptied a bottle of goat's blood in his front balcony. The second time they stabbed all the sofas and beds in the house with an assortment of knives. The third time, when they finally spoke, they brought out guns and proposed to buy off my uncle's share of disputed land for eight lakh rupees.

I did not want to give Aarti all these extra details.

'What kind of college?' she said.

'Engineering.'

'Cool,' Aarti said.

'If I want to be a big man, I have to do big things,' I said.

'You were always a big man to me, Gopal. You know why?'

'Why?'

'Because you have a big heart.' Aarti lightly stroked my hand on the table.

My heart, big or small, skipped a beat at her touch. I quickly launched into small talk. 'How are things with you? How's college?'

'B-o-r-ing. But I am joining an aviation academy.'

'What's that?'

'They train you to become a flight attendant. The classrooms look like the interiors of a plane.'

'Really?' I mused, 'There is so much happening in education.'

'Yeah, most of us only get to be students. Not everyone can open a college,' she teased.

I smiled. 'Long way to go. It's difficult,' I said.

'You have faced more difficult things in life before. You will make it,' Aarti said confidently.

'You think so?' I said.

She nodded. Her nod meant the world to me. I wanted to ask her to date me again. Somehow I thought with my new college plan she might be inclined to say yes. Of course, only my brain comes up with such flimsy theories.

'How's Raghav?' I asked, to bring myself back to reality.

'A bit low, actually,' she said.

I felt a warm glow. 'Really? Why?' I expressed fake concern.

'He lost university elections for general secretary.'

'Oh,' I said. 'Does it matter?'

'It did to him. He lost because he wouldn't horse-trade with other hostels. He wanted to fight fair.'

'I'm not surprised he lost,' I said, spearing a carrot.

'He believes one has to be fair and win. Else, what is the point of winning?' Aarti said.

'Life doesn't work like that, does it?' I said, chewing slowly.

'I don't know. That is how it should work,' Aarti said. 'He's going to contest again next year.'

'Doesn't he do too much?' I said.

'Oh yeah, between his BTech course, magazine and elections, he hardly has any time for me.'

'And you like that?'

'No, but I have no choice. If it makes him happy, so be it.'

We finished our dinner. The chocolate cake arrived. Her eyes lit up. She pulled the plate towards herself. 'Don't steal my cake,' she said and grinned.

'Raghav is such a lucky guy to have you, Aarti,' I said.

'Thanks,' she said and gave a shy smile.

'Aarti, can I ask you something?'

'Yeah?' She looked at me, her spoon poised above the cake.

'Nothing, leave some cake for me if you can,' I said and signalled for the bill.

◆

The doorbell woke me at midnight. I rubbed my eyes and reached for the door, still half asleep. My uncle, aunt and their son, my thirty-year-old cousin Ajay, stood outside.

'Ghanshyam taya-ji?' I said. 'What happened? Please come in.'

My relatives sat on the torn sofa in the front room. They didn't speak for five minutes.

'You have not come so late because you missed me, right?' I said.

'Why are you doing this to us?' Ajay exploded.

'Doing what?' I said. 'Do you want water? Tea?'

'No,' my uncle said. 'Gopal, pay attention to your karma. God is watching. You will have to pay one day. Do not do this to us.'

'Do what?' I said. And why had they come at this time of the night?

'Bittoo hasn't come home from nursery school,' my aunt said and burst into tears. This time they seemed real, unlike the crocodile ones at Baba's funeral.

They had come home because Bittoo, Ajay's four-year-old son whom I had seen only once (in his mother's lap, at my father's funeral), was missing.

'Oh, that is terrible,' I said. 'And this is about my karma?'

'It's those people, who want to buy the land,' my uncle said. 'We know they are with you.'

'What are you talking about?' I said.

My uncle folded his hands. 'Don't do this to us,' he said.

'I am not doing anything. Some people came to me to buy the land too. But I told them I cannot sell it,' I said.

'Really?' Ajay said.

'How can I? It's disputed, right?' I said.

'But the people who came to us don't want to buy. They want us to settle the bank cases, settle the dispute and give it all to you,' uncle said.

'That's strange. So now the question is – do you value the land more or Bittoo? Correct?'

'Shut up,' Ajay said. 'We know it is you who wants to buy it.'

'I don't have money to buy food. How can I buy land?' I scratched my head.

'Who are these people?' my uncle said.

'I don't know. You can go to the police,' I said, 'but they sound like crooks.'

'Avoid the police,' my aunt said.

'They can do anything. Bittoo is a little, young thing, it won't be difficult to hide his body. Anyway, it is Varanasi, dead bodies are easy to dispose of,' I said.

Ajay jumped up from the sofa and grabbed my collar. 'I know you are involved. Your father was straight, you are not,' he said, his eyes wild.

'Leave my collar, brother, right now,' I said in a calm but firm tone.

Ajay's mother tugged at her son's hand. Ajay released me.

'What are they offering?' I said.

'Eight lakhs,' my uncle said.

'That's not bad,' I said.

'That's a fraction of the market price.'

'But more than double of what you offered me,' I said.

'You *are* involved.' Ajay glared at me.

'Go home, taya-ji, and think it over. We all love Bittoo more than the land.'

'Why is this happening to us?' my aunt exclaimed at the door.

'It's all karma. Taya-ji will explain it to you.' I smiled as I shut the door.

◆

It took three nights without Bittoo to make my relatives realise the value of the eight-lakh offer. I received a call from the MLA's office when Mr Ghanshyam Mishra and Mr Ajay Mishra signed the papers.

'Sharma here, PA to Shukla-ji,' the caller said. 'MLA sahib has invited you for dinner tonight.'

'Cheers,' Shukla-ji said as we clinked our whisky glasses together.

Bedi, Sunil and I sat with him in his huge living room. It had three separate seating areas with plush velvet sofas, coffee tables and elaborate lamps and chandeliers. Three waiters served kebabs, nuts and mini-samosas in napkin-lined china plates. I noticed pictures of Shukla-ji's family on the wall.

'Nikhil and Akhil, my sons,' Shukla-ji said. 'Both are studying in the US. Will keep them away for a while.'

Some said Shukla-ji was divorced. Others said he had another family in Lucknow. I didn't feel the need to know.

'Land is a big step,' Bedi said grimly. 'But there's a long way to go. We are meeting the VNN people next week. Meanwhile, we should take care of the trust formalities.'

Bedi explained how VNN, or the municipality, would give us the crucial agricultural-to-educational land re-zoning permit and clear plans so we can commence construction.

'Get the re-zoning done soon. I've not paid eight lakhs for the land to grow rice,' Shukla-ji said.

'We will,' Bedi said. 'They know who is behind this. You are not a small entity, sir.'

'That is true,' Shukla-ji said in a dismissive tone to Bedi for stating the obvious. 'But we have to take care of VNN, no?'

'Yes, of course,' Bedi said. 'It's re-zoning. The land value multiplies five times. Not cheap.'

'How much?' Shukla-ji said.

'Of course, the rate is different for you. I'd imagine ten lakhs.'

'What?' Shukla-ji said, shocked.

Bedi finished his drink in a large sip. 'It's thirty acres, sir. For a normal person it would be forty.'

'See, that is why people like me have to come to education. What is happening in this country?' Shukla-ji said.

'DM has to bless it too. But Pradhan is honest. However, if it is for a college, and VNN recommends, he will approve it,' Bedi said.

'How honest?' Shukla-ji said.

'Honest enough to not take money. But not so honest that he will stop others from taking it.'

'That's good. If you are honest, keep it to yourself,' Sunil said, speaking for the first time that evening.

'Sunil,' Shukla-ji said.

'What, sir?'

'You leave now. I will send something for you. But we will take care of this project from now,' Shukla-ji said.

'Sir, but …' Sunil said.

'You have done your job,' Shukla-ji said and handed him a bottle of Johnnie Walker Black Label.

Sunil took the cue. He thanked him for the bottle, bowed as much as the human spine allowed and left.

'I know DM Pradhan, his daughter is a friend,' I told Shukla-ji.

'Not much of an issue there. Still, good to have his blessings,' Shukla-ji said.

'Sure,' I said.

Shukla-ji went inside his bedroom. He returned with a heavy plastic bag. He gave it to me.

'What's this?' I said.

'Ten lakhs,' he said, 'for VNN.'

'Ten lakhs?' I said. My hands trembled as I held the heavy bag. I had never seen, or lifted that much money.

'It's just a number,' the MLA said. 'Bedi-ji, help the boy. And help yourself too. I don't like empty glasses.'

'Sure, Shukla-ji,' Bedi said and called for the waiter.

'Are people in education happy with money or they want other stuff too?' Shukla-ji asked Bedi.

'Like what?' Bedi asked.

'Girls, if they want to have a good time. I have a man, Vinod, who can arrange that,' MLA Shukla said.

'Oh, will let you know. Money usually does the job though,' Bedi said.

'Good.' He changed track. 'Can Gopal work from your office for a while? Until he has his own?'

'Of course, Shukla-ji.'

The waiters ran to refill our glasses.

'The trust papers are ready. We can sign them this week. But one question, Gopal,' Bedi said.

'What?' I said.

'What's the name of the college?' Bedi said.

I hadn't thought about it.

'I have no idea. Maybe something that signifies technology.'

'And our city,' Shukla-ji said. 'Let me tell people I did this for them when the time comes.'

'GangaTech?' I said.

Shukla-ji patted my shoulder. 'Well done. I like you, Gopal. You will go very far.' Shukla-ji personally filled my glass to the brim with whisky.

17

I flipped through the documents Bedi had plonked on my desk. I sat in an extra room at his education consultancy office.

'Pay to incorporate a trust?' I said.

'Yes, to the Registrar of Companies. Every trust has to be registered there,' Bedi said.

'But why pay a bribe? We are opening a non-profit trust,' I said.

'We are paying a bribe because if we don't the Registrar will stall our approval.' He was irritated.

I sighed in disbelief.

'Anyway, forty thousand maximum. Now, can you please sign here?' Bedi said.

Over the next two hours I signed on every page of the six copies of the forty-page GangaTech Education Trust incorporation document. I cracked my knuckles while Bedi hunted up some more stuff for me to sign.

'What's this?' I said when he handed me a stack of letters. Each letter had a thick set of files attached to it.

'Your application to the University Grants Commission, or the UGC, to open a college. The files contain details about the proposed college.'

I went through the files. It had sections such as course descriptions, facilities offered and faculty hiring plan.

'It is standard stuff, taken from earlier applications,' Bedi said.

I signed the letters. 'So, they send an approval or what?' I said.

'They will send a date for inspection of the site. Once they inspect, they will give you an in-principle approval to start construction.'

'I imagine we have to pay somebody to clear the inspection?' I said.

Bedi laughed. 'You learn fast. Of course, we pay. A thick packet to every inspector. However, right now we pay to obtain an inspection date. First things first.'

My eyebrows went up. 'Joking, right?' I said.

'No, any government work, especially in education, requires a fee. Get used to it.' He then listed out the palms we had to grease in order to open a place to teach kids in our country. Apart from the UGC, we had to apply to AICTE, or the All India Council for Technical Education. They clear the engineering colleges. Also, every private college requires a government university affiliation. For that, we had to get approvals from the vice-chancellor of a state university. Shukla-ji's connections and a generous envelope would do the trick.

'Otherwise the vice-chancellor can create a lot of hassle,' Bedi said, speaking from past experience.

'So, who are these UGC and AICTE inspectors, anyway?' I said.

'University lecturers from government colleges are appointed as inspectors. Of course, since it is such a lucrative job, the lecturers have to bribe to become one,' Bedi said.

'Whom?'

'Senior management at UGC, or someone in the education ministry. Anyway, that is their business. We have to focus on ours. Please inform Shukla-ji we will need funds for all this.'

I nodded.

'Don't forget the VNN meeting,' Bedi said. 'And definitely don't forget the bag.'

'I can't wait to get rid of it,' I said. 'It is scary to keep so much cash in the house.'

'Don't worry,' Bedi said. 'One VNN visit and it will all be gone.'

♦

We reached the Varanasi Nagar Nigam office, opposite Shaheed Udyaan, at six in the evening. The official had told us to come after working hours. If you are willing to pay, government offices can do more overtime than MNCs.

'Welcome, welcome. I am Sinha,' a man greeted us in the empty reception area. He led us upstairs. We climbed up two floors of the dilapidated building. Sinha, deputy-corporator, had known Shukla-ji for over a decade and referred to him as his brother.

'If my big brother wants it, consider it done,' Sinha said. He didn't mention that big brother would need to give little brother a gift.

I took out the maps, property documents and our formal application. Sinha pored over them with a sonorous 'hmmm'.

'We can only start when we have the land re-zoned,' I said.

'Re-zoning is tough,' Sinha said. 'Higher-ups have to approve.'

'How long will it take?' I said.

'You look young,' Sinha said.

'Excuse me?' I said.

'Impatience, the first folly of youth. You are opening a college, what is the hurry?'

'It's still going to take years. But I want to get all the approvals done,' I said.

Bedi signalled me to be quiet. Sinha laughed.

'Don't you have to get the building plan approval too?' the deputy-corporator said.

'Yes,' Bedi said. 'Can your junior officers handle that?'

'Send the documents to me, send everything home. *Everything*,' Sinha said, stressing the last word.

I got the drift. I patted the plastic bag I had kept on the floor.

'I have brought something here,' I said.

'In the office?' Sinha stood up hurriedly. 'Are you crazy?'

I had brought the money to show how serious we were about getting the job done. Obviously, I didn't expect him to take cash over the counter.

'Bedi sir, teach him how it is done. He will be a disaster,' Sinha said, as he led us out of the office.

I hugged the heavy, red plastic bag closer.

'How much, by the way?' Sinha enquired as we came outside.

'Ten,' I said.

'Not for re-zoning and building plan,' Sinha said.

'It's a college, please be reasonable,' I said.

'I am being reasonable. But ten is too less. Fifteen,' Sinha said.

'No concession for Shukla-ji?' I said.

'This is already half of what I take,' Sinha said.

'Eleven?' I said. I was bargaining with him as if I was buying a T-shirt. Of course, the thought of the amount involved numbed me.

'Twelve and a half. Done! Do not embarrass me before my big brother,' Sinha said.

I didn't argue further. I had to make arrangements for the remaining cash.

'You are a good bargainer,' Bedi said to me while dropping me off at Shukla-ji's residence.

◆

'You smash it,' said Shukla-ji, handing me a coconut at the entrance of the college site. A crowd of his sycophants surrounded us.

The *bhoomi pujan* ceremony marked the beginning of construction. I had run around for three months to obtain the two dozen approvals to make this day possible. The UGC and AICTE in-principle approvals had finally arrived. The final inspections would be conducted when the college was ready to open. For now, we had permission to begin construction.

The only other thing we needed were god's blessings. Fortunately, that didn't require a bundle of cash.

I held the coconut in my hand and looked around. Aarti hadn't arrived.

'Do it, son,' Shukla-ji said.

I couldn't wait for her any longer. I guess the day did not mean as much to her as it did to me.

I smashed the fruit, imagining it to be Raghav's head. As it cracked, a sliver of the shell cut my finger. People clapped around me. I took the cut finger to my mouth and sucked the bruise.

'GangaTech Engineering College' – two labourers fixed a metal hoarding in the muddy ground. I should have felt more emotion. After all,

I had slogged for months. However, I felt nothing. Maybe because I knew the exact amount of bribes it took to reach this day. Seventy-two lakhs, twenty-three thousand and four hundred rupees to obtain everything from electricity connections to construction site labour approvals.

Shukla-ji had invited over a hundred guests, including members of the press. We had a caterer who served hot samosas and jalebis in little white boxes.

Shukla-ji addressed everyone from a makeshift dais.

'Three more years, and this dream will be a reality. This is a gift to my city, which deserves the best,' he said.

I sat in the front row. I kept turning around to see if Aarti had arrived. After Shukla-ji's speech the press asked questions. Most were simple, relating to the courses that would be on offer and the upcoming college facilities. However, a few tough journalists did not spare him.

'Shukla sir, are you the owner of this college? How much is your stake?' one reporter asked.

'I am a trustee. I have no stake. It is a non-profit entity,' Shukla-ji said.

'Who is funding the land and construction?'

'Mr Gopal Mishra here owns this land. I want to encourage young talent so I helped him raise some funds,' Shukla-ji said and wiped his forehead with a handkerchief.

'Funds from where?' the reporter continued.

'From various benefactors. Don't worry, somebody has given money, not taken it. Media is so suspicious these days,' Shukla-ji said.

'Sir, what is happening in the Ganga Action Plan scam? You are named in that,' a reporter from the last row asked.

'It is an old and dead story. There is no scam. We spent the money to clean the river,' Shukla-ji said.

This new topic galvanised all the reporters. Everyone raised their hand as they scrambled to ask questions.

'No more questions, thank you very much,' Shukla-ji said.

The reporters ran behind him as he left the site. I stayed back, ensuring that the guests were served the refreshments.

A truck arrived with bricks, iron rods and other construction materials. Behind it, I saw a white Ambassador car with a red light on top.

Aarti got out of the car upon spotting me. 'I am so so so sorry,' she said. 'Are the prayers over?'

'Can the prayers ever be over without Aarti?' I said.

Varanasi
Three More Years Later

18

My arrival went unnoticed amidst loud music and the chatter of people. High-class parties make me nervous and I would have happily skipped Raghav's graduation bash that day if I could. I only went because I didn't want to come across as envious.

I felt no envy. My college, GangaTech, was to open in three months. After three years of working day and night, I had my building ready. I even had faculty recruitment interviews lined up and had obtained a date for the AICTE inspection. A stupid BHU degree meant little when I'd be issuing my own degrees soon.

'Hey!' Raghav said in a slightly tipsy voice. 'Buddy, where were you?'

'Negotiating with a computer supplier,' I said.

Raghav didn't seem to hear.

'For my college. We are setting up a computer centre,' I said.

Raghav raised his hand. 'Good show. Give me a high-five!'

He clapped my hand with his so hard that it hurt.

'You need a drink,' Raghav said. 'There's the bar.'

He gestured towards the dining table, on which were beer, rum and coke. People made their own drinks in plastic glasses. Raghav's parents had agreed to spend the night at some relative's house so that Raghav and his college-mates could have a night of debauchery.

I looked around at Raghav's pals. Thirty boys, most of them wearing glasses and old T-shirts and jabbering about job offers, and only three girls, who – given their lack of fashion sense – had to be from an engineering college.

I got myself a rum and coke. I looked for ice. There was none on the dining table, so I headed for the kitchen. A girl with long tresses, her back to me, was arranging candles on a huge chocolate cake. The cake had a gear-shaped design on it and said 'Happy Graduation' in perky white marzipan letters.

'Gopal!' Aarti said as she saw me struggle with the ice-tray I'd removed from the fridge.

Her voice startled me.

'It's been like,' Aarti said, 'a year?'

I had not kept in touch with her. 'Hi,' I said.

It's not like I wanted to evade her. But I saw no upside to remaining in touch either. I found it more productive to scream at construction workers than hear stories about her dates with her boyfriend. I started avoiding her calls and soon she too drifted away.

'Yeah, I am sorry, my fault,' I said. 'I got very busy at the site.'

She took the ice-tray from me, twisted it to release the ice-cubes and put two of them in my glass.

'I am not asking for an explanation. I understand I am not that important to you now.'

'That is not true. I had my site, you had Raghav,' I said. 'We have our own lives and ...'

'I have a boyfriend. Doesn't mean it is my entire life, okay?' Aarti said.

'Well, he kind of is, isn't he?' I said.

I offered her my drink. She declined. She went back to decorating the cake.

'Nothing like that. No *one* person can be that important.'

'Why?' I said. 'Something wrong?'

'No, no,' she said, too quickly I thought. 'It's great. Raghav's graduated. He has a job offer from Infosys. My aviation course finishes soon. It is still as strong as ever.'

'What?' I said.

'Us.'

'Us?'

'Me and Raghav,' she said.

'Of course,' I said.

She lifted the cake to take it to Raghav.

'I'll keep in touch,' I said.

'That would be nice. I haven't sat in a boat for a year,' she said and smiled.

The confusing, confounding Aarti had returned. What did she mean? Did she miss the boat rides? Did she miss being with me? Was she tossing a bone at me or was she just being witty? I came out of the kitchen, lost in my thoughts.

Everyone gathered around Raghav. He held a knife in his hand. Aarti stood next to him. Raghav cut the cake. Everyone clapped and hooted. I guess graduating from college is a big deal. Raghav fed the first piece to Aarti. Aarti offered a piece to Raghav.

As he opened his mouth, Aarti smeared the cake on his face. Everyone guffawed and clapped hard. I felt out of place. *What the fuck was I doing here? Why did these guys even invite me?*

'Speech! Speech!' the crowd began to demand of Raghav. Aarti took a tissue and wiped his face.

'Well, friends, congrats to all of you on your graduation,' Raghav said. 'We have spent four fabulous years together. As we get ahead with our lives, I am sure we will always have a special place for our campus in our hearts.'

'We will still be together, dude,' a bespectacled boy interrupted him, 'at Infosys.'

Seven people raised their glasses high in the air. They all had offers from the software company.

'Cheers!' they said.

Raghav kept quiet. 'Actually, I have an announcement,' he said. 'I won't be taking up the job offer.'

'What?!' people exclaimed in unison.

'Yes, I have decided to stay here,' Raghav said and draped his arm around Aarti's waist, 'to be near my love.'

'Yeah, right,' Aarti said, wiping a blob of icing from Raghav's cheek. 'Tell them the real reason.'

'That is the real reason,' he chuckled.

'No,' Aarti said, turning to the crowd. 'Mr Raghav Kashyap is staying back to join *Dainik* as a reporter.'

Murmurs of surprise ran through the crowd. Raghav had edited the college magazine, and even done a newspaper internship. However, few knew he had the courage to chuck Infosys to become a newspaper reporter.

Raghav chatted with his friends. Aarti sliced the cake for everyone. The music became loud again. I made another drink and leaned against the wall, wondering if I should leave.

Aarti offered me cake on a paper plate. I declined.

'So, when does your college open?' she said.

'In three months GangaTech starts admissions,' I said.

'Really? Can I apply?' She laughed.

'I'll print you a degree if you want, you do not even have to attend classes,' I said.

'Really?' she said, wagging a finger. 'Yeah, give me an Electronics Engineer degree like Raghav's. But better marks than him.'

'Sure,' I said.

She laughed even more. I had tried so hard the last four years to get over Aarti. Yet, one laugh of hers had set back years of effort. Suddenly it felt like we had never been apart.

I had to leave. 'I better go,' I muttered.

'Why?' she said, 'You just came.'

'I don't fit in here.'

'It's okay. I hardly know these people either. All nerdy engineers. Come, let's go to the balcony.'

♦

We sat in Raghav's balcony. I took little sips of my drink. The breeze blew Aarti's hair in my face. I moved away a bit.

'You finished your course at the aviation academy?' I said.

'Yes, Frankfinn ended two months ago. I am applying to all the airlines. Let's see if they call me for interviews,' she said.

'There's no airline in Varanasi.'

'Yeah, I'll have to move to Delhi or Mumbai. There's even a new low-cost airline in Bangalore. It depends.'

'On what?' I said.

'Where I get a job. Of course, now it is complicated as Raghav's here.'

'He can be a journalist in other cities too,' I said.

'I guess,' she said as she tucked her hair behind her ear. 'But he likes Varanasi. He knows this place and the issues here. How is your drink? Can I take a sip?'

I gave her my glass. 'How much does he get paid for this *Dainik* job?' I said. I had to know how much Raghav made.

She took a few sips and kept the glass for herself. 'A third of what Infosys would give him,' she said.

'Wow. And his parents are okay with it?'

'No way! They went ballistic when he told them. It isn't just about the money, he isn't using his engineering degree. They are still upset.'

'So?'

'So what? He doesn't care. He feels the revolution begins at home. Society changes only when individual family norms are challenged.'

'Revolution?' I said.

'Oh yeah, he is quite into that. The Great Indian Revolution. Oops, I finished your drink. I am so sorry,' she said and touched my arm in apology.

'It's fine. I'll make another one. And you are cool with his career choice?'

'Of course, I believe one should follow their passion. Am I not working towards mine? So an air hostess isn't the same as a revolution, but still, that's me.'

'What exactly is this revolution?' I said, irritated.

'Well, Raghav believes there will be a real people's revolution in India one day, that's his thing.'

'Why?'

'Ask him, he will explain it to you. Wait, I will get us more drinks.'

She went back in. I waited in the balcony. I did not want to be with the smug software types inside. I imagined a day when students from my college would get jobs. I wondered if big software companies would ever visit GangaTech. Of course, we had to open for admissions first.

She came back with a tray. It had two drinks, and a plate with sandwiches, cake and potato chips.

'I thought you might be hungry,' she said. Aarti cannot help but be the caring mother types.

'Thanks,' I said, taking my glass.

'Now tell me, why did you forget me?' Aarti said.

'Who said I had forgotten you?' I said. Our eyes met. It felt awkward after about three seconds. I blinked first.

'I have a mobile phone now. Do you want my number?' she said.

'Sure,' I said. Shukla-ji had given me a cellphone too. We exchanged numbers.

'I'd like to see your college sometime,' she said.

'Let it open. I'll do an inauguration,' I said.

'Is the college your passion?' she said.

'I don't know. It's the best opportunity life gave me.'

'Have you felt passionate about anything, Gopal? It's an amazing feeling,' Aarti said.

I remained silent as I stared at her, my passion.

'Anything?' she said.

'Money, I want to make lots of money,' I said.

She threw up her hands in the air. 'Oh, come on,' Aarti said, 'That's not passion. That's ambition.'

'I don't know, let's go in.' I stood up. I didn't want Raghav to see us alone.

'Stay here,' she said cajolingly and pulled me down by my hand. 'We haven't met for ages. What are you up to? Do you have a girlfriend?'

I shook my head.

'You should get one. It is amazing to be in love. A feeling even better than passion,' she said.

'It's amazing to be in love only when the other person loves you back,' I said. I regretted my statement instantly.

'Ouch! Below the belt.'

'I am sorry,' I said.

'That was so long ago. And Raghav and I are happy. So happy.'

'Should we go back in?' I said.

'If you are willing to open up,' Aarti said, 'you can find someone nice, Gopal.'

'I don't need anyone,' I said and looked away.

She held my chin and turned my face towards her. 'You will own a college. I will be just a flight attendant selling chips, if I am lucky. You can get someone better.'

'Someone better than you?' I said.

'Totally,' she said.

'That is not possible, Aarti,' I said. Before she could answer, I stood up again and returned to the party.

I went up to Raghav and told him I had to leave to meet a contractor. He didn't seem to mind it much. I came outside his apartment and took the stairs down. Aarti came after me. 'Gopal!'

I looked back at her from the steps. 'What?' I said.

'Don't tell me you still have feelings for me?'

I swallowed hard. 'Not at all,' I said and sprinted out.

19

'How long is your break?' I shouted. A group of labourers sat under the banyan tree near the main campus building. 'It's two-thirty, lunch ended an hour ago.'

We had only a week left for the final AICTE inspection. The classrooms needed a last lick of paint. The workers didn't care.

'Your work will be done, sahib,' said one of the workers, folding the newspaper he had been sitting on. He wore a tattered vest and dark trousers with cream paint all over it.

'My college won't open if the inspector is unhappy with us,' I said.

'Who is going to say no to your college?' the worker stood up.

The other workers tightened their turbans. They picked up their brushes and moved to the classrooms. I remained under the banyan tree, exhausted by my daily ritual of hauling up the men every two hours. I glanced down at the newspaper left behind by the workers. A headline caught my attention: 'Varanasi needs more colleges'.

I picked up the newspaper. Under the headline was the writer's name – Raghav Kashyap.

The article talked about how the youth population of Varanasi had grown significantly in the last ten years. At the same time, the number of colleges had not kept pace with the demand. It made recommendations on how the government could make education a priority. He even argued that the government should allow colleges to make a legitimate profit, so that corporate bodies could enter the sector and improve quality. Even though it came from Raghav, I liked the article. It augured well for my business.

The article had a separate box with a list of colleges about to open in Varanasi. It had five names, and I saw GangaTech in the list.

'Wow,' I said to myself, excited. I had never seen GangaTech's name in print. I dialled Shukla-ji's number.

'Well done!' Shukla-ji said. 'Wait and see how much press we get when we open.'

I wanted to call Raghav and ask if he could do a detailed piece on my college. A reputed newspaper talking well about GangaTech could do wonders for our opening.

I didn't have his mobile number. I could easily obtain it from Aarti. However, I didn't want to call her. I took the newspaper to the campus building. My office still didn't have furniture. I sat on a plastic chair and reminded myself to call the carpenter.

I looked at my phone contacts. Aarti always came first, given that her name begins with 'Aa'.

'I am only calling her to get Raghav's number,' I told myself many times before I felt courageous enough to call.

She picked up after four rings. 'Hey, what a surprise,' she said.

'Hi, how are you?' I said. I did not want to exchange pleasantries. However, to jump directly to my query seemed abrupt.

'I'm a little low, but that's okay,' she said. 'How are you? It was nice chatting with you at the party.'

I guess I should have enquired why she felt low. However, I side-stepped it. 'Yeah, listen, do you have Raghav's number?' I said.

'Of course. How come you want it?'

'There's an article of his I read in the paper today, on education. I liked it, wanted to tell him.'

'Oh, sure,' she said. 'He will be so happy.' She read out the number to me.

'Thanks, Aarti,' I said. 'Speak later then?'

'You don't want to know why I am low?' she said.

When a girl asks you that, you'd better say yes. 'I do. Why?' I said.

'Mom and dad won't let me leave Varanasi,' she said.

'Really? How will you fly for an airline then?' I said.

'Exactly. What am I supposed to become here? A boat hostess?'

'Convince them,' I said, for lack of better advice.

'They won't listen. I may have to run away.'

'Are you crazy? They will come around,' I said.

'Will you talk to them?' she said.

'Me?'

'Yeah, why not?'

'Who am I? Raghav will be better, no?' I said.

'Raghav? He doesn't even want me to go. Plus, he is so busy at the newspaper, he won't meet *me*, let alone my parents.'

'You have no other friend? Somebody from the aviation academy?' I said. 'Or maybe even your faculty?'

'You don't want to do it, is it?' she said.

'No, I just ... I just don't think I am the best person to talk to them about this.'

'Fine,' she said. 'Fine' means somewhere between 'whatever' and 'go to hell' in Girlese.

'Okay, the site engineer is calling me,' I lied. 'I will speak to you later.'

I hung up. I checked the duration of the call. I had spoken to her for seven minutes and twenty-two seconds. I felt like calling her again, and advising her on how to deal with her parents. *Maybe I should have agreed to meet her parents; after all, she had chosen me from all the people she knew.* I almost pressed re-dial when I checked myself.

Only pain will come from being close to her. She belongs to Raghav, and there is no place for me in her life, I scolded myself.

I called Raghav. He picked up the phone immediately.

'Hi, it's Gopal,' I said.

'Oh, hi,' he said. 'What's up, buddy? Thanks for coming to the party that day.'

'You are welcome. How's the new job?'

'They are letting me write, even though tame stuff.'

'I read your article today. Pretty good.'

'You read it? Wow. Thanks.'

'You mentioned GangaTech, thanks for that too.'

'Oh, our research team made that table. You are about to open, right?'

'Yes, almost ready. Would you like to visit? Maybe you can do a story specific to GangaTech.'

'Yeah, I could,' Raghav said, his voice hesitant. 'Though the policy might be to not talk about specific institutions.'

'Oh, in that case, forget it,' I said. I didn't want to take a favour from him, anyway.

'But I could do a story on you.'

'Me?'

'Yeah, a young boy from Varanasi opens a college. It is something. And in that interview we can talk about GangaTech.'

'I am more of an employee,' I said.

'MLA Shukla is the real person, right?' Raghav said.

'He is a trustee, yes.'

'And he paid to build the college?'

'Well, he arranged for the funds,' I said.

'From where?' Raghav said.

I didn't like his interrogative tone. 'He knows lots of charitable people,' I said. 'Anyway, do you want to interview me? Either way is fine.'

'Of course, I do. When do you want to do it?'

'I have an inspection next Friday. After that? Maybe the weekend,' I said.

'Sure, I will see you. Where? *Dainik* office?'

'No. Come to my office,' I said. I stressed the last two words. *I have a huge office now, buddy,* I wanted to tell him.

'Oh, sure. Where's your campus?'

'Ten kilometres outside the city on the Lucknow Highway. You will see the board on your right.'

I came out of the campus building. I examined the three-storey structure. We had to paint it gray in the coming week.

My phone rang. It was Bedi.

'Yes, Bedi sir,' I said.

'I've lined up seven solid faculty members for interviews tomorrow. Are you free?'

'I have no choice but to be free. I am on the site all day, can you bring them here?'

'No way. We have to go to their houses. Three other colleges are opening in the area. They all have offers. We have to lure them,' he said.

I sighed. Every day brought a new challenge.

'Fine, I will arrange a car from Shukla-ji's office,' I said.

◆

We reached Prof MC Shrivastava's house in Ashok Nagar at eight a.m. sharp, as instructed by the retired electrical engineering professor from NIT Allahabad. We had to get someone from NIT, if not an IIT, to be the dean. We had almost struck a deal with a retired NIT Bhopal professor. However, he found a better offer closer home in Indore. Prof Shrivastava was AICTE gold standard, with over thirty years' experience. Like all things golden, he didn't come cheap.

'Two lakhs a month?' I asked. 'But we have just started.'

Mrs Shrivastava, the professor's wife, served us tea and *poha* for breakfast. She joined the negotiations. 'Sri Amma College has made an offer. One and a half lakhs, plus a car with a driver,' she said.

'Madam, the university we are affiliated to controls our fee,' I said. 'Plus, we are new. I don't know how admissions will go.'

'Is that our problem?' Mrs Shrivastava asked, quite correctly.

Bedi jumped into the fray. 'Whatever reasonable requirements you have, tell us. We will accommodate,' he said.

'But we have a budget,' I said.

Shrivastava put his spoon down. 'Who are you,' he said to me, 'the owner's son?'

'I am the owner, Gopal Mishra. The college is on my land,' I said.

'And Shukla-ji? Doesn't *he* decide on this?'

'He is a silent trustee,' I said. '*I* decide.'

The professor looked at me for a few seconds, surprised at my defiance.

'Mr Mishra, the dean is most important. I know the AICTE people. With me, consider the inspection done,' Shrivastava said.

'We have a setting in the AICTE too,' I said, 'please understand. If I give you a high package, all other members of the faculty will demand similar levels.'

'You don't have to disclose my salary,' he said.

'How will we keep it hidden? The accounts department will have the details,' I said.

'Pay part of it in cash,' Shrivastava said. Silence descended over the table. He had already provided a solution. A more practical dean would be hard to find.

'How much?' I said.

'Fifty per cent? Maybe more,' he suggested. 'It only saves me taxes. And nobody feels jealous of me. In fact, my on-paper salary will be lower than that of the teachers.'

'We knew we had come to the right place,' Bedi said.

'Fine,' I said.

We settled for a one-lakh-cash-seventy-thousand-cheque package per month. The new dean came on board immediately. He offered to help us hire other faculty, for salaries ranging from thirty to eighty thousand a month, depending on experience and the degrees they possessed.

'I'll charge ten thousand per hire as search fee, apart from my salary.'

'That's fine. When can you start?' I said.

'Anytime,' he said. 'I will come to campus three days a week.'

'Three days?' I said. 'You are the dean of the institute. How can the college work without you?'

'I am the dean, that is why three days. Else, once a week is enough,' he said.

'What?' I said.

'Which faculty goes to teach every day in private colleges? Don't worry, I will tell the AICTE inspectors I am there every day.'

'But who will manage the faculty? Who will ensure that classes are held on time and the students are taught properly?' I said, my heart beating fast. I didn't know if this was how a college dean should be.

'It's a private college. We will manage. Tell him, Bedi-ji, how it works,' Shrivastava grinned.

Bedi finished his cup of tea and nodded. 'Of course. We will figure out the teaching arrangements and all later. Right now our focus is the inspection, and then the admissions. Later on, senior students can teach first-year students. Happens in many colleges.'

Mrs Shrivastava cleared the table. We moved to the drawing room.

'What's your admission strategy?' Shrivastava said.

'We are advertising in all newspapers. Participating in career fairs, also approaching schools and coaching classes,' I said.

'Approaching schools for what?' he asked.

'We'll go to schools and make a presentation on our college,' I said.

'Who cares about the presentation? Did you fix the principals?' Shrivastava said.

'We will, don't worry,' Bedi said.

'We will what?' I said. I hated it when Bedi didn't tell me things beforehand.

'I will explain to you. Let's go, we have other meetings,' Bedi said and stood up. 'Thanks, sir, will see you on Friday.'

Shrivastava came to see us off at the door. 'When do I get my first salary?' he said.

'I will send the cash home,' I said.

We had five more faculty prospects to meet. Shukla-ji had given us an Innova car for exclusive use of the college. We proceeded to Mughal Sarai to meet a retired chemical engineering professor.

'I am so relieved the dean is done,' Bedi said as the car reached the highway.

'He seemed more Mr Deal than Mr Dean to me,' I quipped.

'He has worked in private colleges before. He knows he is in demand. Don't take his tantrums personally,' Bedi said.

'What did he mean by "fix" the school principals?' I said.

'The schools have a big influence on where the child goes next. Many try for an IIT and NIT, most don't make it. Where do they go?'

'Where?' I said.

'That's where we come in. Private colleges can fulfil your dream of becoming an engineer, even if you didn't clear the entrance exam. The problem is, there are so many private colleges now. How does the student choose?'

I asked the driver to decrease the temperature of the air-conditioner, to beat the forty degrees outside. 'How?' I said.

'They go with the school teachers' and principals' advice. Who else can they trust?'

'True,' I said. 'So, we ask the principal to recommend our college?'

'Exactly! You are smart,' Bedi said, probably in sarcasm.

'Do we bribe them too?' I said.

'Yes. But never say that word, especially to school principals. Anyway, it is a straightforward calculation. We give them ten per cent of the fee we take for every admission.'

A defined sum doesn't sound like a bribe.

'We give ten per cent to anyone – coaching classes, career fair organisers or whoever helps us fill up the college.'

'Ten per cent it is,' I said.

'You are working on the media plan, right?' he said.

My thoughts went to our media strategy, then to Raghav, and from there to Aarti. It is amazing how the brain will connect one thought to another until it gets to where it wants to be.

Bedi continued to talk about how we will fill two hundred students for the first batch. I tuned out, looking at the fields outside and remembering Aarti's flowing hair as she took a sip from my drink in Raghav's balcony. Life is a bitch when the only woman you can think of belongs to someone else.

20

I saw Raghav enter the campus from the window of my office. I had screamed at the carpenters to get my office desk and chairs finished in time. Apart from the missing visitors' sofa, my office had become functional. The air-conditioner worked. I increased the cooling to maximum to ensure Raghav noticed it. I surrounded myself with files. He came and knocked on the half-open door.

'Yes?' I said and looked up.

'We did say two o' clock, right?' Raghav said. He wore a white shirt and blue jeans.

'Hi, Raghav. Sorry, I keep so busy, I lose track of time sometimes,' I said.

He sat across me. I sat on the director's chair. I wondered if he noticed how I had a far more plush chair than his.

He took out his notepad, pen and a few printouts. 'I did some research, whatever I could find on the college.'

'You won't find much. We are new,' I said.

'Yes, but I found a lot on one of the trustees, Shukla.'

'Of course, he is a popular politician. But he isn't really involved in the functioning of the college.'

'He's involved in many other things though.' Raghav smoothed out the printout with the questions.

'Tea?' I said.

He nodded. I rang the bell. I had asked the peon to bring tea in the bone china cups we kept for special guests. Not that Raghav counted as special. However, I wanted him to know we had tea in fancy cups.

He looked around the huge twenty-by-eighteen-feet office. I wanted to ask him if anyone in his newspaper had such a big office, but controlled myself.

He noticed an architect's model of the campus behind me. 'Can I take a look?' he said.

'Sure,' I said and jumped up. 'Let me show you all the facilities.'

I explained the campus layout to him. 'The hostels are here. We will keep adding more rooms with successive batches. The classrooms and faculty offices are here, in the main building we are in right now. The labs are in a separate building. All imported equipment.'

'What will be the faculty ratio?' Raghav said, taking frantic notes.

'We are targeting no more than one teacher per fifteen students,' I said, 'which is better than the AICTE norms. One day we want to be better than BHU.'

He looked at me.

'Just as a goal. Who else is there to compare with?' I said.

He shrugged his shoulders in support.

The tea arrived. I had instructed the peon to serve at least five snacks. He brought nuts, biscuits, samosas, potato chips and cut fruits.

'That's not tea. That's a meal,' Raghav said.

'Please have. We can continue the interview later,' I said as the peon served us.

We ate in silence. I didn't want to discuss anything other than the college with him. He picked up his notepad as he ate.

'What kind of investment went into this college?' he said.

'Lots. Engineering colleges aren't cheap,' I said and laughed, avoiding any real figures.

'How much exactly?' he said.

'Hard to say. I had the land, but if you had to buy it, you can imagine the prices,' I said.

'Isn't this agricultural land?' he said.

'Yes, you know that, Raghav. Remember Baba's court case?'

'You managed to get it from your relatives?' he said.

'Yes, but that's not going into the interview, right?' I said.

'No. But tell me, how did this agricultural land get re-zoned?'

'We applied, the VNN approved,' I said.

He continued to take notes.

'Everything is approved,' I repeated, perhaps too defensively.

'Because of Shukla?' he asked.

'No,' I said, somewhat irritated. 'Because we followed procedures.'

'Fine. How much did the college cost apart from the land?' he said.

'I am not sure if I can reveal that. It is, after all, competitive information. But anyone who visits our campus can see it is state of the art,' I said.

'More than five crores?' he persisted. I shouldn't have entered his guessing game.

'Yes,' I said.

'More than ten?' he said.

'How is the actual number relevant?' I said.

'Where did the money come from?' he said.

'From the trustees and their associates.'

'Whose associates? Yours or Shukla's?' he said.

'I gave the land. Shukla-ji arranged for the funds, for the benefit of this town. We are a non-profit trust,' I said.

'Do you know where the MLA arranged the funds from?' Raghav asked, without looking up from his diary.

'No. And I don't see why I should know. It is his and his friends' private wealth.'

'Are you aware of Shukla's involvement in the Ganga Action Plan scam?' he said.

'No, Raghav. I don't want to comment on anything other than GangaTech. If you have all the information, we can end the interview.'

Raghav put away his pen. 'I'm sorry. Yes, I am done. Don't worry, I will do a balanced piece.'

'Thanks, I will see you out.'

We walked together to the campus gate. He had come on an old scooter that belonged to his dad.

'I could have sent my car to pick you up,' I said. 'It is too hot.'

'It's fine. I have to go to many places,' he said and put his helmet on.

'Do you miss engineering?' I said, my first general question to him.

'Not really. Never became one, I guess,' he said.

I felt the time was right to deliver my final punch. 'You are from BHU. You'd look great on our faculty list. Want to join?' I said. Yes, I could hire him. BHU may not have taken me, but I could take their graduates.

'Me? Faculty? No way. Besides, I have a job,' he said and sat on the scooter.

'You don't have to come much. Help me with the inspections, and maybe come once a week,' I said.

He was about to start his scooter, but stopped midway. He mulled over my words.

'We pay well. Maybe more than your newspaper,' I added.

He smiled and shook his head.

'Why not?' I said, irked by his easy rejection.

'I can't be part of a corrupt enterprise,' he said.

'*What*?'

'It is Shukla's college.'

'It is mine,' I protested.

'I know you will run it, but he is behind it, right?'

'So? How can you call us corrupt? We haven't even opened yet.'

'It's built with money made by corrupt practices.'

'I have worked my ass off for three years, Raghav. Three years, Sundays included. How can you make a statement like that?'

'He is accused of stealing twenty crores from the Ganga Action Plan. Government money meant to clean our river.'

'It is an accusation. Not proven,' I said.

'Right after that he made many property investments, including this college. Can't believe you didn't see through it. How can a politician have so much money? He comes from a humble background.'

'Can you prove wrongdoing?' I said.

'Not yet. But are you sure he didn't do anything?' he queried.

I couldn't control myself anymore. 'You are jealous,' I said.

'What?'

'You are jealous that I am doing well. I am not supposed to do well, right? After all, my AIEEE rank was lower than yours. Isn't it, Mr JEE?'

'Easy, buddy. This is not personal,' he said and kick-started his scooter.

'Then what is it, Mr Reporter?'

'It's my job to figure out the truth, that's all.'

Before I could respond, he zoomed off. He left behind a cloud of dust that stung my eyes more than anything ever had in the past year.

◆

The day of the AICTE inspection felt like an exam day. Our faculty of twenty reached the campus at 8:00 a.m. Sweepers scrubbed the floors till the last minute. The IT specialist ensured that the desktops in the computer room worked. We had arranged a dinner at Taj Ganga for the inspection committee. Shukla-ji had promised me he'd come, but backed out at the last minute due to an urgent rural visit. Sweat beads formed on my forehead. I made the fifth trip to the campus gate to check if the inspectors had arrived yet.

'Stand straight,' I hollered at the security guard, 'and salute all guests.'

'Relax, Director Gopal,' Dean Shrivastava said, 'I will handle them.'

They arrived only at eleven. Ashok Sharma, our junior-most faculty member, waited with bouquets at the main building entrance.

The head of the inspection committee shook my hand. 'I am Jhule Yadav, ex-professor from NIT Delhi.'

'I am Gopal Mishra, promoter and director of the college. Meet Dean Shrivastava, ex-director of NIT Allahabad,' I said.

Yadav and Shrivastava exchanged glances, sizing each other up like boxers in a ring. We walked to my office and sat down on the new sofas that smelt of varnish.

'NIT Allahabad?' Yadav asked. 'You had a Barua in Electrical? He went to Stanford later.'

'Yes,' Shrivastava said, 'I hired him.'

'Barua was my student,' Yadav said and slapped his thigh.

Suddenly the lights went out. Everyone sighed as darkness engulfed us. We had power supply issues in the nearby villages. We had no electricity for six hours every afternoon.

'We have a generator,' I said, and went to tell the peon to switch it on.

The office was turning stuffy.

'Should we go outside?' said one middle-aged member of the inspection team.

'Any minute now, sir,' I said. The tube-light in my office blinked as power came back on.

'How many lathe machines are there in your machining lab?' asked an inspector.

'Eight,' Shrivastava said. 'We will take a round later.'

'Shrivastava sir, why walk around in the heat?' Yadav said.

'Your team member asked a question, sir,' Shrivastava said.

Everyone turned to the inspector who had asked the lathe machine question. 'You are?' Shrivastava said.

'Mr Bhansali,' said the inspector.

'Mr Bhansali, why don't we all move to my office for course-related questions? Unless you need the promoter.'

'You look young,' Bhansali said to me.

'I *am* young,' I said.

'What are your qualifications?' he said.

'I have built this college,' I said, 'and I have hired the best faculty.'

'But …' Bhansali said as Shrivastava cut him.

'Let's go, sir. I will answer everything,' Shrivastava said and escorted them out.

When everyone was out, Shrivastava came back into my office. 'Bhansali is new. The other six won't say a word. Lunch is coming, right?'

'Yes, the caterer is already here,' I said.

'Good. And the packets?'

'Packets?'

'Gopal, do I have to explain it? This is AICTE.'

'Oh,' I said. 'You mean the envelopes. Of course, I have them ready.'

'Good. Give it to them after dessert. How much?'

'Two for Yadav, and twenty-five each for the rest?' I said.

'Make it fifty for Bhansali,' Shrivastava said. 'What's for dessert?'

'Moong daal halwa,' I said.

'My favourite!' Prof Shrivastava said and left.

◆

We had booked a private room in Taj Ganga for the AICTE inspection dinner. We had also invited our entire faculty and senior government officials who had helped us in the past. They came with families. This party of a hundred people burnt another hole in GangaTech's pocket.

We hadn't earned a rupee of revenue yet. We had spent six crores already on construction, equipment, faculty, and of course, fixing government officials.

However, Shukla-ji didn't seem to care.

'Relax, we will recover the money,' Shukla-ji said. He handed me a whisky with soda.

I scanned the room. 'We have paid bribes to at least thirty people in this room,' I said.

Shukla-ji laughed.

'What have we done wrong? We only wanted to open a college,' I said.

'It's okay,' Shukla-ji said. 'If we had a straightforward and clean system, these professors would open their own colleges. Blue-chip companies and software firms could open colleges. The system is twisted, they don't want to touch it. That is where we come in.'

'When will we make money? I paid five lakhs today for the inspection.'

'Pay them some more,' Shukla-ji said.

'Who?'

'The inspectors.'

'Why?' I said. 'Shrivastava sir said it is enough. We will get the approval in a week.'

'I want them to not only clear the college, but also say great things about GangaTech,' Shukla-ji said.

'In writing?' I said.

'Yes, which we will use for marketing. Ten thousand more to the minions, fifty more to the main guy. I'll arrange the cash.'

He took out his phone and made a call.

Shukla-ji and I went to the dinner buffet. We filled our plates with food, and came to one corner of the room. 'The cash will arrive in an hour,' he told me.

'Why do you trust me so much, Shukla-ji. I could steal your money.'

'You don't have a family. Whom would you steal for?' he said.

21

The AICTE approval came on time, as promised by Prof Shrivastava. We had one final step before we opened for admissions. We needed the state university affiliation. Mangesh Tiwari, the vice-chancellor, had sat on our application for months.

We were at Shukla-ji's place. 'Affiliation is a simple job. We are offering him double the market rate. Mangesh is turning senile,' Bedi said.

'How much does he want?' Shukla-ji asked.

'It's not about the money. He doesn't like us. Doesn't even take our calls,' Bedi said.

'What is the solution?' I said.

'Use some contacts. Non-political if possible, he is a college batchmate of our DM,' Bedi said.

'I know the DM's daughter. Old school friend,' I said.

'Well, do whatever it takes. I want admissions to open next week. Full-page ads in every paper,' Shukla-ji said.

'Don't worry, next Sunday Varanasi will talk only about GangaTech,' I said.

◆

I had promised myself not to call Aarti. However, I had no choice.

'Look who's calling today!' Aarti chirped.

'You sound happy,' I said.

'Do I? Maybe because you called. I don't really have another reason.'

'Why? What happened?' I said.

'Nothing. I have to find a job in Varanasi.'

'That's not so bad.'

'Will your college have its own plane?' she said.

'Not yet,' I said. 'But if we do, we will make you cabin supervisor.'

She laughed. 'How are you? When will your college actually have students?'

'When we manage to please every Indian government official on this earth,' I said. 'Actually, I had called for some work.'

'What?' she said.

'I wanted to meet your dad.'

'Really? How come?'

'We need some help in getting through to the state university.'

'You want to speak to him now?'

'No, I'd prefer to meet him face to face,' I said.

'Would you like to meet *me* face to face?' she said. 'Or am I still on the blacklist? To be called only in work emergencies.'

'Nothing like that. We can catch up after I meet your dad.'

'Of course, work first,' she said in a sarcastic tone.

'My admissions are stuck, Aarti. It's urgent,' I said.

'Okay, okay, fine. Hold on a second, let me check with him,' she said.

She spoke to her father and picked up the phone again. 'Tomorrow morning at eight?'

'Sure,' I said. 'I will see you then.'

◆

'You never come home now. Not friends with Aarti anymore?' DM Pradhan said.

We sat in his study. A lifesize portrait of Aarti's grandfather, ex-CM Brij Pradhan, stared at me from the wall. DM Pradhan – broad faced with chiselled features, fit and proud – sipped coffee with me.

'Nothing like that, Uncle. Work keeps me busy,' I said.

'I have heard about your college. Shukla-ji's involed in it, right?' DM Pradhan said.

'Yes, and now we are one step away from admissions,' I said and explained the problem with VC Tiwari.

He heard me out and then said, 'Let me see.' He took out his cellphone and called the VC.

'Tiwari sir? Hello, Pratap Pradhan here … Yes, long time. How are you?'

Aarti's father fixed a meeting between us and Tiwari in the afternoon.

'Thank you so much,' I said, preparing to leave.

'You are welcome. Listen, have you paid Tiwari?'

I felt awkward discussing such issues with Aarti's dad, so I kept quiet.

'I know how the education business works. Tiwari talks intellectual, but he wants his share. I hope you guys won't get me involved with that.'

'Not at all, sir,' I said. 'Even I don't deal with that stuff. I only look after the college.'

'So all such work is done by Shukla-ji's men?' Aarti's father asked.

'Yes,' I said as I gazed at the floor.

'Good, you are like me then,' he said. 'Practical enough to leave the people who do the funny stuff alone.'

I nodded and bowed to him before I left his room.

♦

'One chocolate milk shake with ice cream, please,' Aarti said. We had come to the same CCD in Sigra where Sunil had brought me after the career fair debacle.

'Black tea,' I said.

She wore a mauve chikan salwar-kameez. Her father had bought it for her from Lucknow. She removed her white dupatta and kept it aside.

The waiter placed her milk shake on the table. She put her lips to the straw, without touching the overflowing glass with her hands. 'I often spill this. I better be careful,' she said.

Wisps of her hair brushed the table as she sipped her drink. The entire café checked her out.

'We should totally do this more often,' she said, 'coffee meetings. Even though neither of us is having coffee.'

'I don't think so,' I said.

'Why? You don't like meeting me?' she said. 'So much for being my best friend for over ten years!'

'Raghav won't appreciate it,' I said.

'What is wrong in meeting for coffee? Besides, Raghav is too busy to be bothered by such things.'

'Of course, big reporter now. I met him,' I said as I lifted my cup.

'You did,' she said, still sipping her milk shake as her eyebrows shot up.

'He interviewed me, for his paper.'

'What for?' she said.

'Local boy starts college.'

'It's true. Quite an achievement.'

'Yeah, for a loser like me.'

'I didn't say that,' she said. 'Hey, you'd like something to eat?'

Before I could answer she ordered two chocolate chip muffins. If Aarti had a choice, there would be nothing but chocolate to eat in the world.

'How's your job-hunt going?' I said.

'I have an offer. I am not sure I want to take it.'

'Really? What is the offer?'

'Guest relations trainee, Ramada Hotel. They are opening up in Cantonment.'

'Five-star, isn't it?'

'Yeah, they came to meet dad for some work. Dad found out about the vacancy, I applied and now they want me to start next month.'

'Go for it. I know you, you can't sit at home,' I said.

'You know me better than most people, Gopal,' she said, 'but …'

'What?' I said.

The muffins arrived but she didn't touch them. I noticed her eyes. They had turned moist. A tear trickled down her cheek.

'Aarti, are you okay?' I passed her a tissue.

She wiped her eyes and returned the eyeliner-stained tissue to me. 'Once I join, my parents will say – this is a good job, close to home, stay here. If I sulk at home, maybe they will let me try for some airline.'

I scoffed at her. 'What is the need to cry for this? You've got a good job. You have done a course in hospitality ...'

'Aviation, not hospitality.'

'Fine, but a flight attendant also serves guests, like hotel staff. And a guest relations trainee has better scope for growth. Trainee today, officer tomorrow, maybe GM of the hotel some day. You are smart. You will rise.'

She sniffed a few times to control herself.

'You think so?' she said, her eyes even more beautiful when glistening with tears.

I couldn't respond, so lost was I in the details of her face.

'What? Did the eyeliner spread?' she laughed. 'I am so stupid, crying away like a baby.'

'No, you are not. You wouldn't have got the job otherwise,' I said.

'Should I take it?'

'Why not? Quit if you don't like it. What does Raghav say?'

'Nothing.'

'Meaning?'

'I haven't met him since the offer. I called him, but he said I should do whatever I want. He is in some village this week for a story.'

'It's good for both of you if you stay here,' I said.

'Well, he didn't say that at all.'

'I am sure he realises it.'

'I don't think he cares so much about my issues, unless I am involved in a corruption scandal,' she said.

I smiled like she had intended me to. I asked for the bill.

'So, coffee friends?'

'We are friends,' I said.

'Cool. It's not officially open, but I will show you the hotel sometime. It's pretty grand.'

'Sure,' I said.

'When can I see GangaTech?' she said.

'Two more weeks,' I said, 'I promise. It's almost done.'

We walked to her car.

'I laughed, I cried. It is so nice to meet you,' Aarti said.

'Same here, I didn't cry though,' I said.

She laughed again. She hugged me and held me slightly longer than usual.

'Old friends are old friends, Gopal. Boyfriends and all are fine, but they never understand you like old friends can.'

I hated the word 'friends' but didn't say anything, just waved goodbye.

My phone rang. Bedi.

'The VC has called us for a meeting. The phone call from the DM worked. They know each other from childhood,' he said.

'Old friends are old friends,' I said.

22

For GangaTech's opening I wore a suit for the first time in my life. I supervised the decorations. We slept in my office the night before. We had turned three classrooms into admission centres. I stayed up to ensure we had forms, pens and information booklets.

Shukla-ji had gone all out too. He had managed to convince the Chief Minister to come and inaugurate the college. Two state ministers would accompany him. The security officials of the politicians had already visited us the day before. Since we didn't have an auditorium yet, we had erected a makeshift podium inside a tent for the speeches.

'Two thousand invites sent, sir, to all prominent families in Varanasi,' Ajay, from the chemical engineering faculty, told me.

We had promised lunch. Hence, we expected at least half of the invitees to turn up. Given the distance, we had arranged four buses for the general public, and a dozen cars to ferry the media to and fro.

I had spent ten lakhs on full-page ads in leading city newspapers, three days in a row. You only get one shot at a launch. Shukla-ji wanted the city to know he had built an institution.

Work ended at 5:30 a.m. I lay down on the office sofa for a power nap before the function. Shukla-ji's call woke me up at six-thirty. I rubbed my eyes, disoriented.

'Good morning, Shukla-ji,' I said.

'*Did you see the newspaper?*'

I realised he must have seen the full-page ads and called in excitement. After years of waiting, finally the day had come. 'No, I am in campus. The paper hasn't arrived yet,' I said.

'How did this happen?' Shukla-ji said.

I wondered why he didn't sound happy. Maybe he is not a morning person, I thought. 'The ads look nice, don't they?'

'Not the ads, you idiot. I am talking about the article in *Dainik*.'

Shukla-ji had never called me names before. Sure, I worked for him. But he had never raised his voice at me until now.

'What article?' I said, my hand going to my sleep-deprived, throbbing temples.

'Read the paper and call me.'

'Okay. How do the ads look?'

I only heard a click in response.

I shouted for the peon and asked him to fetch all the newspapers. In an hour I had them on my desk.

Every paper had our full-page colour ad. The campus photograph looked beautiful. I saw my name at the bottom of the ad. Shukla-ji's harsh words rang in my head.

I flipped through *Dainik*. On page six I found the article.

The headline said: '**New engineering college opens in city – with corruption money?**'

'What the fuck!' I said to myself as I read further.

Raghav Kashyap, Staff Reporter

I couldn't believe he had done this. The first few lines seemed harmless.

The city of Varanasi, also called the City of Learning, can boast of another engineering college of its own. The GangaTech College of Engineering, set in a fifteen-acre campus on the Lucknow Highway, opens its gates for admissions this weekend.

Raghav had indeed mentioned the facilities we offered, the faculty profile, the branches of engineering available and the selection process. The half-page article also carried a picture of Shukla-ji and me. I had never seen my picture in a newspaper. However, I couldn't savour the moment as I continued to read the article.

Interestingly, MLA Raman Lal Shukla is one of the trustees of GangaTech. He has helped fund the college. Shukla also owns land around the GangaTech campus, estimated to cost between five and ten crores. Where did Shukla obtain these funds from? Incidentally, he floated the college three years ago, around the same time that his name came up in the Ganga Action Plan scam. Is this college an attempt to clean up his reputation? People come to the Ganga to clean their sins. Is Shukla trying to clean away his sins against Ganga?

'Fuck you,' I said as I finished the article.

I crumpled the newspaper. This could not be happening to us. Not on the day of admissions. Not on any day. Shukla-ji called again. I hesitated but picked up.

'I saw it,' I said.

'How the hell did this happen? Who is this behenchod reporter Raghav? He really interviewed you?'

'He is my … f … friend … from school,' I said, stammering. 'He had promised a balanced piece.'

'This is balanced? He has shoved it up my ass.'

'I am really sorry, Shukla-ji. Don't worry, other papers don't have this story.'

'*Dainik* is the biggest and most influential. The CM has already cancelled his visit.'

'What?' I said, shocked. 'Who will inaugurate the college? We have a stone plaque in his name.'

'I don't know. The peon can inaugurate it for all I care,' Shukla-ji said.

'Please be calm, Shukla-ji,' I said. 'Really, we have to find someone in the next three hours.'

The MLA took a deep breath. 'The state minister for education is still coming. He can inaugurate it.'

'And the plaque?'

'Put a sticker on it, Gopal. Do I have to tell you everything?'

'Sorry, Shukla-ji. I will fix it,' I said.

I began a round of follow-ups. Most of the invitees confirmed their presence. A free lunch beats corruption allegations any day.

'May I come in, sir?' I heard a female voice as I finished a call.

I looked up. 'Aarti!'

'Am I disturbing you?' she said. 'I am early.'

She had come at nine, an hour before the scheduled inauguration. Even in my stressed state, I noticed she had dressed up for the occasion. She wore a bottle green salwar-kameez with a purple and gold border.

I continued to stare at her, my mouth half open. 'May I come in, Director sir?' she said.

'Huh? Yeah, of course,' I said. 'Wow, you look …'

'What?' she said.

'You look so formal,' I said. Stunning, is what I wanted to say.

'Oh, I thought you might say I look nice.'

'That's obvious, Aarti.'

'What's obvious?'

'You always look good,' I said.

'Yeah? I don't hear that so much these days.'

'Why? Your boyfriend doesn't say it?' I asked with a sting in my voice, thoughts of Raghav's article not leaving my head.

She sighed. 'Unless I dress up in newsprint I don't think he would notice.'

I smiled. And started to check the list of school principals to see if I had missed anyone.

'You seem busy,' Aarti said. 'Should I wait outside?'

I would have never let Aarti go, but I had tons of calls to make.

'Will you be okay outside?' I said.

'Yes, mom is here. Dad couldn't come. He is on tour.'

'Oh,' I said. 'Let me wish her at least.'

We walked outside. Her mother was sitting in the front row, one of the first guests in the tent.

'Hello, aunty,' I said, my hands folded.

'Congratulations, Gopal. What a lovely campus,' she said.

'It's still under construction,' I said, gesturing at a waiter to bring tea and snacks.

'Don't worry about us,' Aarti said. 'You do your function. Attend to all the high-profile guests.'

She hugged me before I left. I noticed her mother's eyes on me.

I folded my hands once more and excused myself.

◆

The inauguration ceremony went off smoothly, though without the CM the event lost some of its sheen. The state education minister unveiled the college plaque, his name stuck over the CM's on the black granite stone. There were murmurs among the media members regarding the CM's absence.

'The CM had to cancel in the last minute due to a crisis,' Shukla-ji said as he came on stage. He kept his speech to less than a minute. The press scrambled to ask questions. They all wanted to talk about the *Dainik* article. However, the MLA dodged them all from podium to gate.

'My apologies, no questions today. I have to visit villages. The farmers need me. Mr Gopal Mishra will take it from here.'

Within minutes, he had left the campus in his car. He called me from the highway.

'I want to speak to the bloody editor of *Dainik*,' he said.

'Sure, I will set it up,' I said. 'By the way, the admission forms are going well.'

'Do the bastards know how many ads we give them?' he went on.

'Shukla-ji, on the admissions …' I said.

But he had already cut the call.

◆

We hoped to fill the remaining seats with an ad campaign.

'We want to advertise all year,' I told the marketing head of *Varanasi Times*. 'We expect a bigger discount.'

I had spent the whole day doing the rounds of newspapers to book more ads. I sat in the office of Amar Trivedi, marketing head of *Varanasi Times*.

'Why don't you make us your media partner?' he said.

'What's that?' I said.

'For a little extra fee we publish positive articles about your college. We get news, you get an image. It is a win-win partnership,' he said.

'How do I know they will be positive?' I said. Once bitten, twice shy.

'You send us the articles,' Amar said.

I asked him to send me a formal proposal.

After *Varanasi Times*, I went to Bansphatak to visit the *Dainik* office.

'Welcome Gopal-ji,' Sailesh Gupta, the sales manager at *Dainik*, greeted me at the building entrance.

I flashed him a curt smile. We went to his office.

'What will you have, sir?' he said.

I shook my head.

'Tea? Coffee??'

'Articles full of lies?' I said.

'What?' he said.

'Sailesh, I signed you the biggest cheque among all the places we advertised in. And what did you do? On the day of our launch?'

Sailesh understood my context and shifted his gaze.

'I have five lakhs more to spend next week. Tell me why I should not make *Varanasi Times* happy and give them this?' I waved the trust's chequebook at him.

'Gopal bhai,' Sailesh said in a low voice, 'what are you saying? We are the number one newspaper.'

'So? You fuck us?'

'Gopal bhai, I didn't do it.'

'College made with corrupt money! You have made money from us too.'

'It is the editorial. They are stupid, impractical people,' Sailesh said.

I banged my fist on the table.

'I want to meet your editor-in-chief. If you want me to book any ads after this,' I said.

Sailesh glanced at my chequebook. He stood up.

'Let's go,' he said. I followed him to the editorial floor.

In his glass cabin, Ashok Kumar, the editor-in-chief, was in a meeting with some sub-editors. Sailesh went in, the sub-editors came out. Sailesh signalled for me to enter.

Ashok scanned me from tip to toe. 'You are from MLA Shukla's office?' he said.

'I am the director of GangaTech College,' I said and offered my hand. He shook it in a cursory manner and asked me to sit down.

'I saw the full-page ads,' Ashok began, looking a bit puzzled about my presence in his cabin.

'Did you see the article you did on us?' I said.

'I am sure I must have. Who did it?' Ashok said. He put on his spectacles and turned to his computer to search.

'Sir may not remember the reporter,' Sailesh told me. 'Should we search by date?'

'Raghav Kashyap wrote it,' I said.

'The new hire?' Ashok said, upbeat for the first time. He quickly located the article on his computer. He turned the monitor towards us. 'This one?'

I nodded.

'I must congratulate the reporter. He's new, yet his stories are getting noticed.'

'If you write nonsense you will get noticed,' I said.

'What happened Sailesh-ji. Why is your client so upset? We have done a half-page profile on their college,' Ashok said.

'Why the last two paras? And the headline?' I butted in.

'What?' Ashok said and skimmed the article again. 'Oh, the corruption stuff. What is the big deal in that?'

'It affects our image,' I said, bringing down both my palms forcefully on the table.

Ashok didn't appreciate my display of emotion. He stared at me. I removed my hands from the table.

'If you are so concerned about image, why did you open a college with MLA Shukla?' Ashok said.

Sailesh realised this wasn't going well.

'Sir, GangaTech is expected to be our biggest account,' Sailesh said.

'So, we should stop reporting news in a fair manner?' Ashok said.

'The allegations have not been proved,' I said. 'A three-year-old dead issue is brought out on the day of the opening. Is that fair?'

'Ashok sir, let's talk in private for two minutes,' Sailesh said.

I stood outside the office as they spoke. I looked around. I asked a peon where Raghav Kashyap sat. I saw his tiny cubicle. It occupied less space than the sofa in my office. I saw Raghav. He was typing furiously on his computer, unaware of the world around him.

Sailesh called me back in. 'Don't worry, it is all settled. Ashok sir will speak to the MLA directly. We will sort it out. Please, let's continue our association,' Sailesh said.

'Okay,' I said. 'What about the reporter?'

'What about him?' Sailesh said. 'He is a trainee.'

'I want him to apologise to me,' I said.

Sailesh looked at Ashok.

'That's up to him,' Ashok said. He picked up the phone and asked his secretary to send Raghav in.

Five minutes later, Raghav knocked on the door.

'Sir, you called me?' Raghav said, then saw me. 'Hey, Gopal. You here?'

'You guys know each other?' Ashok said, one eyebrow raised.

'He interviewed me,' I said.

Raghav seemed surprised by my terse statement. He realised I didn't want to establish any prior connection.

'What's the matter?' Raghav said, as he noticed the serious mood in the room.

Sailesh recounted our earlier discussion.

'Apologise?' Raghav said. 'Gopal, you want me to apologise to you?'

'Do you guys know each other from before?' Ashok said, catching on to the undercurrents.

'We went to the same school,' I said.

'And sat at the same desk. Close friends,' Raghav said. 'Why don't you tell them that?'

Why don't I tell them you took my girl, you asshole, I wanted to say. *Or that you are so jealous of my success that you planted a stinker article?*

'These corruption allegations are unfounded. And there is no need to mention them in a college profile,' I said.

'I had to be balanced,' Raghav said. 'Shukla is a known crook.'

'Nonsense,' I said, my voice loud.

'Mr Gopal, let's not raise our voice. Raghav, you don't have to be an activist in every story,' Ashok said.

'Sir, I hardly wrote anything. I didn't probe the building violations in the college.'

'There are no violations. All our plans are approved,' I said.

'And how did Shukla get these approvals? Anyway, I didn't mention any of that.'

'Even the Ganga Action Plan is old news, Raghav,' Ashok said. 'Unless you have new, solid evidence, no point repeating it. We can't keep spoiling someone's name.'

Raghav ran his fingers through his hair distractedly. 'Fine, I won't do it until I find something solid. May I leave now?'

'You haven't apologised to Gopal sir,' Sailesh said. 'GangaTech's our client.'

'Editorial only apologises for genuine errors,' Raghav said.

'Or if your chief editor tells you to,' Sailesh said, his voice firm.

Raghav looked at Ashok. Ashok kept quiet.

'Sir, how can you …' Raghav began.

'Raghav, let's get it over with. I have to sign off the next edition in one hour,' Ashok said, turning back to his computer screen.

Silence for ten seconds or so.

'I'm sorry,' Raghav said on a sigh.

'It's okay,' I said, but Raghav had already stomped out of the room.

23

'You and Raghav had an argument?' Aarti said. She had called me late at night, her preferred time.

'He told you?' I said.

'I suggested that the three of us meet up and he almost bit my head off,' she said.

'No way! I like your head,' I said.

'The hotel opens next week. I thought I would take permission and show you guys the place beforehand. It is so beautiful,' she said.

'You can show him separately,' I said.

'What happened?' Aarti said. 'You met him, right? Why doesn't anybody tell me anything?'

'It was work-related, don't worry. All settled now.'

'If you say so. Can you come around tomorrow?'

'Of course.'

'Good night, Director saheb!'

◆

I waited for Aarti at the Ramada Hotel entrance. The security wouldn't let me in. Aarti arrived and flashed her staff card and I followed her in. She wore a maroon Banarasi sari, her uniform. 'Aarti Pratap Pradhan – Guest Relations Trainee,' her badge said.

'Wow, you look so different,' I said.

'Different? Formal? Is that all you say?' she mocked.

'No … You look great. But I didn't expect to see you in a sari,' I said.

'Didn't expect what? That your stupid classmate from school could get a real job?' she wiggled her eyebrows, hands on hips.

'Yeah. You *are* quite stupid,' I pretended to agree, which made her punch my arm playfully.

We entered the hotel lobby. Construction workers were using noisy polishing machines on the already shiny Italian marble. Smell of paint pervaded the air. She took me to a restaurant with plush velvet chairs.

'This will be our bar – Toxic.'

The hotel would ensure that even as people visited the city to wash their sins, they'd commit new ones. We walked around the hotel to see the rest of the facilities.

'So, why won't people tell me anything?' she said.

'What?' I said.

'What happened between Raghav and you?'

'The college didn't like a story the newspaper did. He apologised. End of story.'

I gave her a two-minute summary of what had happened, making her swear that she would never tell Raghav I told her. She told me she hadn't even told Raghav she was meeting me, so there was no question of telling him anything. That's what human relationships are about – selective sharing and hiding of information to the point of crazy confusion.

We found ourselves in an ethnic-theme restaurant. 'Aangan, for Indian cuisine,' she explained. She took me to the gym next. I saw the treadmills with TVs attached to them.

'Imported?' I said.

She nodded. 'Sometimes I feel so guilty,' she said. Girls can handle simultaneous multi-topic conversations with ease.

'Why?'

'I spoilt your friendship with Raghav,' she said.

'That's not true,' I said.

She sat down on a bench-press. I took a balancing ball and used it as a stool.

'All three of us used to be *friends* in our childhood. What happened?' she said, her eyes filling up.

'Life,' I said. 'Life happened.'

'Without me, things wouldn't be so bad between the two of you,' she said.

'No, that's not true. I didn't deserve you. Raghav had nothing to do with it,' I said.

'Never say that,' Aarti said, her voice echoing in the empty gym. 'It's not that you don't deserve me. You are a great guy, Gopal. And we click so well.'

'But you don't feel that way about me, I know, I know. I am hungry. Where are we having lunch?'

'It's not that,' she said.

'What?'

'It's not like that with girls. It's sometimes about timing, and sometimes about how much you push.'

'I didn't push enough for a relationship?' I said.

'You pushed too much,' she said and wiped her eye.

I didn't know if I should console her. One, she belonged to someone else. Two, we sat at her workplace.

I picked up a 20-pound dumbbell instead. I found it heavy. However, I pretended to lift it easily in front of Aarti. Raghav could probably lift twice as much, I thought. *Why did I always compete with Raghav on every damn thing?*

'I am sorry,' I said. 'I'm sorry if I put too much pressure.'

'You came at a time when I didn't feel ready for anything. You wanted it too much. You wanted to lean on me. I didn't think I could be a strong enough support.'

'What is this? My performance evaluation day?' I said. I did a set of five with the dumbbell before keeping it down.

'I am just saying … I don't know why. I guess I really need to talk.'

'Or need to be heard,' I said.

We looked at each other.

'Yes, exactly that. How well you know me, Gopal.'

'Too well,' I said and smiled.

'You want to see the rooms before we have lunch?' she said.

'Sure. Where are we eating?' I said.

'At the staff canteen,' she said.

We took stainless-steel elevators to the third floor. She had a master key card to every room.

'I am not supposed to bring anyone to the hotel, by the way,' she confided.

'So?' I said, wondering if it meant we should leave.

'I am telling you how important you are. I am risking my job for you.'

'If they fire you, I will hire you.'

Our eyes met. We burst into laughter. We had not shared such a moment in years. We used to laugh like this in school – in sync and for the silliest of things – a burping kid in class, her mimicking the teachers, me pretending to sleep during History period.

She opened room number 3103. I had never seen anything so luxurious in my whole life. 'Cool,' I said.

'Isn't it?' She sat on the large bed with its six cushions of bright red silk. 'This bed is heaven! Sit and see.'

'Are you sure?' I said.

'Sit, no,' she said.

We sat next to each other, me on the edge of the bed.

'It's nice,' I said, as if I was a mattress inspector by profession.

'It's more comfortable lying down,' she said.

I looked at her, aghast. She saw my expression and started to laugh, holding her stomach.

'I am not saying let's,' she said. 'Since when did you become so serious?'

We spent the next twenty minutes playing around with light switches and bathroom taps. I had never been with her in a solitary place like this. It was going to my head. And I sensed a slight tension in the air. Maybe the tension was only on my side.

'Let's go.' I checked my watch. I had to be back in the campus soon.

'Okay,' she said and shut the washbasin tap.

We stepped out of the room. A man in a crisp new suit saw us come out.

'Aarti?' he said, surprised.

The colour vanished from Aarti's face.

'Sir,' she said. I read the tag on the man's suit. Binayak Shastri, Banquet Manager.

'What are you doing here?' he said.

'Sir,' she said, 'this is Mr Gopal Mishra. He is a client.'

'We haven't opened yet,' he said, still suspicious.

'Hi,' I said, offering him my hand. 'I am the director of the GangaTech group of colleges.'

He shook my hand.

'We are thinking of doing a college event here,' I said.

We walked towards the elevator. I was hoping he would ask no further questions when he said, 'What kind of event?'

'A dinner for the top companies that we call for placement,' I said.

Aarti avoided eye contact with everyone.

'Sure, we will be happy to assist you,' Binayak said, as he handed me his card.

I guessed that our staff-canteen lunch plan had to be dropped.

'I am running late, but my team will get in touch with you,' I said as we came to the lobby.

Aarti gave me a professional smile and disappeared behind the reception desk. Binayak chose to wait with me till my car arrived.

'How come you wanted to see the rooms?' Binayak asked.

'We will have guest faculty. Maybe from abroad,' I said. At that moment, thankfully, my driver drove into the porch.

24

Over the next two months we managed to fill a hundred and eighty seats out of the two hundred in our first batch. For the first time, I actually handed money to Shukla-ji's accountant. Many students paid their fee in cash. Farmers' kids, in particular, brought money in gunny bags, with bundles of notes accumulated over the years.

'Make my son an engineer,' a farmer pleaded with folded hands.

It made life so much easier. For the job and dowry market a B.Tech degree never hurt. Dean Shrivastava and his gang of twenty faculty members took care of the classes. I kept myself busy with projects such as getting the hostel mess operational, hiring new staff and ensuring that the remaining construction work continued as per schedule. I had a limited social life. Once a week I had dinner with faculty members, mostly to discuss work. A couple of times, I ended up at Shukla-ji's place.

'You are the director of the institute. How can you still stay in your tiny old house?' he said one day, after too much whisky.

'The faculty bungalow will be ready soon. I sleep in the office most of the days,' I said.

Aarti, however, had come back into my life, as the only non-work person I spent time with. Ramada opened, she joined work and sat prettily at the Guest Relations desk in the lobby. On her first day of work I sent her a box of chocolates and flowers. Maybe I shouldn't have, but I felt the day was important to her. I made sure the bouquet had only white roses for friendship – no red ones.

Hey, thanx. Really sweeeet of u!! :) came her SMS.

I read the message fifty times. I finally composed a reply. U r welcome. For a gr8 future career woman.

She replied after ten minutes. Why r u being so nice to me?

I had no answer. I used a women's trick. When in doubt, send a smiley.

I sent three. :) :) :)

She messaged: Meet up after work? 7 p.m. CCD?

Sure, I replied promptly.

I drove down from the campus to Sigra to meet her. She told me about her day at work. She had helped settle five Germans into the hotel, arranged three cars for a ten-member Japanese delegation and sent a surprise birthday cake to an American in his room. She seemed happy. I didn't think she missed being an air hostess.

'So we met today. What do you do in the evenings otherwise?' she said.

'Not much. Stay on campus. Work,' I said.

'That's horrible. What about friends?' Aarti said.

I shrugged. 'I have colleagues in the college. That's company enough.'

She patted my hand. 'You should have friends. Look at me, I have you.'

'What about Raghav?' I said.

'He works late at the newspaper. He has no time …' she said, withdrawing her hand. She did not tell me how Raghav would feel about our regular meetings, which is what I had really asked. She only told me Raghav would not find out.

'You *have* to meet friends after work.' She sounded like she was convincing herself.

'I probably bore you to death with my hotel stories but …'

'You never bore me. Even if you don't say a word,' I said.

With that, Aarti and I became friends-who-meet-after-work. We met twice a week, sometimes thrice. We ate at new restaurants, visited cafés, took walks in the Ravidas Park and occasionally watched movies.

We had some unspoken rules. We didn't have long chats on the phone, and mostly texted each other. We never visited the past or talked about touchy topics. I would never touch her, even though she would sometimes hold my arm mid-conversation. At movie theatres, we would enter and leave separately. That's what boys and girls did in Varanasi, anyway. When Raghav called, I would quietly step away so I couldn't hear her. Finally, when Raghav finished work, she would leave.

I couldn't figure out why I'd started to hang out with her. I had become a buffer until her boyfriend got free from work. I guess I wanted a break from work too. And, of course, when it came to Aarti, my reasons went for a toss anyway.

'So, Raghav has no idea we meet?' I asked her one day.

She shook her head, and wiped her coffee moustache.

♦

Raghav stayed out of my life after the inauguration day debacle. However, he couldn't stay off his old tricks for long.

'Varanasi Nagar Nigam eats, builder cheats'
Raghav Kashyap, Staff Reporter

I woke up to this headline a month after we opened. He often wrote about black-marketeer ration shop owners, LPG cylinders sold illegally, the RTO officer taking bribes and other routine Indian things nobody gives a fuck about. I would have ignored this article too, had he not mentioned GangaTech.

I skimmed a few lines.

The article said, 'Surprisingly the inappropriate approvals and the resultant illegal construction are right there in front of our eyes. Unlike other corruption cases where the wrongdoing is hidden (like the Ganga Action Plan scam), here the proof is for all to see. Farms are turned into colleges, which then flout all norms to construct as much as possible. Colleges will soon have malls next-door. Politicians, meant to protect us and prevent all this, are often the culprits. This is not all, the city has new hotels, residential towers and office buildings where the VNN has taken its cut. We have proof to compare the vast difference between what is allowable and what VNN approved ...'

A box next to the article listed the controversial approvals.

I read the list:

1. The V-CON apartment building, a ten-storey tower on a low-flying zone.
2. Hotel Vento, construction of which has taken over a neighbourhood park.
3. GangaTech College – Farmland mysteriously approved. College buildings constructed beyond permissible floor-space index.

I threw the newspaper away. I had improved my relations with Shukla-ji with great difficulty. I had told him that the reporter had apologised to me and that this would never happen again. I knew Raghav was taking revenge for the 'sorry' that day. He must have obtained GangaTech's building plan from his shady sources in VNN.

I took out my phone. Before I could call him, however, Shukla-ji called me.

'I don't know how this happened,' I said.

'Behenchods these *Dainik* people are,' Shukla-ji said.

'This reporter has to stop ...' I said.

'It's not the reporter. The opposition must be doing this.'

'I don't know, sir.'

'Or maybe someone in my own party? Jealous bastards wanting to spoil my name.'

'I don't think so, sir.'

'What?'

'It is the reporter. I know him from before. He's the crusader-activist types. Plus, he had to apologise to me. He is taking revenge.'

'Who?'

'Raghav Kashyap, the name is there in the article.'

'I'll fuck his happiness,' Shukla-ji said.

'Should I call him?' I said.

'Don't. I'll speak to his seniors.'

I said, 'What about the article. Does it affect us?'

'If VNN calls, direct them to me,' Shukla-ji said.

♦

No VNN officials called. Instead, they came straight to my college. The officials didn't come alone, they came with two bulldozers.

Students peeped from classroom windows as the sounds of the earthmover disrupted classes. I came running to the gate.

'Open the gates, we have come for demolition,' said a man wearing cheap sunglasses and a yellow plastic helmet.

'What?' I said.

'We have orders,' said the VNN official. He took out a folded piece of paper from his pocket.

My heart beat fast. 'What will you demolish?'

'The main building. There's illegal construction here,' he said, his tone defiant.

The harsh morning sun hit our faces. 'Can we talk?' I said.

He shook his head.

I took out my phone. I called Shukla-ji. He didn't answer.

'This is MLA Shukla's college. What is your name, sir?' I said.

'Rao. I am Amrit Rao. I don't care whether you say MLA or PM.'

I coaxed him to be patient for ten minutes. He turned the ignition off on the bulldozers. I asked the peon to get soft drinks with ice for everyone. I continued to try Shukla-ji's number. He answered at the eighth attempt.

'What is it, Gopal? I had to call the CM. These stupid articles are the biggest headaches.'

'Sir, we have bulldozers here.'

'What?' Shukla-ji said.

I handed the phone to Rao, who repeated his mission to the MLA. However, he became silent as the MLA spoke at the other end. Rao stepped aside to have a lengthy animated conversation with Shukla-ji for ten minutes.

Rao returned my phone. 'Here, Shukla-ji wants to speak to you.'

'Sir?' I said, still dazed.

'How much cash do you have in the office?' Shukla-ji wanted to know.

'Not sure, sir. Around two lakhs in the safe.'

'Give it to him. Put the notes in an empty cement bag, topped up with sand.'

'Yes, sir,' I said.

'His colleagues should not see it. He has a solid reputation.'

'Okay, sir.'

'And he has to break something. He can't go back without demolition pictures.'

'What?'

'Is there anything partially constructed you don't need immediately?'

'Sir, the students are going to see the demolition,' I said.

'No choice. This reporter friend of yours has kicked us right in the ...'

'He's no longer a friend, sir,' I said.

'He's fucked. Anyway, tell me what can be broken easily and will cost the least to fix?'

'The machining lab. We can put the machines somewhere else,' I said.

'Do that. Then draw a cross sign with chalk outside the lab. Let them do the rest. Don't forget the cement bag.' Shukla-ji hung up.

I signalled the security guard to open the gates. Rao gave me an oily smile.

25

'I can't do a movie today. I have to leave in ten minutes.' Aarti frowned as she stepped into my Innova.

I had come to pick her up at the hotel with tickets for the 7.30 p.m. show of *Rock On*.

'Can you get a refund?'

I tore up the tickets.

'Gopal!' she said. 'What are you doing? You shouldn't have bought tickets without asking me.'

'Why are you distraught?'

'It's about Raghav. I have to be with him.'

'What?' I said.

'Don't talk about Raghav. Whose rule is that, Mr Mishra?'

'Mine. But I want to know why you are cancelling the plan.'

'I'll tell you. Can you drop me home?'

'DM's bungalow,' I told the driver.

'Keep it to yourself, okay?' Aarti said. 'He told me not to tell anyone. I can trust you, right?'

'Do I have to answer that?' I said.

'Fine. Raghav lost his job,' she said.

'What?' I said. A surge of warm joy ran through me.

'I'm shocked. *Dainik* considered him a star reporter,' Aarti said.

'Did they give a reason?' I said. The reason was sitting next to her.

'I don't know. He didn't say. He just said the management asked him to leave.'

'Recession?' I said in a mock-concerned voice. 'They cut staff in tough times to save costs.'

'How much can you save by firing a trainee reporter? And *Dainik* is doing well.'

The car reached Aarti's home.

'Is he at your place?' I said as she stepped out.

She shook her head. 'I'll go meet him. I wanted to come home and change.'

'How did he sound? Upset?' I said.

'Very, very angry,' Aarti said and rushed off.

◆

I shouldn't have called him. However, I couldn't resist calling Raghav at midnight. I wanted to see if he would remain defiant in his unemployed state. I held a tall whisky glass in my right hand and the phone in my left.

I thought he wouldn't take my call. However, he picked it up soon enough.

'Do you need another apology?' were his first words.

'Hi, Raghav,' I said, my voice calm. 'How are things?'

'Quite good. What is bothering you that you called?'

'Don't be upset with me,' I said.

'You only get upset with people you care about,' Raghav said.

'You cared about your job.'

'Bye, Gopal,' he said.

'I told you not to write shit about us,' I said.

'I don't need to ask you how to do my job.'

I took a big gulp of whisky. 'Oh yeah, how can you? BHU pass-out, taking advice from an uneducated man like me.'

He remained silent as I filled my glass again. The whisky made me feel more confident than ever before.

'It's not about education, Gopal. It's the person you have become. I can't believe it!'

'Rich. Successful. Hard to believe, huh? The person who cleared JEE is unemployed.'

'I'll find a job, Gopal. And tell that MLA of yours – just because he could get a trainee fired from *Dainik* doesn't mean he can silence the truth.'

'I could give you a job, Raghav. Want to work for me?'

I only heard a click in response.

◆

'Revolution 2020,' Aarti said, chin in hands and both her elbows on the table.

We had come to the Ramada Hotel coffee shop. It was an off-day for her. She could visit the restaurants as a customer in regular civilian clothes. Waiters smiled at her in recognition, and she greeted them back. Ever since Raghav lost his job, she hadn't met me too often as she wanted to be with him. Finally, on her weekly holiday I coaxed her to meet up.

'What's that?' I said.

'Don't ask questions. Revolution 2020 – when I say this to you, what comes to your mind? What could it be?'

She blinked a couple of times as she waited for me to reply. I noticed how appealing she looked even in a simple orange T-shirt and black jeans.

'A new restaurant? Is Ramada opening one?'

She laughed.

'What's so funny?' I said. 'What is this Revolution 2020?'

'It's a new newspaper. Raghav's.'

'His own newspaper?' I said, startled.

'Yeah. He decided not to take up another job.'

Even if he wanted Raghav could not get a media job in Varanasi, at least in the top papers. Shukla-ji had informed all the major editors. Aarti, of course, didn't know this. She didn't even know why Raghav had lost his job.

'Raghav said *Dainik* didn't give him a reason. Is that fair?' she said.

'There's politics in organisations. He will learn to fit in,' I said.

'He doesn't want to fit in. He wants to change journalism. Give it some teeth,' Aarti said.

We ordered our coffee. Alongside, the waiters also gave us freshly baked cookies and muffins.

'Did we order all this?' I said.

'Contacts,' she said and winked at me.

'How can he start a newspaper?' I said. 'You need money.'

'It's not money. It's the content that matters,' Aarti said and took a sip. A sliver of foam was left behind on her lip.

'Aarti, you really believe this? You are a practical girl.'

'It's fine, Gopal. You opened a college. Why can't he do this?'

'I had a backer – MLA Shukla, who had cash and connections.'

'He hates him. Raghav says Shukla is the most corrupt leader Varanasi has ever had,' Aarti said.

'That's speculation,' I said. 'Is there any successful person who hasn't been criticised? Shukla is high-profile and rising. People are trying to bring him down.'

'Okay, can we please not discuss politics?' Aarti said. 'The political gene ended in my family with my grandfather.'

'You could join,' I said. 'People still remember your grandfather.'

She raised her hand and pumped her fist to make a mock-slogan gesture. 'Vote for me, I will give you free cookies with coffee.' She smiled. 'No, thanks. I am happy in Ramada.'

I smiled back. 'Anyway, so how exactly is he going to start his ... revolving what?'

'*Revolution 2020*. That's his goal. That India must have a full-blown revolution by 2020. Power will be with the youth. We will dismantle the old corrupt system and put a new one in place.'

'And he's going to do that from Varanasi?' I sounded as skeptical as I felt.

'Yes, of course. Kids from big cities are cushioned against the system. They have decent colleges, get good breaks. The revolution has to start from a small city.'

'He's definitely got you on board,' I said.

'What better place to start than the city that cleanses?' she said.

She spoke in an enthusiastic voice. Maybe this was what she liked about Raghav. His passionate approach to life, even if it was outlandish and fantastic. Girls don't like reality that much. Or practical questions.

'How does this newspaper work? Who pays for the printing, paper and promotion while the revolution comes?'

She sobered quickly. 'So it isn't exactly a newspaper to start with. It is like a newsletter. Just one big sheet.'

'Okay?' I egged her on.

'On one side of the paper will be matrimonials. People from Varanasi love fixing marriages. So he will put ads for local brides and grooms on that side. Free at first, and charge later. Maybe some job ads too.'

'Why wouldn't people advertise in established newspapers?'

'*Revolution 2020* ads will cost much lower and will be extremely local. You can find brides and grooms down your own street.'

I nodded.

'On the other side, Raghav will do local news stories. And since it is not a proper newspaper, he can be edgier and do more sting operations.'

'He loves doing that,' I agreed.

'So that's it. Printing costs are low, as there is only one big sheet to begin with. He will contact temples for the initial ads, so let's see. Do you like the name?'

I shrugged my shoulders. She bit into a muffin.

'Everyone has their thing, Gopal,' Aarti said, her mouth full. 'You have your college. This is his.'

'It will never make money,' I said.

'So?' She waved her muffin at me. 'Money isn't everything.'

'Easy to say that when you are eating cakes in a five-star hotel,' I said.

She grinned and kept her muffin down.

'I like money,' I said.

'Nothing wrong with that. My deal is simple. Money or revolution, everyone should follow their heart.'

'Sometimes your heart can lead you to a dead end,' I said.

She paused and looked at me as she digested my statement. 'Ahh,' she pretended to marvel, 'nice. Striking below the belt again, are we?'

'Of course not,' I said. I asked for the bill, which came with a twenty per cent staff discount.

We came to the lobby. 'Do you have to leave soon?' I said.

'Not super-soon, why?'

'I haven't rowed for a year,' I said.

26

Phoolchand, my favourite Assi Ghat boatman, recognised me from a distance. He looked amused to see me in a formal suit. He untied the boat for us. I helped Aarti on board and tipped him an extra hundred bucks. He slid a small paper packet in my hand.

'What's this?'

'Good stuff. I have sourced it from the Aghori sadhus. You have a matchbox?'

I understood what he had given me. Aarti did too, and gave me a sly smile. I bought a few cigarettes and matchbox from the paan shop.

I dipped the oars into the water, and together Aarti and I floated away.

'It's been ages. I have missed this, Raghav,' she said.

'Gopal,' I corrected without looking at her.

'What? Did I say Raghav? Oh, sorry. I am so sorry. I didn't mean to …'

'It's okay,' I said.

I rowed to the opposite bank of the river. The oars felt rough. My arms were not as strong as they used to be, when I did this on a regular basis. The main ghats of Varanasi are packed end to end with temples and ancient structures. The soft sandy shore on the other side of the river looked desolate. A small tea kiosk was the lone hub; it served the occasional tourists who went there on a boat. I anchored the boat to a tree stump. The evening sun turned the Varanasi skyline orange.

'Let's take a walk,' said Aarti, raising her face to feel the breeze.

We viewed the buzzing ghats on the opposite side. We could see the frantic activity, but not hear a thing. We strolled for a while, then went to the kiosk and sat on stools to order tea.

'Are you going to smoke what Phoolchand gave you?'

'If you don't mind,' I said.

She shrugged. I opened the pack of cigarettes. I teased the tobacco out of one of them, and pushed the dried marijuana in. I lit it and took a puff.

'May I try?' she said.

I shook my head.

Her phone rang. She took it out from her bag. The screen flashed 'Raghav calling'.

'Shh! Quiet,' she signalled to me. 'Hi,' she said into the phone. She listened as Raghav spoke for a while.

'That's great. Yes, put the pandit-ji's picture in the paper. He will be so happy. He will give you all the marriage listings,' she said and grinned.

'Yes,' she continued, 'still at the hotel. This is a terrible industry, they make you work on an off-day … Yes, a whole bus of French tourists has arrived.'

She mimed at me to be patient. I nodded as I watched the sky turn dark.

'Yes, baby, I miss you,' Aarti signed off. She reached for the joint.

'What?' I said.

'Give me a puff.'

'Are you crazy?'

'Why? Just because I am a girl? True colours of a Varanasi man, eh?'

'You will reek of it.'

'I'll go straight to the shower. And what are all the Banarasi paans for? I'll have a fragrant one before I go,' she said.

I passed her the joint. She took a few puffs. 'It doesn't seem to have any effect on me,' she grumbled.

We finished our tea and stood up. She walked close to the water.

'Come, let's see the aarti lamps in the water,' she said.

'It's late,' I said. 'We'd better go.'

'I like it here. Come,' she said and sat on the sand. She patted the ground next to her.

I sat down beside her. 'Your phone will ring again,' I said.

'Whatever,' she said. 'When he worked at *Dainik*, he never called. Now it is a break, so he does. Wait until his *Revolution 2020* starts.'

'Is he serious about it?' I said disbelievingly.

'Oh, yeah. The first issue comes out in two weeks,' she said.

I finished my joint and contemplated the holy river. The world came to wash away their sins in Varanasi. Did they ever stop to think about Varanasi for a moment – about what its people would do with all the sins they left behind? The grass had turned me philosophical.

I flexed my fingers, preparing myself for the tough ride back. Aarti took my right hand into her lap and started to massage it.

I looked at her in surprise.

'Nice?' she said.

I didn't say anything. Not a thing. I didn't withdraw my hand either. A full moon emerged in the sky.

'It's *purnima*,' she said softly.

The sand beneath us, her face and the moonlight…. Suddenly she began to blink furiously.

'You okay?' I asked.

She shook her head, still blinking. A particle of sand had blown into her eye. I withdrew my hand from her grasp and cupped her face.

'Open your eyes,' I said.

She shook her head again.

'Open, Aarti,' I said. I cradled her head with both hands.

She opened her right eye. I blew into it. 'You okay?' I said.

She nodded, her eyes shut again. I heard her sniff.

'Are you hurt?' I said.

She began to sob. She rested her forehead on my shoulder.

'What's wrong, Aarti?'

'I'm scared for Raghav. I hope he doesn't fail in life.'

I held the back of her head. She buried her face in my chest. It felt strange to console her about her boyfriend. However, I liked the feel of her against me.

'He'll be fine. I hate him, but Raghav is capable. He'll be fine. He is a little impractical but not bad at heart,' I said.

She lifted her head, her face turned up to me trustingly.

I stroked her hair. 'I miss how you cared for me,' she said.

Our faces were only a breath apart. The proximity stunned me. I couldn't speak.

'I have no one to talk to when I am low. Thank you,' she said.

Droplets from the Ganga splattered on us. I felt compelled to move my face forward. My lips met hers. She didn't kiss me back. She didn't move away either. But soon – too soon – she pushed me away.

'Gopal!' she said.

I didn't say anything. I kind of expected it. In fact, I wanted her to yell at me more.

'I'm sorry,' I said. I looked away. In the distance I saw the aarti diyas wobble on the water, as if admonishing me.

'Let's go. I am late,' she said. She was up in a split second and was taking rapid strides towards the boat. I paid the tea-shop owner and ran to catch up with her.

'I have to row you back. You can't run away,' I said.

She kept silent. She refused to even look at me. Okay, I admit I had done wrong, but she didn't have to treat me like this. A few moments ago she had massaged my hands and buried her face in my chest. She sat as far as possible from me in the boat.

I slapped the oars hard on the water as I rowed back.

'I said sorry already,' I said midway.

'Can we not talk please?' she said.

The boatman noticed our sour moods.

'Didn't like the *maal*?' Phoolchand asked. I didn't respond.

Aarti walked on.

'Where are you going? I will drop you home,' I said.

'I'll take an auto,' she said and disappeared from my sight.

27

Even Baba's death hadn't left me so sleepless. But Aarti's flight from Assi had me staring at the office walls at 4 a.m. two nights after the boat ride. I was too nervous to call or message her though I could think of nothing but her. Her face, her drenched eyes and her lips on mine ... I couldn't focus on the contractor's plans for my upcoming bungalow's bathrooms. I sat through faculty meetings like a zombie, staring at my phone non-stop.

'Expecting a call, sir?' Dean Shrivastava said.

I shook my head, only to check my phone again. *How can god give girls so much power? How can they turn productive, busy and ambitious men into a wilting mass of uselessness.*

'Sir, so you are okay with us conducting mid-terms next week?' said Anmol, the civil engineering professor.

'Yes,' I managed to respond while wondering what I'd do if she didn't call *ever*.

On my third sleepless night my phone beeped at two in the morning.

A message from her: Don't call or message me.

What made her send this message? I hadn't called or messaged.

I was sitting there holding the phone when my phone beeped again.

Ever, said her next message.

She isn't sleeping and she is thinking of me – my optimistic, irrational brain kicked into action. *Why did she send these messages? What do they mean in Girlese? Since Girlese often means saying the opposite of what is meant, did this mean – call me?*

Okay, I replied. I waited for an hour but got no response.

Soon I drifted off into a dream about boat rides.

✦

A fluorescent pink A3-sized sheet fell out of the morning paper. I thought it was a flyer for a travel agency or tuition classes. However, it had a masthead like a newspaper. Aha, I smirked, Raghav's attempt to change the world.

Revolution 2020, it said in big, bold font. Below was a letter from the editor, headlined: '**Because Enough is Enough**'. I read on.

> What do you say about a society whose top leaders are the biggest crooks? What do you do in a system where almost anyone with power is corrupt? India has suffered enough. From childhood we are told India is a poor country. Why? There are countries in this world where an average person makes more than fifty times that an average Indian makes. Fifty times? Are their people really fifty times more capable than us? Does an Indian farmer not work hard? Does an Indian student not study? Do we not want to do well? Why, why are we then doomed to be poor?

I laughed at Raghav's self-indulgent trip. I sipped my morning tea and continued to read.

> This has to stop. We have to clean the system. Che Guevara, the great revolutionary, once said, 'Power is not an apple that falls from a tree into your lap. Power has to be snatched from people who already have it.' We have to start a revolution, a revolution that resets our corrupt system. A system that shifts power back into the hands of the people, and treats politicians like workers, not kings.
>
> Of course, this won't happen overnight. This also won't happen until the real suffering begins. As India's young population increases, we will need more good colleges and jobs. Soon, there won't be enough. People will realise who is fooling them. It could take ten years. I call it Revolution 2020, the year in which it will

happen, the movement that will finally shake the muck off India. When the Internet will connect all colleges across the country. When we will go on strike, shut down everything, until things are fixed. When young people will leave their classes and offices and come on to the streets. When Indians will get justice and the guilty will be punished.

And it will all begin in Varanasi. For that reason, we bring you *Revolution 2020*.

Yours truly,
Raghav Kashyap
Editor

I smiled as I saw a crudely sketched map of India under the article. It had a dot on Varanasi, with arrows connecting it to various cities. The map had a little 'Revolution 2020 potential plan' attached to it. In various cities, it listed the main colleges that would lead the revolution there.

My accountant came into my office for my signatures on the month-end accounts. My amused expression puzzled him.

'What happened, sir? Reading jokes?' he said.

I nodded.

The front page also carried an exposé on cremation shops in Varanasi selling ordinary wood as sandalwood after spraying it with synthetic perfume.

My accountant saw the pink-coloured paper.

'Is this an ad? A poster?' he said.

'I have no idea,' I said.

I turned over the *Revolution 2020* page and couldn't help but laugh. In contrast to the bombast in the front, the back page had matrimonial ads! I read one out aloud.

'Wanted beautiful/educated/fair/homely virgin for twenty-five-year Kayasth Brahmin engineer working in stable government job. Girl must be willing to stay in joint family and respect traditional values.'

I handed Raghav's paper to my accountant.

'Searching for a girl, sir?' he said.

I looked how I felt – offended.

'Sorry, sir,' he said. 'Sir, we have more requests for admissions,' he sought to change the subject.

'We are full,' I said, 'you know that. We have as many students as we are authorised to take.'

'Sir, if the AICTE can adjust ...'

I sighed. 'How many more?'

'Five, ten ...' he said. 'Twenty at the most.'

'Take them in,' I said. 'I'll manage the AICTE when the time comes.'

'Yes, sir,' he said and left the office.

I picked up the pink rag, ripped it apart, bundled up the shreds and threw them in the dustbin.

◆

Every Friday I made rounds of the classes. I kept a three-day stubble to look old enough to be a director. I entered a classroom where a maths class was in progress.

The professor stopped lecturing when he sighted me. The entire class of forty students stood up. It felt good. I could go to any of the eight classrooms and the same would happen. Money, status and power – however evil people may say these are – get you respect in life. A few years back I was begging at career fairs for an admission. Today, hundreds stood up to attention when I arrived.

'Good afternoon, Director sir,' the professor said.

I nodded in response. A boy in an ill-fitting shirt in the front row blinked rapidly when I addressed him. 'What is your name?'

'Manoj, sir,' he said.

'Where are you from?' I said.

'Sarnath, sir,' he said.

'Parents work there?' I said.

'We have land, sir. My father is a farmer.'

I immediately softened. 'You don't want to be a farmer?'

He didn't answer, afraid of how he might be judged by the response. I understood.

'Any problems at GangaTech?' I said.

'No, sir,' he said nervously.

'Don't feel shy, tell me,' I said.

'Too much English, sir,' he said. 'I don't understand it well.'

'Learn it. The world won't let you live otherwise. Okay?' I said.

He nodded.

I turned to the professor. 'Sorry to disturb you,' I said.

The professor smiled. He reminded me of Mr Pulley in Kota.

◆

A dozen documents awaited my attention when I returned from my rounds. My phone beeped.

Aarti had sent a message: Saw R2020?

Yes, I texted back.

What do you think? she wanted to know.

I didn't respond. I started going through the documents. My phone beeped again.

She had texted: ?

Good luck for the revolution, I said.

Thanks, came her reply.

I wondered if that meant the end of conversation.

You are welcome, I said anyway.

Good to know, she said.

What? I said.

That I am still welcome, she said.

I didn't know what to say to that. Girls can come up with the simplest of messages that have the most complex meanings.

I typed out another message: I am sorry about that evening. I was pondering whether to send it when my phone beeped again.

Sorry about that evening, her message said.

I gasped at the coincidence. I deleted what I had composed and typed again. It's fine. I shouldn't have crossed the line.

I had a reply within seconds: Don't worry about it.

Perplexed, I kept my phone away.

What exactly did she mean? Why can't girls be direct? Don't worry about it? Is she just being formal? Or did she mean it is okay I kissed her, and that I need not worry about it ever again? Most important, had we closed the chapter or opened a new one?

I wanted to ask her all these questions but did not have the guts.

I didn't want to keep things hanging either. One kiss, and her silence thereafter, had devastated me. I didn't want to kiss her just once. I wanted to kiss her a million times, or however many times it was possible for a person to kiss another person in a lifetime. I did not want to talk to her in cryptic messages. I wanted to have her by my side all the time.

I didn't give a fuck about Raghav anymore. He had anyway become borderline cuckoo, with his pink newspaper. Aarti deserved better, and who could be better than me? Our college would make a crore this year. Raghav would never see a crore of his own in his entire fucked-up honest revolutionary life. These intense thoughts darted about in my head like little birds let loose from their cage.

'Enough is enough,' I spoke out loud and forced myself to pick up the phone.

'I LOVE YOU,' I typed and kept my thumb on the send button.

But I deleted the text. I replaced it with a softer 'I MISS YOU', but erased that as well.

I went back to my files but found it hard to read even one sentence. I closed my eyes. Immediately, I remembered the warmth of her body when I had held her, the locks of her hair that brushed against my face in the breeze, and relived the moment when I had kissed her.

My phone rang. She had called me. A part of me didn't want to, but I picked it up in one ring.

'Hi!' she said.

'Aarti!'

'Yeah?' she said.

'I crossed the line that day,' I said.

'Don't keep saying that.'

'Is it okay, really?' I said.

'Really. How did you like the paper? Be honest.'

I was shocked at how effortlessly she switched the topic.

'Kayasth Brahmin grooms on one page, mega-revolution on the other. Isn't it strange?'

'I told you. That's how the paper becomes viable,' she said.

'What do the readers feel about that?' I said.

'The response is mind-blowing. Raghav's ex-boss from *Dainik* had c ... called to congratulate him,' she stammered in her excitement.

'Well, what do I know about newspapers? If people from *Dainik* like it, it is probably good,' I said flatly.

'You have seen nothing yet. Raghav is working on some big stories.'

'Great,' I said, my tone bland.

'Sorry, I didn't mean to talk only about him. Just thrilled about the first issue. I put a few copies in the hotel lobby too,' she confessed with a giggle.

'I am sure the tourists will love to see how fucked-up our country is,' I said.

'Or they may like the matrimonials,' Aarti pointed out. That evening by the river seemed to be a distant memory for her. *How can girls pretend that nothing happened? Do they erase stuff from their brains, brush it aside, or are they just good actors?*

'Aarti,' I said.

'What?'

'What if I …' I said and paused.

'What if I what?' she said.

She had put it out there. I could either chicken out and say lame crap like 'What if I said you are amazing,' like I had over the years. Or, I could be a man and say what I really wanted to, even if it meant she may never talk to me again. For once, I chose the latter option.

'What would you do if I kissed you again?'

'Gopal!' she said, her voice hushed.

'Don't sound so surprised. We did kiss, remember?'

'I don't know what happened,' she said. How could she not know what had occurred?

'Don't avoid the question,' I said.

'What?' Aarti said, a rare hesitation in her voice.

'What would you do if I kissed you again?' I repeated.

'I don't know,' she said.

She hadn't said yes. However, she hadn't hung up the phone in disgust either.

'I might,' I said.

'Don't!'

'I just might.'

'Can we talk about something else?' she said.

'Are we meeting?' I said.

'Where?' she said. Again, no yes or no. She didn't even say when. She simply asked the location. It meant she wanted to meet me. Even after I had warned her that I wanted to kiss her, she wanted to meet me. A dozen smileys filled up my head.

'I'll pick you up at work. What time do you get done?'

'Six. Not today though. Raghav has some friends over. First issue and all.'

'Party?'

'Kind of. A low-key affair. Raghav doesn't have money to party. Everything has gone into the paper.'

'You want me to give some money?' I said, enjoying every syllable of my sentence.

'Stop it, Gopal. So, tomorrow at six?'

'I will call you,' I said.

'Oh, okay. Where are we going?' she said.

'Somewhere private,' I said.

She paused for a second.

'Where we can talk,' I added.

'Let me know then.'

28

'You are in 2105, Mr Mishra'

I had booked a room at Ramada for five thousand a night.

'Any help with your luggage, sir?' the lady at the reception asked me.

'I only have this,' I said, pointing to my rucksack.

The receptionist smiled at me. She walked with me to the centre of the lobby and to the guest relations desk.

'This is Aarti,' the receptionist said, 'and she will guide you to your room.'

Aarti looked up from her computer. Her jaw dropped.

'Hello,' I said as nonchalantly as possible.

'Oh, hi … I mean, good evening,' she said, flustered.

'Aarti, this is Mr Gopal Mishra, director of GangaTech. He is in 2105. Please escort him to his room.'

'Sure, sure,' Aarti said, still in shock.

She stood up. We walked towards the elevator. A housekeeping staff member entered the elevator with us. We couldn't talk. She only spoke in the second floor corridor.

'Gopal, what are you doing here?' she whispered. She continued to walk two steps ahead of me.

I had my story ready. I couldn't tell Aarti I had booked a room just for us.

'We had a senior guest faculty coming from London.'

'So?'

'He cancelled last minute. We had already paid for the room. So I thought, why not enjoy the hospitality of Ramada?'

'What? You should have told me. I could have got you a refund.'

'Forget it. I have never stayed in a five-star hotel before. I'll try it out.'

We reached 2105. She opened the room with the magnetic key card. She looked beautiful in her uniform, a formal sari, with her hair – every strand of it – locked in a bun.

I dumped my rucksack on the bed.

'You need help with the features of the room?' she said.

'No,' I grinned. 'Someone already showed me.'

'You are crazy, Gopal,' she said. 'Anyway, I better go.'

I sat on the single-seater sofa in the room. 'Stay,' I said.

'I can't. I am on duty.'

'After six? It's five-thirty already,' I said.

'I can't be in a guest's room!'

'You know this guest,' I said. 'Two minutes?'

She went to the door and closed it as much as possible without locking it. She sat on a chair by the desk and stared at me.

'What?' I said.

'You didn't plan this?' she said.

'What plan? The faculty cancelled,' I said.

'What's the name of the faculty?' she said.

'Mr Allen,' I said.

'Oh, really? Which college?'

'He's from …' I said and hesitated.

'See. Stop fibbing,' she said.

'How will I know the college? The dean would know. All I know is, we had a room, and I took it.'

She shook her head.

'Let's hang out here after you finish,' I said.

'How?' she said. 'It's not allowed.'

'You only do things you are allowed to?' I said.

'No,' she said, 'but ...'

'You don't have the guts,' I said.

'That's not the case,' she said and stood up. 'And you know it.'

'Nobody will find out,' I said. 'Finish work and come. We will eat here. Leave in an hour or so.'

'If room service sees me?' she said.

'You hide in the toilet when they come,' I said.

'That's weird,' she said.

'Okay, I will order before you arrive. Sandwiches?'

She bit her lower lip and mused over my suggestion for a few seconds. 'Fine,' she sighed. 'But you have to check no staff is around when I come or leave.'

'Sure, I will stand in the corridor. Will give you the green signal on the phone.'

She walked to me and whacked me lightly on the side of my head. 'The things you make me do!' she said and left the room.

◆

I ordered a club sandwich, chocolate cake and a bottle of wine. I also took a shower, using more shampoo and hot water than I normally do in a week.

She called me at 6:30 p.m. 'Check the corridor.'

I came out of the room. 'It's fine,' I said into the phone, turning my head left and right to scan the corridor.

Two minutes later, we were both in the room with the door firmly locked. She had already changed into a white button down shirt and jeans downstairs after her shift.

'You are stupid, you know that, right?' she said, plonking herself on the bed and holding a hand dramatically to her chest. 'My heart is beating so fast!'

'Relax,' I said.

She laughed. 'You are lucky they haven't installed corridor CCTVs yet. Can't pull this stunt after that.'

'So, right timing,' I said. 'Hungry?'

I opened the silver cover on the sandwich plate.

'Starving,' she admitted.

I added some french fries and salad to the sandwich. 'Come, let's eat.'

'I am too exhausted to move. I stood in heels for eight hours. Can I eat on the bed?'

'Sure,' I said. I passed her the plate. I poured a glass of red wine.

'You ordered a full bottle of wine?' she said.

I shrugged.

'When did you start drinking wine?' she said.

'Shukla-ji made me try everything,' I said.

'You like wine?'

'I usually have whisky. But I thought you might like wine.'

'I do. But I shouldn't drink. This is my place of work.'

'One glass …' I insisted.

She gave a brief nod and took the glass.

'Raghav doesn't drink much. He is such a bore sometimes,' she said and took a sip. 'Nice. What is it?'

'Jacob's Creek from Australia,' I said, emphasising the country of origin. It had cost me two thousand bucks, but I didn't mention the price.

'It's good. It will hit me soon.'

'Relax, my driver will drop you home,' I said.

She held her sandwich tight with both hands and ate like a famine victim.

'Slow down,' I said.

She said with food in her mouth, 'I haven't had anything since breakfast.'

'Even in school you used to stuff your face,' I teased.

'Provided you left any food for me!'

'Hey, I stole your tiffin *once*, and that too half of it. I am still serving my sentence,' I said.

'Oh, really?' she said. 'The teacher punished you for only one period.'

'But I am still stuck with you,' I said, looking totally depressed.

She picked up a french fry from her plate and threw it at me. She missed. It fell on the sofa.

'Oops, pick it up, please. I can't dirty my own hotel,' she said.

29

She kicked off her shoes and sat crosslegged on the bed. I went to pour her more wine.

'I'll get high,' she said but extended her glass. She sipped and checked the time. The bedside clock said 8:30 p.m.

'How long can you stay?' I said.

'Until nine,' she said. 'Half an hour more.'

'Ten?' I said.

She shook her head. 'Mom will ask a hundred questions. Unless ... I tell her I have to do a double shift,' she said.

'Tell her that,' I said immediately.

'I have to stay for eight more hours then. Till 2 a.m.'

'Perfect,' I said.

'Are you crazy?' she said. 'I can't be in your room till two!'

'Why not?' I said. 'When do we ever get to catch up like this?'

'If my boyfriend finds out ...' she said and went quiet. She leaned back against the headboard.

'Finds out what?' I said.

We had finished half the bottle. I poured myself some more wine.

'That I am in another man's room for so many hours, he will kill me,' she finished.

'He will?'

She grinned. 'Not literally. But he would get, like, really mad. Break something.' She picked up a pillow and threw it at me, playing the part of a possessive boyfriend.

'He will kill you if he finds out it is me,' I told her.

'He's not finding out,' Aarti said.

I got off the sofa and came next to the bed.

'You are doing that double shift,' I said, pointing to her phone.

'You sure?' she said. 'I will eat your head till two in the morning!'

'That's what you've done all your life,' I said.

She hit me with the other pillow. I caught it and kept it aside. She placed a finger on her lips, signalling me to be quiet. She called home.

'Mom?' she said. 'Yes, I am still at work. Double shift, what to do?'

Her mother spoke for a few seconds. Aarti continued: 'Stupid Bela was to do this shift. She has made some excuse for not coming. Ever since her engagement, she bunks so much.'

Her mother spoke again. Aarti looked irritated.

'Why should I get engaged because Bela did? Yes … I will one day, mom … Okay, fine … Yes, the hotel car will drop me ... Bye.'

She kept her phone on the bed, and looked exasperated.

'You okay?' I said.

'I think at some point a switch flicks in the heads of Indian parents. From "study, study, study" they go "marry, marry, marry".'

'You don't want to?'

'I will,' she said, and patted the bed. 'Why are you standing like a show-piece?'

I sat on the bed, careful to sit a little away from her.

'You are paying a lot for this room. Please be comfortable.'

'Huh?' I said.

'It's my job to make our guests comfortable,' she said and smiled a guest-relations smile. Even with the specks of red wine on her teeth, her smile was downright beautiful.

I bent to take off my shoes and socks. 'You don't need to call Raghav?'

She shook her head. 'He won't even realise it. He is working on a big story,' she said. She poured herself some more wine.

'If he calls?' I said.

She placed her hand on my mouth. 'If he does, you go shh ... and I will deal with it,' she said.

Her touch was like a spark.

She removed her hand. 'So Mr Director, how is work, life, everything?'

'Everything is work. It isn't easy to run a college,' I said.

'Only work?' She imitated her mother, 'What? You should get married. Why aren't you married by now?'

We laughed and clinked our glasses together.

'I will have to get engaged soon though,' she said. 'The pressure is building.'

'How about Raghav?' I said.

'Obviously, he is not ready at the moment. He'll do it if I push him,' she said.

'Are your parents okay with him?' I said.

'They love him. My father broke the family tradition of politics to join services. He admires Raghav's passion.'

'Even though he doesn't make money?'

'He will. One day he will,' Aarti vowed. 'And why are you talking like my relatives?'

She picked up the remote and switched on the television.

'This is so boring,' she said and flicked through the news channels. She stopped at Channel V, where an item girl danced to a remixed video.

'She has totally done her lips,' she said, 'and a nose job, and possibly a boob job.'

'What?' I said, shocked at her choice of words.

'Boob job. To fix your boobs, make them bigger,' she said.

I looked as shocked as I felt.

'You are my best friend,' she said and playfully punched my arm. 'I can totally be myself with you.'

She flipped channels again and suddenly we were watching *When Harry Met Sally* from somewhere in the middle.

'Men and women can't be friends,' Billy Crystal said to Meg Ryan, a toothpick in his mouth.

'Of course, they can be. Look at us,' Aarti said impatiently and increased the volume. 'I love this movie.'

'You have seen it?' I said.

'Yeah, have you?'

I shook my head. I didn't watch English movies.

'Come, let's watch. I'll tell you what happened so far.'

I moved closer to her. I dimmed the room lights from the bedside panel while she summarised the plot for me. Harry and Sally went about their lives, meeting and fighting several times but never really connecting even though it seemed obvious that they should. We watched the movie in silence.

'Wow, we finished the bottle,' she observed after a while. She lifted a pillow, placed it in my lap and rested her head there for the rest of the film.

'You comfortable?' she asked, looking up at me from my lap, her eyes twinkling in the TV light.

I hesitated a little, then placed my hand lightly on her head and gently stroked her hair. She didn't object. It felt wonderful to be with her. I couldn't think of a happier moment than this in my life so far.

'Aarti?' I said.

'Yeah?' she said, her eyes still on the TV.

'Is it okay for you to lie in my lap like this?'

She nodded, her eyes on the screen.

'Why did you run away from the river that day?' I said.

'I don't want to talk about it. Watch the movie, no,' she said.

'Will you run away again?' I said, my voice heavy.

She sensed the tension in me. She muted the television and sat up.

'You okay, Gopi?' she said, the words slightly slurred. The TV light flickered over our faces.

'Run now if you want to,' I said, my voice barely making it out of my throat. 'Because if you stay for a while in my life and then go ...'

I had spoken too much. The Australian wine had managed to open up an Indian heart.

'Shut up,' she said and placed her palm on my mouth again, 'Drama queen. Sorry, drama king!'

But I meant it, I couldn't bear to be away from her.

'I am lonely too, Gopal,' she said, 'so lonely.'

'Why?'

'Raghav has no time. My parents can't see why I want to work. They can't understand why the DM's daughter has to slog. All my girlfriends are getting married, planning kids and I am not. I am weird.'

'You are different,' I corrected her.

'Why am I different? Why can't I just be normal – satisfied to be at home, waiting for my husband?'

'That's not normal. That's backward.'

'Raghav stresses me out. I want to support him. But he can't seem to get his act together. He rejected a tie-up with a newspaper for the sake of independence. How is he ever going to make money like this?'

'I thought you said he will one day,' I said.

'I put on a brave face. But I can discuss my fears with you, no?' she said.

'Of course, you can,' I said and caressed her cheek.

We turned to the TV screen. One night Sally was feeling low. Harry comes over to her house. He comforts her. They end up kissing. I don't know if the scene motivated me or the wine or the fact that I felt I might not get another chance. I leaned over to kiss Aarti. She looked up at me in surprise. However, she did not protest. Just stared.

I kissed her again, this time more insistently. Nothing for two minutes and then she was kissing me back. We kissed again and again. I kissed her lips, her cheeks, her forehead, her nose, her ears and her lips again. I switched off the lights.

When I hugged her again, she said, 'This is wrong.'

'I know,' I said, 'but I can't stop.' My hand reached for her shirt buttons.

'No,' she said and gripped that hand hard.

I slid my other hand under her shirt. Thank god, men have two hands; nobody could make out otherwise. My palm was, at last, on her breast.

'Gopal, you realise what is happening?' she said.

I shook my head.

'We shouldn't …' she said.

I shut her up with another kiss. She wriggled a little, but I kept kissing her. She started to respond. Slow at first, then matching and finally outpacing me.

'This isn't right, Gopal,' she panted, biting my lower lip.

I answered in kisses. The movie had ended. I heard shampoo commercials in the background as I tugged at her top to take it off.

'Don't, Gopal!' she whispered but raised her arms to make my job easier.

I removed my shirt. This time when we embraced, her warmth and softness melted into me.

'I care for you so much …' I said.

'Stop talking,' she said, interrupting my garbled speech.

I gently pushed at her shoulders to make her lie back on the bed. I removed the rest of my clothes.

She looked away.

'What?' I said.

She shook her head, without making eye contact.

I slid next to her. She kissed me passionately, but whenever I paused to look into her eyes, she turned away.

I reached down to unbutton her jeans. She halted me one last time.

'I have a boyfriend,' she reminded me.

'I have lived with that for years,' I said.

'I am not that kind of girl, Gopal,' she said on a sob.

'You are an amazing girl,' I said, my finger dipping into her navel. I paused to kiss her there. 'The most amazing girl in the world.'

I placed her hand on my body. I went back to undoing her jeans. Girls wear the most unremovable, tight jeans in the world. I found it impossible to take them off without her help.

'Could you?' I said, after a five-minute struggle.

My request brought forth a giggle. She wriggled to take them off. I waited and then drew her close to me.

'Gopal,' she said, and held me close. Passion repressed for years came forth unleashed. I bit her and kissed her all the time that I was becoming one with her.

I knew my life would no longer be the same again. What happened only magnified my love for her. They say men withdraw after sex. But I wanted to draw her close, cuddle and keep her with me forever. Spooning her tightly, I kissed her hair as she looked ahead with no particular expression.

'You are wonderful, Aarti. Every bit of you is wonderful.'

She half-smiled. I raised myself on an elbow.

'Did you like it?' I said.

She nodded but looked elsewhere.

'Look at me,' I said. She did turn her eyes to me, but looked past me.

'Are you okay?' I said.

She nodded.

We lay down again. A little red LED beeped on the ceiling.

'What's that?' I said, worried it could be a camera.

'Smoke alarm,' she said.

We remained silent for a few minutes.

'I can't live without you, Aarti,' I said.

'Don't say that, please,' she said.

'It's true. I love you,' I said.

'Please, stop!' she said and sat up on the bed, covering herself with the bedsheet.

'What's the matter?' I said, holding her arm through the sheet.

Her phone beeped. She looked at the message. She let out a deep breath as she punched a reply.

'Can I wear my clothes?' She slid away from me.

'Huh?' I said. 'Sure.'

She draped the bedsheet around her, picked up her clothes and went to the bathroom. I switched on the lights. A confused mix of emotions stewed in me.

She obviously cares for me, for no girl will do what she did otherwise. Yet, why was she acting distant? Does she expect me to tell her I will be there for her now? Or is she regretting it? Is this going to bring us closer or take us further apart?

I was naked and confused. I couldn't resolve my confusion, but I could at least wear my clothes. She re-entered the room while I was buttoning my shirt.

'I better go home,' she said decisively.

The bedside clock said 0:00 a.m.

'Don't you have to stay till 2 a.m.?' I asked.

'I'll say the shift ended earlier. In either case, they would be too sleepy to check the time now,' she said.

Sit with me, I wanted to say. I wanted to talk. I wanted her to know how much this meant to me. *Isn't this what girls want, anyway, to talk*?

'Will you call your driver?' she said.

'Stay for five minutes,' I begged. 'Please?'

She moved to the sofa. I sat on the bed.

'Why are you so tense?' I said. 'I am your Gopal. Don't you care for me?'

'You still need proof?' she asked.

I came next to her. I held her hand. It felt cold.

'I don't want you to feel ashamed about it,' I said. 'This is special. We have to be proud of it.'

'But I am in a relationship,' she said.

'With a guy who is never there for you?' I said.

She turned to me in surprise.

'I haven't ever commented about you and Raghav. That doesn't mean I don't notice. Aarti, you deserve better. You deserve all the joys of life.'

'I am a simple girl, Gopal,' Aarti said, biting her lip.

'Even a simple girl needs love, security, attention, support. Right?' I said.

She kept quiet.

'The simple girl will get married someday. She will need to know if her husband will be able to raise a family with her,' I said. I had remained defensive for years. With Aarti by my side, I felt confident to go on the offensive.

'I am tired. I want to go home,' she said and stood up.

I called my driver. I offered to come down with her. She declined. She came close to me before she left. I expected a kiss but there was only a brief hug. The door shut behind her. Her scent lingered in the room for hours and in my heart for days.

30

We didn't talk to each other for two days after the Ramada night. I couldn't control myself any longer and finally called her. She couldn't speak to me as her parents were around her. However, she agreed to meet me at CCD the next morning before work.

'I am sorry I freaked out,' she said, taking little sips from her extra-hot black coffee. She wore a crinkly purple skirt and a white printed top. Her wet hair told me she had just taken a shower. 'I have twenty minutes before I leave for work,' she said.

'What happened to you that night?' I said.

'Well, you know what happened,' she said.

'You have to come to me, Aarti,' I said. I placed my hand on hers.

'Gopal!' she said, and pulled her hand away.

'What?' I said. I wanted her to look at me with shy eyes, smile at our shared experience, and squeeze my hand tight. None of it happened.

'People know us,' she said instead. Steam from our coffee cups rose between us. The café felt warm, compared to the chilly December morning outside.

'Do you love me?' I said, desperate for her confirmation. *She had to love me. How could she not?*

Aarti let out a breath of frustration.

'What is the matter with you? At least accept your feelings now,' I said.

'Do you want to know what I feel?' she said.

'More than anything else,' I said.

'Guilt,' she said.

'Why?' I said, almost in protest. 'Wasn't it wonderful? Isn't this love?'

'Gopal, you have to stop using the word "love", okay?' she said.

Girls cannot be understood. Period. I became quiet.

'Raghav did me no wrong,' she spoke after a minute, staring outside the window.

'So this is about Raghav …' I said as she cut me.

'Can you listen? Simply listen, okay?' she said, her gaze stern. I had to comply. Men are born on earth to listen to girls. So, I nodded.

'He only wanted to make a living while doing the right thing. It's not easy,' she said.

I nodded again, hoping like hell I didn't come across as fake.

'I shouldn't have cheated on him. I am a terrible person.'

I nodded again.

'You think I am a terrible person?' she said.

I kept quiet.

'Say something,' she shouted.

'You told me to listen,' I said.

'So do that,' she said.

'What?' I said.

'Say something,' she said. There's something about male-female conversation. I don't think one side ever gets what the other side intends.

'Aarti, you are a sensible girl. You don't do stuff unless you want to.'

'What are you trying to say?' she said.

'You never said yes to me despite my attempts for years. Something made you do it that night.'

'I made a mistake,' she said.

I must admit, her saying this felt like crap. The most special day of my life classified as a mistake for her. I controlled my anger.

'Was it? Why did you come to meet me today?' I said.

'It's just coffee,' she said, her eyes shifty.

'Aarti, don't lie. Not to me. If your feelings have changed, there's nothing to be ashamed of,' I said.

Tears rolled down her cheeks. I picked up a tissue and leaned forward to wipe them. She looked around, and composed herself.

'Gopal, in every relationship, there is a weaker person and there is a stronger person. The weaker person is the one who needs the other person more.'

'True,' I said.

'It's not easy being the weaker one in the relationship. Not all the time,' she said.

'I know the feeling,' I said.

She looked at me.

'I am sorry. I am listening,' I said.

'My parents are pressurising me to get married. I can't fight them forever,' she said. 'Raghav doesn't seem to understand that.'

'He doesn't want to marry you?' I said.

'Only in a couple of years. He avoids the topic. Sometimes it is about not being settled, sometimes about work being too dangerous, mostly he is too busy. What about me?'

I nodded. Sometimes your best chance with women lies in adequate nods. I made mine just right, with a measured swinging of the head.

'He loves me, I know. Every now and then, he sends a sweet SMS. It's nice.'

I realised she was thinking aloud. I pretended to listen but focused on her triangular purple earrings that bounced mildly when she spoke. She finished her pros and cons after five minutes.

'Thanks for listening,' she said.

'Why me?' I said.

'What do you mean?' she said.

'Why did you sleep with *me*? Sure, you had some problems with Raghav. But why me?'

She looked at me. She had softened a little after venting out.

'Because I like you,' she said.

'You do?' I said.

'Of course, I do. And I know what I mean to you. I swear I would be so happy if you found another girl.'

'I can't,' I said.

'Can't what?'

'I can't be with another girl. It's you or nobody,' I said, looking her straight in the eye.

'You realise how guilty that makes me feel?' she said.

'So you feel guilty if you sleep with me and if you don't?'

She gave a wry smile. 'Its not easy being a girl. We feel guilty about everything.'

'Don't be confused. Come to me,' I said.

'What about Raghav?' she said. 'He needs me at this stage.'

'He does what he wants to. Why shouldn't you?'

'That's work. He never stops me from work. Infidelity is different.'

'You inspire me, Aarti,' I said. 'I can't tell you how much I want to do in life if you are by my side. I want to expand my college. We can open an aviation academy, MBA, maybe medicine.'

'You don't need me for that,' she said.

'I want you for myself. Without you, there is no me,' I said. 'People break up all the time, Aarti. You guys are not married. We will be so happy.'

'And Raghav?' she said.

'He will be fine. He'll find someone, a journalist or activist or something,' I said.

She laughed.

'What?' I said.

'I like you, Gopal. But why do you try so hard?'

'Sorry,' I said stiffly. 'I don't have the right moves or the right lines all the time.'

'Shut up, this isn't about the moves.'

'Will you be mine?' I said, extending my hand.

'Please don't pressurise me.'

I took my hand back.

'Not at all,' I said.

She checked the time. She had to leave. I called my driver, who slowly rolled up in a black Mercedes.

'Wow!' she said. 'Is that yours?'

'No, it belongs to the trust. It is for Shukla-ji. We just took delivery.'

We got into the car. The black leather felt warm. 'It's got seat heaters,' I said, showing her the controls.

'One day, Mr Gopal, you will have your own,' she said as we reached the hotel.

'Car or girl?' I winked at her.

'Both, hopefully,' she said and winked back.

'When can we meet,' I said, 'alone?'

'Gopal!'

'We don't have to do anything. In fact, I don't want to do anything.'

'Famous last words from every guy,' she said and walked into the hotel.

Guards saluted the black Mercedes as it drove out of the hotel gate.

◆

'Where are your parents?'

She drew the curtains in her room. 'Hospital. It's dad's knees again.'

Aarti and I continued to meet, though seldom in public places. Mostly, she would call me home when her parents were out. Even with half a dozen servants in the house, her room had privacy. Two months had passed since the night at Ramada. Her guilt for cheating on Raghav had subsided somewhat, or at least she hid it well from me. I stopped asking her if she loved me as it only moved her away from me.

Girls are contradictory. They will say they like communication, but on certain topics they clam up. If they like you, they would prefer you sense it rather than make them say it.

'Grapes?' she said as she offered me a tray of fruit.

'Feed me,' I said as I sprawled out on her easy chair.

'Shut up,' she said and shoved the tray towards me.

She sat on the chair across me. We had an unwritten rule – we stayed away from her bed.

'Once?' I said.

'What is this?' she said and stood up. She picked up a bunch of grapes and brought it close to my mouth. As I parted my lips, she pushed the whole bunch inside.

'That's not how you feed kings,' I said, struggling to talk as juices squirted from my mouth.

'All you boys are the same. First you chase, but when you get the girl, you want to be kings,' she said.

'You are my queen, my dear,' I said.

'Cheesy. Corny. Horrible,' she said.

I gave her a grape-stained kiss.

'The maids are around!'

'They knock. You know that,' I said.

I wanted to kiss her again, but she pushed me away.

'I am horrible to you, isn't it?' she said.

'It's okay,' I said.

'Too much physical stuff messes up my head. You don't want me to be low for weeks, right?'

'It's okay, I don't want to either,' I said.

'Really?' she said, surprised.

Guys always want to do things. Yet, she knew I wasn't lying. I had never asked her to come to my campus where we could be totally alone. Neither had I attempted another Ramada-like rendezvous.

'Really,' I said, my tone serious.

'You don't want to?' she said. She was wearing a saffron salwar and a white kameez. I wanted her more than any woman, or for that matter anything, in the world. Still, I had a condition.

'Not until Raghav is out of your system,' I said.

'What?' she said.

'That night at Ramada I had your body, not your soul. I don't want it to be like that again.'

'You don't get people out of your system overnight,' she said.

'I know. But are you trying?'

'I don't know,' she said. 'No matter how much I deny it, the fact is I meet you almost everyday.'

She sat on the armrest of my chair.

'So, are you ready to call it off with him?' I said.

As I finished my sentence, her phone rang. 'It's him,' she said.

I became quiet.

'Hey,' she said to him. She sat close enough for me to hear Raghav's voice on the other end.

'We hit five thousand copies,' he was saying.

'Congratulations!' Aarti said.

'We will get proper brands to advertise soon. What are you doing?'

'I came home early,' Aarti said.

'Parents?'

'Mom's taken dad to the hospital. His knees are killing him. He'll have to replace both of them.'

'That's awful,' he said.

I played with Aarti's hair as she spoke to Raghav. She made a face at me to make me stop. I didn't.

'So what else? Doing anything in the evening?' she said.

'Finalising the big Monday issue. It's going to be crazy,' he said.

'Okay,' Aarti sighed. I brushed back the hair falling on her face. She grabbed my hand as she spoke.

'I could meet you for a midnight coffee,' Raghav said.

'Have to be with dad. And every time I go out late, mom wants to get me married the next week.'

'You are so young,' Raghav said.

'My family doesn't get all that. Cousins my age are married,' she said.

'Can we not start a fight again?' Raghav said. 'I'm exhausted.'

'I'm not,' Aarti said.

'I love you, bye,' Raghav said smartly.

'Do you?' Aarti said.

'Aarti, c'mon. I have to hang up. I do love you. Say it, no,' Raghav said.

'Love you. Bye,' she said.

I withdrew my hand from her face.

'What?' she said.

'This is what I mean by getting him out of your system,' I said.

'It was just a simple chat,' she said.

'You said "love". With me you don't like that word.'

'I wanted to be normal. That's how we end calls,' she said. She walked up to the window and stared outside.

'I'm sorry, it's not easy hearing you say that to another man,' I said.

'It's not easy being a cheat,' she said and turned all teary-eyed.

I took her in my arms.

'At some point he will find out,' Aarti said, her face buried in my chest. 'I just want to tell him myself.'

'Will you be with me?' I said.

She gave a barely perceptible nod, without lifting her face.

'I will love you forever, Aarti,' I said.

She hugged me tight. After a while she looked at me. 'Should I tell him?' she said.

I shook my head.

'I will,' I said. I wanted to rub it in his face.

31

It took just a mini-van to move my stuff from my old house to the brand new director's bungalow. I had clothes, my father's old books and family pictures. The contractor purchased the rest. I didn't need a three-bedroom duplex bungalow, but the director couldn't hole up in a hostel room. I stood in the lawns of the new house, supervising the move early morning. A truck with the new purchases – furniture, carpets, appliances, utensils and furnishings – drove into the compound.

A labourer held up some old photographs of my father. 'Where should I keep these?' he said. In one framed picture Baba sat under a tree smoking a hookah and watching the fields. I, all of five years, sat naked next to him. My father's farmer friend had taken that black and white picture with a camera his son had sent him from abroad. I picked up that picture and saw my father's face. Unlike the Baba I remembered, the person in the picture looked young and healthy. I saw the tree and tried to gauge its location in the current campus. I couldn't.

I hadn't cried over my father once in the four years after his funeral. Yet, I didn't know why I felt so overwhelmed that day. Baba would've loved to see me move into such a big house. He probably died thinking his loser son would never get anywhere in life. If only he could see this! *Gopal doesn't cry. Gopal fights the world,* a voice inside told me.

'Put them up in the front room,' I said.

We finished the move by ten in the morning. My first guest, I had planned, would be the person who made this possible – Shukla-ji. I had invited him for lunch. I hurried the hostel chef. The gas stove at my new home didn't work, and the chef wanted to go to the hostel kitchen to prepare the dishes.

'Bring the stove here!' I shouted. 'MLA sir is coming. I can't trust the hostel cooking.'

Of course, I also wanted Aarti to be one of my first guests. However, I had promised myself that Aarti would come to my new house as my girlfriend, not someone else's girlfriend having a parallel affair with me.

She SMSed me: 'How's the move gng? When do i c the place?'

I replied: 'U can come anytime but i won't let u leave. Let me meet Raghav first.'

'R u sure? Am so nervous about u meeting him.'

I was composing a reply to her when my phone rang. I picked up Shukla-ji's call.

'Sir, we are making puris. Come hungry, okay?' I said.

'Come home, Gopal,' he said.

'I am home. My new home. I mean, this is also your home.'

'I'm screwed,' Shukla-ji said , his voice unusually tense.

'What?'

'Come to my place. Your fucker friend, I won't spare him. Come right now.'

'What happened? We have lunch …' I was saying but he cut the call.

The chef arrived panting at my house, carrying the heavy stove on his shoulders.

'It will take only an hour,' he said reassuringly to me.

'Lunch has been cancelled,' I said and walked out of the house.

My phone beeped. Another SMS from Aarti.

'U should let me decorate the house. After all, hotel industry & all.'

I sent her a smiley and kept the phone back in my pocket.

'MLA Shukla's place,' I told the driver.

◆

MLA Shukla's men stood in a circle in Shukla-ji's verandah. They looked mournful, as if someone had just died. Pink-coloured papers lay strewn on the coffee table.

'Where's Shukla sir?' I said.

One of his party workers pointed to his office. 'Wait here. He is on an important call,' he said.

'What happened?' I said. The party worker did not respond. He looked pointedly at the pink papers. I picked one up.

Revolution 2020, said the masthead, as pompous as ever. A miniature map of India, showing the so-called command centres of the revolution, was the logo.

'MLA makes money by making holy river filthy!' said the headline. A poor quality, black and white picture of Shukla-ji occupied a quarter of the page.

'₹25 crores sanctioned for Dimnapura Sewage Treatment Plant. MLA pockets ₹20 crore,' said the sub-headline.

'These are all old, done to death, bullshit allegations, right?' I said. Raghav liked to stir things up, but surely nobody would give a fuck about his rag.

No one in the room responded to me. Half the party workers couldn't read the paper anyway. The others seemed too scared to talk. I read on.

Early Monday morning in Navabaga, a group of children walk towards their school waist-deep in sewage water. It is a gut-wrenching sight to see filthy water everywhere. Stink pervades the air. People of the neighbourhood don't know what happened. They do know that this hadn't happened before the government implemented the Ganga Action Plan (GAP). Yes, the same plan meant to clean up our holy river has ended up spreading more filth around our city.

How? Well, because none of the projects meant to clean up the river were implemented. The Navabaga flooding apart, the river is filthier than ever. To give you an idea, the presence of fecal coliform, a form of bacteria, should not be more than 2,000 units/litre. At the ghats, the fecal coliform levels are 1,500,000 units/litre. Not only is our river dirty, we are living with serious health hazards.

I saw Shukla-ji come out of his office. I rushed to him. He signalled me to wait and I saw that he was still on the phone. He picked up a few files and returned to the office. I continued to read.

Revolution 2020 found many truths about the GAP scam. However, the most shocking one is about MLA Raman Lal Shukla's Dimnapura Sewage Treatment Plant in Varanasi. Built at a cost of ₹25 crores, the plant remained dysfunctional for years. When finally made operational, it never cleaned the water. We have startling facts, with proof, on what happened inside the plant.

'The opposition has done this,' one party worker said to another. I sat down to finish the article.

When untreated water reached the plant, eighty per cent of it was diverted downstream into the Varuna river, and dumped right back without any cleaning. The remaining twenty per cent of water was released at Dimnapura plant's own exit, untreated. When the inspectors took the input and output measurements at points before and after the plant, it showed an eighty per cent drop in pollutants. Meanwhile, the water dumped into the Varuna river met the Ganga a few kilometres later. The net effect – no treatment of water at all and the river remaining as polluted as ever. Shukla took credit for the plant showing an eighty per cent drop in pollutants. The construction company, AlliedCon, is owned by the MLA's uncle, Roshan Shukla, who made fake invoices for pumps that were never purchased (scans below).

'We will kill this newspaper,' a party worker whispered in my ear as he saw me read with such concentration.

The bottom of the page had several images. These included fake invoices for pumps amounting to ₹15 crores. However, the actual site pictures showed no such pumps installed. A scanned letter from the pump manufacturer showed they never supplied the pumps. The ownership structure of AlliedCon confirmed links to Shukla-ji's family. Finally, the paper had a picture of the Varuna river, with a dot to show the exact point where the effluents were released.

'The CM is coming down from Lucknow,' a party worker announced and worried murmurs rippled around the room.

I could tell Raghav had worked hard on the story. He had suffered earlier for doing a story without evidence. This time he had left nothing to chance. The fake invoices, contractor-MLA link, and the audacity to dump the dirty water right back into the revered Ganga didn't spell good news for Shukla-ji. Locals would be livid. A politician stealing is bad enough, but to rob from the holy river is the worst sin.

'It's not even a real newspaper,' Shukla-ji's PA was discussing the matter with someone. 'Couple of thousand copies, nobody will pay attention to it.'

The low circulation of *Revolution 2020* had become the MLA's only hope. Party workers had removed as many copies from the newsstands as they could. However, *Revolution 2020* came free, like a brochure inside newspapers. It would be impossible to get rid of it completely.

Aarti was calling. I stepped out to the lawns.

'Saw *R2020* today?' she said. I didn't know the paper had an acronym.

'I have it in my hand,' I said.

She breathed audibly before she spoke again. 'Is it too much?' she said.

I sneered, 'It's Raghav. When is he not too much?'

'It is shocking, isn't it? They dump the dirty water elsewhere in the river and claim to have cleaned it!'

'He is taking on big people. He should be careful.'

'But he is only speaking the truth. Someone has to stand up for the truth.'

'I just said he needs to be careful,' I said.

'I don't want him to be in trouble,' she said, scared.

'He doesn't like to stay out of it,' I replied.

'Is he in trouble?' she said, pausing after every word.

'How would I know?' I said. I heard the noise of traffic outside the house.

'C'mon, Gopal, you and MLA Shukla ...' she said and paused.

'I'm not involved in any scam, okay?' I screamed.

Horns blared outside as I walked towards the gate.

'I didn't say that,' she said softly. 'I just don't want Raghav to be in danger. I may not be faithful to him, but I don't want him to get hurt.'

'Hold on for a second, Aarti,' I said.

I came to the gate. My eyes popped as I saw the scene. Six vans from different TV channels had parked themselves outside the house. The guards were struggling to keep the reporters out, as they stood there airing live with the MLA's house as backdrop.

'What's going on?' I asked the guard.

'They want to come in,' the guard said. 'They know the CM is coming.'

'Everything okay?' Aarti asked anxiously on the phone.

'Yeah, so far.'

'Promise me Raghav won't get hurt.'

'It's not in my hands, Aarti,' I said, exasperated. 'I don't even know what will happen. It's a small paper. Maybe the story will die.'

'It won't,' she said.

'What?'

'All the mainstream newspapers and channels are in *Revolution 2020*'s office,' she said.

'Fuck,' I said, as a fleet of white Ambassador cars approached the house. Photographers went berserk as they took pictures of everyone around, including me.

'Will Raghav be okay? Promise me.'

'Aarti, I have to go.'

I jogged back to the house.

32

Everyone stood in attention as the CM entered the house. The aura of power could be sensed along every inch of the MLA's bungalow. Shukla-ji came running and greeted the CM with folded hands.

'Who called the media?' the CM said, his voice purposeful.

'What?' Shukla-ji said, as clueless as anyone else in the room.

'Let's go inside,' the CM said. The two leaders disappeared into MLA Shukla's office. The CM's minions mixed with the MLA's minions in the hall. Even the minions maintained a hierarchy. The CM's minions stood with their heads held high, while the MLA's minions looked at the floor. I didn't fit in anywhere.

I sat on a wooden chair in the corner of the room.

'Gopal,' Shukla-ji's booming voice startled me. I looked up. He asked me to come into his office.

Once in, the MLA shut the door.

'Gopal, sir. He runs my college, my trusted man. Bright and ...'

'You know the person who did it?' the CM asked me, with no interest in my qualities or capabilities.

'Raghav Kashyap, sir. Friend once, not anymore.'

'You couldn't shut him up?' the CM said.

'We had him fired from *Dainik*. He started his own rag after that,' I said. 'Nobody cares about it.'

'The media has sniffed it out. The rag doesn't matter much, but if he gives interviews or provides all the evidence to the media, it is going to be bad.'

'He is already doing that,' I said.

Both of them looked at me with accusing eyes.

'My sources told me. I am not in touch with him,' I clarified.

'We can't *handle* him?' the CM asked. 'How can you open a college without handling people?'

I understood what he meant by 'handling'.

'He can't be bought, sir,' I said. For a second I felt proud of Raghav. It felt like a good thing to be – someone who can't be bought.

'What do you mean by *can't be*? Everyone has a price,' the CM said.

'He doesn't,' I said. 'I have known him for years. He's mad.'

'Well, he does want to live, doesn't he?' Shukla-ji said. I noticed his eyes were red.

I looked at the CM. He shook his head.

'Shukla-ji is not in the right frame of mind,' he said.

'No, CM sir, I will not …' Shukla-ji began.

'Calm down, Shukla-ji,' the CM said, his voice loud. 'Do you have any idea what has happened?'

The MLA looked down.

'You didn't even make a plant? Ten per cent here and there doesn't matter. But what were you thinking shoving the dirty water into Varuna? This is Mother Ganga. People will kill us,' the CM said.

I offered to leave the room but the CM told me to sit right there.

'We have elections next year. Raman, I have always respected your space and never interfered. But this will take us down.'

'I will fix it, CM sir,' Shukla said, 'I will, I promise you.'

'How? By killing the journalist?'

'I said it in anger,' Shukla-ji said, his tone apologetic.

'Anger makes people do a lot of unpredictable things. It makes voters throw out governments. I know when a scam report has teeth, and when it doesn't. This one does.'

'Tell me what to do, sir,' Shukla-ji said, 'And I will do it.'

'Resign,' the CM said and got up to leave.

'What?' Shukla-ji said, his face looking bleached.

'It's not personal. Resign with grace and maybe you will come back.'

'Else?' the MLA said after a pause.

'Don't make me fire you, Shukla. You are a friend,' the CM said. 'But the party is above friendship.'

Realisation slowly dawned on Shukla-ji. He clenched his fists in anger.

'It happens. You will be back,' the CM said.

He then walked out briskly with his minions. The press was waiting outside for the CM to give a statement. I followed the CM's workers to the gate.

'I came for a routine visit,' the CM told the reporters.

'What is your view on the Dimnapura Plant scam?' a reporter shouted hoarsely.

'I am not fully aware of the situation. It looks like a smear campaign. Our party is clear on corruption. Even if there are allegations, we ask our leaders to step down.'

The CM jostled past the reporters and sat in his car.

'So will MLA Shukla resign?' one of the reporters managed to jam the mike close to the CM's face.

'That is for him to decide,' the CM said, hinting at the inevitable.

The CM's car left. I wondered what would happen to my GangaTech. I went back to Shukla-ji's room.

'We will destroy the newspaper office,' a party worker was saying to Shukla-ji.

Shukla-ji did not respond.

'Tell us what to do, Shukla-ji. What did CM sir say?' another minion said.

'Leave me alone,' Shukla-ji said. Party workers got the message. They scuttled away within seconds. Soon only he and I remained in his big house.

'Sir?' I said. 'Do you need me?'

Shukla-ji looked at me. He no longer had his trademark ramrod posture. He slouched on the sofa, elbow on the armrest and face in his palm.

'The CM is a behenchod,' he said.

I kept quiet.

'When he needed his election funding, he came to me. I did his dirty work, distributing liquor all over the state. Now he screws me.'

'You will come out of it, Shukla-ji, you always do.'

'Nobody gives a fuck about cleaning the Ganga. Everyone made money on that plan. So why *me*?'

I didn't have an answer. I felt a tinge of guilt. Maybe Raghav did it to Shukla-ji because he wanted to get even with me. Or maybe it was my imagination. Raghav would expose anyone he could.

'You run GangaTech properly, okay? I don't want any mud from here to reach there,' he said.

'Of course, sir,' I said. 'Anyway, you are here, sir. We have big growth plans.'

'They'll lock me up,' he said calmly, decades in politics making him wise enough to forecast events.

'What?' I said, shocked.

'Once I resign, I have no power. Many MLAs have made money in the GAP scam. Before it spreads, they will lock me up to show they have taken action.'

'You are the MLA, Shukla-ji. The police cannot touch you,' I said.

'They will if the CM asks them. I will go in for a while. Pay my dues if I ever want a comeback.'

The thought of my father-figure and mentor going to jail unsettled me. I had very few people in life I could call my own. Shukla-ji counted as one of them.

'Wait here,' Shukla-ji said and got up. He went into his bedroom and returned with a set of keys.

'Keep it,' he said. 'I can't be seen with such flashy stuff.'

I picked up the keys. They belonged to the black Mercedes.

'Your new car? I can't.' I placed the keys back on the table.

'Keep it for me. You are like my son. I will also move some money into the trust. Make the college big.'

'Alone? How can I do that alone?' I said, my voice choked. 'You haven't even come to my house.'

'I can't step out of here. My relatives are waiting outside with their cameras,' he said.

Shukla-ji spent the next hour explaining to me his various bank accounts and businesses. He had his people running them, but he was telling me in case of an emergency. 'GangaTech is my cleanest business, and can aid my comeback one day.'

He wrote out his resignation in front of me and asked me to fax it to Lucknow.

The fax machine beeped as the transmission started. 'He fucked us, eh?' Shukla-ji said.

'Who?' I said.

'Your friend. I had him fired. He got me fired.'

'He tried to ruin my life. I will ruin his life,' I vowed.

33

Every newspaper of Varanasi city carried the Dimnapura Plant scam story on the front page the next morning. Shukla-ji, whose resignation became public, had become the new villain in town and Raghav Kashyap the new hero. Everyone spoke highly of the stupid pink paper. Local television channels covered the scam for hours on end.

I flicked through the channels on my new forty-inch LCD television. I paused when I saw Raghav being interviewed.

'It took us two months of secret work to get all the evidence on the scam. Everyone knew this MLA was shady, but there just wasn't proof. Our team did it,' Raghav said smugly. He had lost weight, and looked sleep-deprived with his unshaven face and dishevelled hair. Yet, he had a glint in his eye.

'Who is your team?' the reporter asked him.

'Well, we are a small newspaper called *Revolution 2020*. There are four of us, including me. We don't have much experience but we are passionate about our work.'

'What are you passionate about?'

'Making a difference. Changing India for the better. That is what we live for,' Raghav said.

'Is it true that you believe India will have a revolution in the year 2020?'

'Yes, but we all have to work towards it and make sacrifices for it.'

'What exactly will the revolution be for?'

'A society where truth, justice and equality are respected more than power. Such societies progress the most.'

'Can you explain that?'

'Power-driven societies resemble animal societies. "Might is right" is the rule of the jungle and applies to beasts. And beasts do not progress, humans do.'

I turned off the TV. I couldn't take his bullshit anymore. Neither could Shukla's men.

Nitesh, one of the party workers, called me in the morning.

'You smashed what?' I said on the phone.

'His only computer is in pieces. We took hammers and broke the printing press too.'

'Nobody saw you?'

'We went at night. Ransacked the office. Bastard. He's finished.'

I got ready for work. I saw the Mercedes parked outside. I had a less than 300-yard commute to the office. Yet, I wanted to go in my new car.

I thought about Raghav. After yesterday's bravado and all that attention, a plundered office was all he was left with.

He had no job, no business and soon nobody would give a fuck about his paper after this story died.

'Where, sir?' the driver said.

'Office,' I said.

I made up dialogues to say to Raghav in my head.

'The average-looking dumb Gopal Mishra, the boy you had preached to, saying, "you can try again next year", is sitting in a Mercedes. You have a broken printing press. And you think you are handsome, right? Well, soon I will make your girlfriend mine. The girl you stole from me.'

'Sir,' the driver prompted. We had reached office.

I entered my office. I sank into the leather chair and closed my eyes. I visualised Raghav's face when I told him, 'Aarti is with me.' It would be amazing. I had planned it all. I would go to his office. I would drop the Mercedes keys on his table. I even had some lines ready.

'Sometimes losers get ahead in life. Never forget that,' I said out loud, to practise for D-day.

I still didn't have the right lines to break the news about Aarti being mine. I decided to try a couple of them.

'Buddy, I am sorry to say this but Aarti is mine,' I mumbled.

That didn't sound manly enough.

'Aarti and I are a couple. Just wanted you to know,' I tried a casual one. Couldn't quite pull it off.

How do you come up with a suitable sentence to convey something you have meant to say for years? I wanted my words to bomb-blast him, to hit him like a lethal weapon. I wanted him to know that he had made me feel inadequate all my life. I wanted him to burn with jealousy seeing my car, my life, and hurt like hell for losing the girl he stole from me. I wanted to tell him 'I am better than you, asshole,' without actually saying it.

Aarti's call disrupted my thoughts.

'They attacked his office,' she said, her voice disturbed.

'Oh, really?' I acted surprised.

'*Revolution 2020* can't be published. The press is broken,' she said.

I scanned the files on my desk. I didn't care if the stupid rag came out or not.

'You there?' Aarti said.

'MLA Shukla could be jailed,' I said.

'He should, isn't it? He stole money and dirtied the river.'

'Are you on his side or mine?' I said to Aarti, irritated.

'What? How is this about sides?' she said.

'Are you with me?' I said.

'Huh?' she said.

'Are you?'

'Yes. But shouldn't we wait to tell Raghav till he settles down?'

'Will he ever settle down?' I said.

She went quiet.

'Come home,' I said.

'Your place?' she said. 'You are finally showing me your new home?'

'Yes.'

'Tomorrow? I have a morning shift, will be done by three.'

'I'll send my car,' I said.

◆

I kept one eye on the TV and another on the porch as I waited for the Mercedes to arrive with Aarti. The afternoon rain had slowed down traffic, and the car took longer than it should have. Images of Shukla-ji's arrest flickered on TV.

'I have done no wrong. I will be out soon,' he proclaimed on one of the channels. He had pre-empted his own arrest to win some public sympathy. He had called me before going to jail. He seemed relaxed. Perhaps he had cut a deal with the party. Or maybe he didn't realise that the party had made him the fall-guy.

'It's not so bad. If I pay, jail is like a hotel,' he had told me.

I saw the black car approach. My heart beating fast, I rushed out.

34

She stepped out of the car. She had come in her work sari.

'Wow, you have a bungalow?' she said. It's not "mine", it's "ours", I wanted to tell her, but didn't.

She hugged me but looked serious.

'All good?' I said.

'Raghav's exposé has created complete chaos. Even my family has been affected,' she said.

'What happened?' I said. 'But what is this, first come in!'

She came in and stepped on the new silk carpet I had laid out in her honour. She saw the huge TV, the velvet sofas and the eight-seater dining table. For a moment, she forgot about Raghav.

'Your college is doing this well?' she said, wide-eyed.

'This is only the beginning,' I said, and came forward to hold her. 'With you by my side, see where I take it. University status in three years.'

'Big man, Gopal. You have become a big man,' she said.

I shook my head. 'For you, I am the same,' I said. I kissed her on the forehead.

I offered to show her the house. We went upstairs and saw each of the three bedrooms. My room had a king-size bed with a twelve-inch mattress. Next to the bed, I had kept a rocking chair similar to Baba's.

She kept quiet throughout my guided tour. Every time I showed her something, like the marble tiles or the split air-conditioner, she looked suitably awed. However, she seemed more interested in watching the excitement on my face than the fittings.

I threw myself on the bed. She sat on the rocking chair. We looked at the window as rain splattered on the panes.

'It's raining,' she said, excited.

'It's an auspicious sign. The first time you came to our house,' I said.

She raised an eyebrow.

'It is ours, not mine. I made it for us,' I said.

'Shut up. You didn't know we would be together when construction started,' she said and grinned.

I smiled. 'Correct. But I have done it up for us. Else, why would I need such a big house?'

'You are the director. It's not a joke,' she said.

'You want to talk about Raghav?' I said. I sensed she needed to.

'We don't have to,' she said and shook her head, putting on a brave smile.

'Come here,' I said and patted the bed.

She hesitated, but I extended my hand. She held it as I pulled her gently down. I kissed her, and she kissed me back with closed eyes. It wasn't frantic or sexual. It was, if at all it is possible to kiss like that, chaste and pure. However, we kissed for a long time, our pace as gentle as the rain on the window. I felt her tears on my cheeks. I paused and held her shoulders. She hugged me and buried her face in my chest. It was what Aarti always did, and I loved it when she did that. It made me feel protective.

'What's up, my love?' I said to her.

'I am happy for you, Gopal. I really am.'

'Us. Say happy for us,' I said.

She nodded, even as she fought back tears.

'I am happy for us. And I don't want to ruin your moment of showing me your house.'

'It's fine,' I said.

'You have worked so hard to get here. You deserve this,' she said.

'What do you want to talk about?' I said.

She shook her head and composed herself. I waited for her to talk.

'I'm fine. Girls are emotional. You will get used to my drama,' she said.

'I live for your drama,' I said.

She smiled.

'How's Raghav?'

'They ruined his office,' she said.

'Politicians are vindictive. Is he hurt?' I said.

'No, thank god. The computer and the machines are all broken. He is trying to bring the issue out but there's no money.'

'He wants money? He can ask me,' I said. I wished he would come and beg me on bended knees.

'You know he'll never do that. He won't even take money from me.'

'So?' I said.

'He's trying to figure stuff out.'

'Are you still with me?' I said.

'Gopal!' she said.

'What?'

'I wouldn't be sitting on your bed. I wouldn't be, you know …'

'Okay, okay,' I said. I took a pillow and sat against the headrest. She sat on her haunches, facing me.

'You have to stop asking me so much. Please understand this is difficult for me,' she said.

'What?' I said.

'Breaking up with him, especially at this time. And *you* want to break the news to him.'

'That's life, Aarti,' I said. I planned to go meet Raghav next week.

'One should be sensitive …' she said.

'Nobody was sensitive to me when I didn't clear my entrance exam two years in a row. Nobody gave a fuck when Baba died. I lived with it. Aarti, he will learn to face life.'

'You men … why are you so competitive all the time?' she said.

'Me? Raghav is nothing compared to me today. Why would I compete with him?'

'We can still wait a few months …' she said but I cut her.

'I can't bear you to be someone else's girlfriend,' I said, my voice loud.

'Really?' she said, patting my cheek.

'Not for another second,' I said.

I tugged at the loose end of her Ramada sari, bringing her close to me. We kissed. The rain grew insistent, noisy, thumping the window rhythmically. We kissed and, naturally, my hand went to her blouse.

'Mr Director,' she smiled, 'I thought you said you didn't want to have me until he was out of my system.'

'Isn't he?' I said.

'Almost,' she said, closing her eyes.

'Well, maybe this will help get the remaining bits out,' I said and brought her lips to mine again.

I plundered her neck, planting as many kisses as the raindrops on the window. We undressed with a lot more awareness than the previous time.

'These are my work clothes, please keep them carefully,' she said as I tried to fold the never-ending sari.

Our naked bodies felt toasty in the cold weather. We huddled under the quilt and explored each other for hours. The rain stopped, started and stopped again. She wanted to get closer to me, perhaps to justify leaving Raghav. I wanted to show her how much she meant to me. I could give up this oversized house, the black car, the entire college for her.

This time she looked me in the eye as she surrendered herself.

We dozed off.

'It's six o' clock,' she said, peering into her mobile phone on the side-table.

'Ten more minutes,' I said, nuzzling her shoulder.

'Lazy bones, wake up,' she said. 'And I am famished. Such a big house and nothing to eat!'

I sat up. Still groggy, I said, 'There's food. The cook made so many things for you. Let's go downstairs.'

'It's power, Aarti,' I said. 'Means a lot in this country.'

'I don't care about power. I don't need it. I am happy,' Aarti said.

I looked into her eyes. She seemed sincere.

'Are you happy with me?'

'I will be. We have to resolve some stuff, but I know I will be,' she said, more to herself than to me.

She left soon after that. Her parents had visitors, more party officials, who also wanted to meet Aarti. I dropped her home, so I'd get some more time with her.

'You'll be alone on the way back,' Aarti pointed out.

I shrugged.

'Thanks for a lovely day,' she said as we reached her house.

'My pleasure,' I said. 'Have a good dinner with the politicians.'

'Oh, please. Shoot me in the head,' she said. Both of us stepped out of the car. I leaned on the bonnet as she walked towards her gate.

'Sure you don't want to become an MLA?' I said from behind.

She turned to me. 'No way,' she said. 'Maybe my husband can, if he wants to.'

She winked at me before skipping towards her house.

I stood there, surprised. Was she implying something? Did she want me to be the MLA? More specifically, did she want me to be her husband?

'Aarti, what did you say?' I said.

But she had already gone into her house.

◆

I hadn't known that the Varanasi Central Jail had private rooms. I went to meet Shukla-ji in his cell. As requested, I brought him three boxes of fruits, two bottles of Johnnie Walker Black Label and a kilo each of salted cashewnuts and almonds. The cop who frisked me for security collected the parcel and promised to deliver it. I thought the MLA would meet me in the waiting area, but I could go right up to his cell.

He sat in his room, watching a small colour TV and sipping cola with a straw.

'Not bad, eh?' he said. He spread his hands to show me the fifteen-by-ten-feet cell. It had a bed with clean sheets, a desk and chair, closets and the TV. Yes, it didn't seem awful. It resembled a government guesthouse more than a jail. However, it couldn't be compared to Shukla-ji's mansion.

'It's terrible,' I said.

He laughed.

'You should have met me in my early days in politics,' he said. 'I have slept on railway platforms.'

'I feel so bad,' I said. I sat on the wooden chair.

'Six months maximum,' he said. 'Plus, they get me everything. You want to eat from the Taj Ganga?'

I shook my head.

'How is the car?' he said.

'Great,' I said.

'College?' he said.

'Going okay. We have slowed down a bit. We don't have the capital,' I said.

'I will arrange the money,' Shukla-ji promised.

'Take it easy, Shukla-ji. Keep a low profile. Things can wait,' I said.

He switched off the TV. 'Your friend fucked us, eh?' Shukla-ji said.

'He's not my friend. And he is finished now. And you will be back,' I said.

'They won't give me a ticket next time,' he said pensively.

'I heard,' I said.

'From who?' Shukla-ji looked surprised.

I told him about my friendship with Aarti, the DM's daughter, and what she had told me. I didn't tell him about her relationship with Raghav, nor did I give details about her and me.

'Oh yes, you have known her for long, right?' he said.

'School friend,' I said.

'So her father won't contest?' Shukla-ji said.

I shook my head. 'Neither will the daughter. She hates politics. So maybe you still have a chance,' I said.

'Not this time,' Shukla-ji dismissed. 'I have to wait. Not right after jail.'

'They'll find someone else then?'

'The DM's family will definitely win,' he said. 'People love them.'

'They aren't interested,' I said.

'How close are you to her?' His sharp question had me in a dither.

I never lie to Shukla-ji. However, I didn't want to give him specifics about Aarti and me either.

I kept quiet.

'You like her?' he said.

'Leave it, Shukla-ji. You know I am immersed in my work,' I said, evading the topic.

'I am talking about work only, you silly boy,' Shukla-ji said.

'What?' I said, amazed by how the MLA sustained his zest for politics even in jail.

'You marry her. If that broken-legged DM can't contest and the daughter won't, the son-in-law will.'

'What? What makes you say that?'

'I have spent twenty-five years in Indian politics. It is obvious that is what they will do. Wait and watch, they will marry her off soon.'

'Her parents are pestering her for marriage.'

'Marry her. Contest the election and win it.'

I kept quiet.

'Do you realise where your GangaTech will be if you become an MLA? I will be back one day, anyway, maybe from another constituency. And if both of us are in power, we will rule this city, maybe the state. Her grandfather even served as CM for a while!'

'I haven't thought about marriage yet,' I lied.

'Don't think. Do it. You think she will marry you?' he asked.

I shrugged my shoulders.

'Show her mother your car and money. Don't take dowry. Even if the daughter doesn't agree, the mother will.'

'Shukla-ji? Me, a politician?'

'Yes. Politician, businessman and educationist – power, money and respect – perfect combination. You are destined for big things. I knew it the day you entered my office,' he said.

Shukla-ji poured some Black Label whisky into two glasses. He asked the guard to get ice. I kept quiet and sat thoughtfully while he prepared the drinks. Sure, power is never a bad thing in India. To get anything done, you need power. Power meant people would pay me money, rather than me paying money to get things done. GangaTech could become ten times its size. Plus, I loved Aarti anyway. I would marry her eventually, so why not now? Besides, she had somewhat hinted at it. I let out a sigh.

I fought my low self-esteem. *It's okay, Gopal*, I told myself. *You are meant for bigger things. Just because you didn't get an AIEEE rank, just because you didn't remember the molecular formula, doesn't mean you can't do great things in life.* After all, I had opened a college, lived in a big house and had an expensive car.

Shukla-ji handed me the drink.

'I can get the girl,' I said.

'Cheers to that, Mr Son-in-law!' Shukla-ji raised his glass.

36

'Busy?' I said.

I had called Aarti at work. A tourist was screaming at her because the water in his room was not hot enough. Aarti kept me on hold while the guest cursed in French.

'I can call later,' I said.

'It's fine. Housekeeping will take care of it. My ears are hurting!' Aarti said, rattled by all the screaming.

'You will own a college one day. You won't have to do this anymore.'

'It's okay, Gopal. I really like my job. Sometimes we have weirdos. Anyway, what's up?'

'How did the dinner go?'

'Boring. I dozed off on the table when the fifth guy wanted to inform me of the Pradhan family's duty towards the party.'

'Any conclusion on the ticket?'

'It's politics, Director sir, things aren't decided so fast. Anyway, election is next year.'

'You said something when you were saying bye,' I said.

I could almost see her smile. 'Did I?' she said.

'Something about your husband becoming the MLA?'

'Could be, why?' she said, her voice child-like.

'I wonder if I could apply?' I said.

'For the husband or MLA?' she said.

'I don't know. Whichever has a shorter waitlist,' I said.

Aarti laughed.

'For husband the queue is rather long,' she said.

'I am a bit of a queue jumper,' I said.

'That you are,' she said. 'Okay, another guest coming. Speak later?'

'I'm going to visit Raghav soon.'

'I have stopped talking to him,' she said. She didn't protest against my proposed meeting with him. I took it as her consent.

'Intentionally?' I said.

'Yeah, we had a bit of a tiff. I normally fix things up, I didn't bother this time.'

'Good,' I said. 'So what's the tourist saying?'

'She's Japanese. They are polite. She will wait until I finish my call.'

'Tell her you are on the phone with your husband.'

'Shut up. Bye.'

'Bye,' I said and kissed the phone. I opened the calendar on my desk and marked the coming Friday as the day for my meeting with Raghav.

◆

I pressed the nozzle of a Gucci perfume five times to spray my neck, armpits and both wrists. I wore a new black shirt and a custom-made suit for the occasion. I put on my Ray-Ban glasses and looked at myself in the mirror. The sunglasses seemed a bit too much, so I hung them from my shirt pocket.

I had taken the day off on Friday. Dean sir wanted to bore me with a report of the academic performance of the students in the first term. I needed an excuse to get out anyway.

All the best. Avoid hurt as much as possible, Aarti had messaged me.

I assured her that I would handle the situation well. From her side, she had messaged him a 'we need to talk' equivalent and he had responded with a 'not the best time' message – exactly the kind of stuff that irked her about him in the first place.

I told my driver to go to Nadeshar Road, where Raghav's place of work was.

One could easily miss the *Revolution 2020* office in the midst of so many auto-repair shops. Raghav had rented out a garage. The office had three areas – a printing space inside, his own cubicle in the middle and a common area for staff and visitors at the entrance.

'May I help you?' a teenager asked me.

'I am here to meet Raghav,' I said.

'He's with people,' the boy said. 'What is this about?'

I looked inside the garage. Raghav's office had a partial glass partition. He sat on his desk. A farmer with a soiled turban and a frail little boy sat opposite Raghav. The father-son duo looked poor and dishevelled. Raghav listened to them gravely, elbows on the table.

'It's personal,' I told the teenager before me.

'Does he know you are coming?'

'No, but he knows me well,' I said.

Raghav noticed me then and stepped out of his cabin.

'Gopal?' Raghav said, surprised. If he was upset with me, he didn't show it.

Raghav wore a T-shirt with a logo of his newspaper and an old pair of jeans. He looked unusually hip for someone in a crisis.

'Can we talk?' I said.

'What happened?' Raghav said. 'MLA Shukla sent you?'

'No,' I said. 'Actually, it is personal.'

'Can you give me ten minutes?' he said.

'I won't be long,' I said.

'I am really sorry. But these people have travelled a hundred kilometres to meet me. They have had a tragedy. I'll finish soon.'

I looked back into his office. The child now lay in his father's lap. He seemed sick.

'Fine,' I said and checked the time.

'Thanks. Ankit here will take care of you,' he said.

The teenager smiled at me as Raghav went inside.

'Please sit,' Ankit said, pointing to the spare chairs. I took one right next to Raghav's office.

I chatted with Ankit to pass time.

'Nobody else here?' I said.

'We had two more staff members,' Ankit said, 'who left after the office was ransacked. Their parents didn't feel it was safe anymore. As it is, salaries are delayed.'

'Why haven't you left?' I said.

Ankit shook his head. 'I want to be there for Raghav sir,' he said.

'Why?' I said.

'He is a good person,' Ankit said.

I smiled even though his words felt like stabs.

'The office doesn't look that bad,' I said.

'We cleaned it up. The press is broken though. We don't have a computer either.'

'You did such a big story,' I said. 'They fired an MLA because of you guys.'

Ankit gave me a level look. 'The media ran with the story because they wanted to. But who cares about us?'

'How are you operating now?' I said.

Ankit opened a drawer in the desk. He took out a large sheet of paper with handwritten text all over it.

'Sir writes the articles, I write the matrimonials. We make photocopies and distribute as many as we can.'

'How many?' I said.

'Four hundred copies. It's handwritten and photocopied; obviously not many people like that in a paper.'

I scanned the A3 sheet. Raghav had written articles on the malpractices by ration shops in Varanasi. He had hand-drawn a table that showed the official rate, the black market rate and the money pocketed by the shopkeeper for various commodities. I flipped the page. It had around fifty matrimonials, meticulously written by hand.

'Four hundred copies? How will you get ads with such a low circulation?'

Ankit shrugged and did not answer. 'I have to go to the photocopy shop,' he said instead. 'Do you mind waiting alone?'

'No problem, I will be fine,' I said, sitting back. I checked my phone. I had a message from Aarti: 'Whatever you do. Be kind.'

I kept the phone back in my pocket. I felt hot in my suit. I realised nobody had switched on the fan.

'Where's the switch?' I asked Ankit.

'No power, sorry. They cut off the connection.' Ankit left the office.

I removed my jacket and undid the top two buttons of my shirt. I considered waiting in my car instead of this dingy place. However, it would be too cumbersome to call the driver again. I had become too used to being in air-conditioned environs. The hot room reminded me of my earlier days with Baba. As did, for some reason, the little boy in the other room who slept in his father's lap.

I looked again from the corner of my eye. The farmer had tears in his eyes. I leaned in to listen.

'I have lost one child and my wife. I don't want to lose more members of my family. He is all I have,' the man said, hands folded.

'Bishnu-ji, I understand,' Raghav said. 'My paper did a huge story on the Dimnapura plant scam. They broke our office because of it.'

'But you come and see the situation in my village, Roshanpur. There's sewage everywhere. Half the children are sick. Six have already died.'

'Roshanpur has another plant. Maybe someone cheated the government there too,' Raghav said.

'But nobody is reporting it. The authorities are not doing anything. You are our only hope,' the farmer said. He took off his turban and put it on Raghav's desk.

'What are you doing, Bishnu-ji?' Raghav said, giving the turban back to the hapless man. 'I am a nobody. My paper is at the verge of closing down. We distribute a handful of handwritten copies, most of which go into dustbins.'

'I told my son you are the bravest, most honest man in this city,' Bishnu said, his voice quivering with emotion.

Raghav gave a smile of despair. 'What does that mean anyway?' he said.

'If the government can at least send some doctors for our children, we don't care if the guilty are punished or not,' the man said.

Raghav exhaled. He scratched the back of his neck before he spoke again. 'All right, I will come to your village and do a story. It will be limited circulation now. If my paper survives, we will do a big one again. If not, well, no promises. Okay?'

'Thank you, Raghav-ji!' There was such hope in his eyes, I couldn't help but notice.

'And one of my friends' father is a doctor. I will see if he can go to your village.'

Raghav stood up to end the meeting. The man stood up too, which woke up his son, and bent forward to touch Raghav's feet.

'Please don't,' Raghav said. 'I have a meeting now. After that, let's go to your village today itself. How far is it?'

'A hundred and twenty kilometres. You have to change three buses,' the farmer said. 'Takes five hours maximum.'

'Fine, please wait then.'

Raghav brought them – the man and his weak and sleepy son – outside the office.

'Sit here, Bishnu-ji,' Raghav said and looked at me. 'Two minutes, Gopal? Let me clean up my office.'

I nodded. Raghav went inside and sorted the papers on his desk.

The man sat on Ankit's chair, facing me. We exchanged cursory smiles.

'What's his name?' I said, pointing to the boy who was lying in his lap once again.

'Keshav,' the farmer said, stroking his son's head.

I nodded and kept quiet. I played with my phone, flipping it up and down, up and down. I felt for the duplicate Mercedes key in my pants pocket. I had especially brought it for the occasion.

'Baba, will I also die?' Keshav said, his voice a mere thread.

'Stupid boy. What nonsense,' the farmer said.

I felt bad for the child, who would not remember his mother when he grew up, just like me. I gripped the key in my pocket harder, hoping that clutching it will make me feel better.

Raghav was dusting his desk and chair. His paper could close down in a week and he had no money. Yet, he wanted to travel to some far-flung village to help some random people. They had broken his office, but not his spirit.

I clutched the key tighter, to justify to myself that *I am the better person here.*

I realised the boy was staring at me. His gaze was light, but I felt disturbed, like he was questioning me and I had no answer.

What have you become, Gopal? a voice rang in my head.

I restlessly took out the sunglasses from my pocket and twirled them about. I suddenly noticed that the eyes of the boy, Keshav, were moving with the sunglasses. I moved them to the right, his eyes followed. I moved them to the left, his eyes followed. I smiled at him.

'What?' I pointed at my fancy shades. 'You want these?'

Keshav sat up, feeble but eager. Though his father kept saying no, I felt a certain relief in handing over the sunglasses.

'They are big for me,' the boy said, trying them on. The oversized glasses made his face look even more pathetic.

I closed my eyes. The heat in the room was too much. I felt sick. Raghav was now on the phone.

My mind continued to talk. *What did you come here for? You came to show him that you have made it, and he is ruined? Is that the high point of your life? You think you are a better person than him, because of your car and suit?*

'Gopal!' Raghav called out.

'Huh?' I said, opening my eyes. 'What?'

'Come on in,' Raghav said.

I went into his office. I kept my hand in my pocket, on my keys. According to the plan, I was to casually place the keys on his table before sitting down. However, I couldn't.

'What's in the pocket?' Raghav said as he noticed that my hand would not come out.

'Oh, nothing,' I said and released the keys. I sat down to face him.

'What brings you to *Revolution 2020*? Have we upset your bosses again?' Raghav chuckled. 'Oh wait, you said it is personal.'

'Yeah,' I said.

'What?' Raghav said.

I didn't know what to say. I had my whole speech planned. On how Aarti deserved better than him, and that better person was I. On how I had made it in life, and he had failed. On how he was the loser, not me. And yet, saying all that now would make me feel like a loser.

'How's the paper?' I said, saying something to end the awkward silence.

He swung his hands in the air. 'You can see for yourself.'

'What will you do if it closes down?' I said.

Raghav did not smile. 'Haven't thought about it. End of phase one I guess.'

I kept quiet.

'Hope I won't have to take an engineering job. Maybe I will have to apply …' Raghav's voice trailed into silence.

I could tell Raghav didn't know. He hadn't thought that far.

'I'm sorry, Gopal,' Raghav said, 'if I have hurt you in the past. Whatever you may think, it wasn't personal.'

'Why do you do all this, Raghav? You are smart. Why don't you just make money like the rest of us?'

'Someone has to do it, Gopal. How will things change?'

'The whole system is fucked up. One person can't change it.'

'I know.'

'So?'

'We all have to do our bit. For change we need a revolution. A real revolution can only happen when people ask themselves – what is my sacrifice?'

'Sounds like your newspaper's tagline,' I mocked.

He had no answer. I stood up to leave. He followed me out. I decided not to call my car, but to walk out into the lane and find it.

'What did you come here for?' Raghav said. 'I can't believe you came here to check on me.'

'I had work in the area. My car needed servicing. I thought I will visit you while it gets fixed,' I said.

'Nice of you to come. You should check on Aarti too sometimes,' he said.

I went on red-alert at the mention of her name.

'Yeah. How is she doing?' I said.

'Haven't met her in a while, but she seems stressed. I have to make it up to her. You should call her, she will like it,' he said.

I nodded and came out of his office.

37

I lay down in my comfortable bed at night. However, I could not sleep a wink. There were three missed calls from Aarti. I didn't call back. I couldn't. I didn't know what to say to her.

How did it go? she messaged me.

I realised she'd keep asking until I told her something. I called her.

'Why weren't you picking up?' she said.

'Sorry, I had the dean at home. He left just now.'

'You met Raghav?' she asked impatiently.

'Yeah,' I sighed.

'So?'

'He had people in his office. I couldn't bring it up,' I said.

'Gopal, I hope you realise that until I break up with him, I am cheating on him with you. Should I talk to him?'

'No, no, wait. I will meet him in private.'

'And I need to speak to my parents too,' she said.

'About what?'

'I have three prospective grooms lined up for meetings next week. All from political families.'

'Have your parents gone insane?' I exploded.

'When it comes to daughters, Indian parents are insane,' she said. 'I can stall them, but not for long.'

'Okay, I will fix this,' I said.

I pulled two pillows close to me.

'See, this is what happens after sex. Roles reverse. The girl has to chase now.'

'Nothing like that, Aarti. Give me two days.'

'Okay. Else I am speaking to Raghav myself. And in case he asks, nothing ever happened between us.'

'What do you mean?' I said.

'I never cheated on him. We decided to get together, but only did so after the break-up. Okay?'

'Okay,' I said.

Sometimes I feel girls like to complicate their lives.

'He will be devastated otherwise,' she finished.

I ended the call and lay down on the bed, exhausted.

My eyes hurt due to the extra white clothes people had worn for the funeral. I looked at people's faces. I could not recognise any of them.

'Whose funeral is it?' I asked a man next to me.

We stood at the ghats. The body, I saw, was small. They took it straight to the water.

'Why are they not cremating it?' I asked. And then I realised why. It was a child. I went close to the body and removed the shroud. It was a little boy. In sunglasses.

'Who killed him?' I screamed but the words would not come out ...

I woke up screaming at the white ceiling of my bedroom and the bright lights I had forgotten to switch off. It was 3:00 a.m. Just a nightmare, I told myself.

I tossed and turned in bed, but could not go back to sleep.

I thought about Raghav. The guy was finished. His paper would shut down. He would find it tough to get a job, at least in Varanasi. And wherever he was, Shukla's men could hurt him.

I thought about Aarti – my Aarti – my reason to live. I could be engaged to her next week, married in three months. In a year, I could be an MLA. My university approvals would come within the space of a heartbeat. I could expand into medicine, MBA, coaching, aviation. Given how much Indians cared about education, the sky would be the limit. Forget Aarti becoming a flight attendant, I could buy her a plane. If I played my cards right, I could also rise up the party ranks. I had lived alone too long. I could start a family, and have lots of beautiful kids with Aarti. They would grow up and take over the family businesses and political empire. This is how people become big in India. I could become really big.

But what happens to Raghav? The dead-alive Keshav asked me. *I don't care,* I told him. *If he went down, it is because of his own stupidity. If he were smart, he would have realised that stupid bravado will lead to nothing. There would be no revolution in this country by 2020. There wouldn't be one by 2120! This is India, nothing changes here. Fuck you, Raghav.*

But Keshav was not done with me. *What kind of politician will you be, Gopal?*

'I don't want to answer you. You are scaring me, go away,' I said out aloud, even though there was nobody in the room. Really, I knew that.

What about Aarti? A voice whispered within me.

I love her!

What about her? Does she love you?

Yes, Aarti loves me. She made love to me. She wants me to be her husband, I screamed in my head until it hurt.

But will she love you if she knows who you really are? A corrupt, manipulative bastard?

'I work hard. I am a successful man,' I said aloud again, my voice startling me.

But are you a good person?

The clock showed 5:00 a.m. Day was breaking outside.

I went for a walk around the campus. My mind calmed a little in the fresh morning air. Little birds chirped on dew-drenched trees. They didn't care about money, the Mercedes or the bungalow. They sang, for that was what they wanted to do. And it felt beautiful. For the first time, I felt proud of the trees and birds on the campus.

I realised why Keshav kept coming to me. Once upon a time, I was Keshav – sweet, innocent and unaware of the world. As life slapped me about several times, and thrashed the innocence out of me, I had killed my Keshav, for the world didn't care about sweetness. Then why didn't I crush Raghav completely yesterday? Maybe that Keshav hasn't died, I told myself. Maybe that innocent, good part of us never dies – we just trample upon it for a while.

I looked at the sky, hoping to get guidance from above – from god, my mother or Baba. Tears streamed down my face. I began to sob uncontrollably. I sat down under a tree and cried for an hour. Just like that.

Sometimes life isn't about what you want to do, but what you ought to do.

◆

Shukla-ji was eating apples in the jail verandah. A constable sat next to him, peeling and slicing.

'Gopal, my son, come, come,' Shukla-ji said. He wore a crisp white kurta-pyjama that glistened in the morning sun.

I sat on the floor. 'Had a small favour to ask you,' I said.

'Of course,' he said.

I looked at the constable. 'Oh, him. He is Dhiraj, from my native place. Dhiraj, my son and I need to talk.'

The constable left.

'I've told him I'll get him promoted,' Shukla-ji said and smiled.

'I have come with a strange request,' I said.

'Everything okay?'

'Shukla-ji, can you help me hire some … call girls? You mentioned them long ago.'

Shukla-ji laughed so hard, apple juice dripped out of his mouth.

'I am serious,' I said.

'My boy has become big. So, you want women?'

'It's not for me.'

Shukla-ji patted my knee and winked conspiratorially. 'Of course not. Tell me, how old are you?'

'I will turn twenty-four next week,' I said.

'Oh, your birthday is coming?' he said.

'Yes, on November 11,' I said.

'That's great. You are old enough. Don't be shy,' he said, 'we all do it.'

'Sir, it's for the inspectors. We have a visit next week,' I said. 'I want to increase my fee. They control the decision.'

He frowned. 'Envelopes won't do it for them?'

'This one inspector likes women. I have news from other private colleges in Kanpur.'

'Oh, okay,' Shukla-ji said. He took out his cellphone from a secret pocket in his pyjamas. He scrolled through his contacts and gave me a number.

'His name is Vinod. Call him and give my reference. Give him your requirements. He'll do it. When do you need them?'

'I don't have the exact date yet,' I said and began to stand up.

'Wait,' Shukla-ji said, pulling my hand and making me sit down again. 'You also enjoy them. It gets harder after marriage. Have your fun before that.'

I smiled absently.

'How is it going with the DM's daughter?'

'Good,' I said. I wanted to say bare minimum on the topic.

'You are going to ask her parents? Or give her the love bullshit?'

'I haven't thought about it,' I said. 'I have to go, Shukla-ji. There's an accounts meeting today.'

Shukla-ji realised I didn't want to chat. He walked me to the jail exit.

'Life may not offer you the same chance twice,' he said in parting.

The iron door clanged shut between us.

38

The calendar showed tenth November – my last day as a twenty-three-year-old. I spent the morning at my desk. The students' representatives came to meet me. They wanted to organise a college festival. I told them they could, provided they got sponsors. After the student meeting, I had to deal with a crisis. Two classrooms had water seepage in the walls. I had to scream at the contractor for an hour before he sent people to fix it.

At noon my lunch-box arrived from home. I ate bhindi, dal and rotis. Alongside, I gave Aarti a call. She didn't pick up. I had back-to-back meetings right after lunch. I wouldn't be able to speak to her later. I tried her number again.

'Hello,' an unfamiliar female voice said.

'Who's this?' I said.

'This is Bela, Aarti's colleague from guest relations. You are Gopal, right? I saw your name flash,' she said.

'Yeah. Is she there?'

'She went to attend to a guest. Should I ask her to call you?'

'Yes, please,' I said.

'Oh, and happy birthday in advance,' she said.

'How did you know?' I said.

'Well, she's working hard to make your gift … oops!'

'What?'

'Maybe I wasn't supposed to tell you,' Bela said. 'I mean, it's a surprise. She's making your birthday gift. It's so cute. She's also ordered a cake … Listen, she will kill me if she finds out I told you.'

'Relax, I won't mention it to her. But if you tell me, I can also plan something for her.'

'You guys are so sweet. Childhood friends, no?' she said.

'Yeah, so what's the plan?'

'Well, she will tell you she can't meet you on your birthday. You will sulk but she will say she has work. However, after work she will come to your place in the afternoon with a cake and the gift.'

'Good that you told me. I will be at home then and not in meetings,' I said.

'You work on your birthday?' she said.

'I work all the time,' I said. 'Is she back?'

'Not yet, I will ask her to call you,' she said. 'But don't mention anything. Act like you don't know anything.'

'Sure,' I said and ended the call.

It was time. I called Vinod.

'Vinod?' I said.

'Who's this?' he said.

'I am Gopal. I work with MLA Shukla,' I said.

'Oh, so tell me?' he said.

'I want girls,' I said.

He cut the call. I called again but he didn't pick up. I kept my phone aside.

After ten minutes I received a call from an unknown landline number.

'Vinod here. You wanted girls?'

'Yes,' I said.

'Overnight or hourly basis?'

'Huh?' I said. 'Afternoon. One afternoon.'

'We have happy-hour prices for afternoon. How many girls?'

'One?' I said doubtfully.

'Take two. I'll give a good price. Half off for the other one.'

'One should be okay.'

'I'll send two. If you want two, keep both. Else, choose one.'

'Done. How much?'

'What kind of girl do you want?'

I didn't know what kinds he had. I had never 'ordered' a call girl before. Did he have a menu?

'S … somebody nice?' I said, like a total amateur.

'English-speaking? Jeans and all?' he offered.

'Yes,' I said.

'Indian, Nepali or white?' he said. Varanasi wasn't too far from the Nepal border.

'You have white girls?' I said.

'It's a tourist town. Some girls stay back to work. Hard to find, but we can do it.'

'Send me Indian girls who look decent. Who won't attract too much attention in a college campus.'

'College?' Vinod said, shocked. 'We normally do hotels.'

'I own the college. It's okay.'

Vinod agreed after I told him about GangaTech, and how he had to bring the girls to the director's bungalow.

'So when do you need them?'

'Two o'clock onwards, all afternoon, till six,' I said.

'Twenty thousand,' he said.

'Are you crazy?' I said.

'For Shukla-ji's reference. I charge foreigners that much for one.'

'Ten.'

'Fifteen.'

I heard a knock on my door.

'Done. At two tomorrow. GangaTech on Lucknow Highway,' I whispered and ended the call.

'The faculty meeting,' Shrivastava said from the door.

'Oh, of course,' I said. 'Please come in, Dean sir.'

I asked the peon to place more chairs for our twenty faculty members.

'Students tell me it's your birthday tomorrow, Director Gopal,' the dean said. The faculty went into orgasms. It's fun being the boss. Everyone sucks up to you.

'Just another day,' I said.

'The students want to cut a cake for you,' the dean said.

'Please don't. I can't,' I said. The very thought of cutting a cake in front of two hundred people embarrassed me.

'Please, sir,' said Jayant, a young faculty member. 'Students look up to you. It will mean a lot to them.'

I wondered if the students would still look up to me if they knew about my specifications to Vinod.

'They have already ordered a ten-kilo cake, sir,' Shrivastava said.

'Make it quick,' I said.

'Ten minutes, right after classes end at one,' the dean said.

The faculty meeting commenced. Everyone updated me about their course progress.

'Let's look at placements soon,' I said, 'even though our passing out batch is two years away.'

'Jayant is the placement coordinator,' the dean said.

'Sir, I am already meeting corporates,' Jayant said.

'What is the response?' I said.

'We are new, so it is tough. Some HR managers want to know their cut,' Jayant said.

'Director Gopal, as you may know …' the dean began but I interrupted him.

'HR managers want a cut if they hire from our colleges, correct?' I said.

'Right, sir,' Jayant said.

Every aspect of running a private college involved bribing someone. Why would placements be an exception? But other members seemed surprised.

'Personal payout?' gasped Mrs Awasthi, professor of mechanical engineering.

Jayant nodded.

'But these are managers of reputed companies,' she said, still in shock.

'Mrs Awasthi, this is not your department. You better update me on applied mechanics, your course,' I said.

✦

The maids had prepared a lavish dinner with three subzis, rotis and dal. I didn't touch it. I lay in bed and checked my phone. Aarti hadn't returned my calls all day. However, I didn't call her again.

I thought again about my plan.

At midnight, Aarti called me.

'Happy birthday to you,' Aarti sang on the other line.

'Hey, Aarti,' I said but she didn't listen.

'Happy birthday to you,' she continued to sing, elevating her pitch, 'happy birthday to you, Gopal. Happy birthday to you.'

'Okay, okay, we are not kids anymore,' I said.

She continued her song.

'Happy birthday to you. You were born in the zoo. With monkeys and elephants, who all look just like you,' she said. She sang like she did to me in primary school.

Corny as hell but it brought tears of joy to my eyes. I couldn't believe I had made my plan.

'Somebody is very happy,' I said.

'Of course, it is your birthday. That's why I didn't call or message you all day.'

'Oh,' I said.

'What "oh"? You didn't even notice, did you?' she sounded peeved.

'Of course, I did. Even my staff wondered why my phone hadn't beeped all day in office.'

I got off the bed and switched on the lights.

'Anyway, I thought hard about what to give you, who has everything.'

'And?'

'I couldn't figure out.'

'Oh, that's okay. I don't want anything.'

'Maybe I will buy you something when we meet,' she said.

'When are we meeting?' I said, even though Bela had told me her plans.

'See, tomorrow is difficult, I have a double shift.'

'You won't meet me on my birthday?' I said.

'What to do?' she said. 'Half the front-office staff is absent. Winter arrives and everyone makes excuses of viral fever.'

'Okay,' I said. I must say, she could act pretty well. I almost believed her.

'Happy birthday again, bye!' she said.

A number of birthday messages popped into my inbox. They came from various contractors, inspectors and government officials I had pleased in the past. The only other personal message was from Shukla-ji, who called me up.

'May you live a thousand years,' he said.

'Thanks, you remembered?' I replied.

'You are like my son,' he said.

'Thank you, Shukla-ji, and good night,' I said.

I switched off the lights. I tried to sleep before the big day tomorrow.

39

'Enough, enough,' I said as the tenth student fed me cake.

We had assembled in the foyer of the main campus building. The staff and students had come to wish me. The faculty gave me a tea-set as a gift. The students sang a prayer song for my long life.

'Sir, we hope for your next birthday there will be a Mrs Director on campus,' Suresh, a cheeky first-year student, announced in front of everyone, leading to huge applause. I smiled and checked the time. It was two o' clock. I thanked everyone with folded hands.

I left the main building to walk home.

Happy birthday!: Aarti messaged me.

Where are you?: I asked.

Double shift just started. ☹, she sent her response.

Vinod called me at 2:15. My heart raced.

'Hi,' I said nervously.

'The girls are in a white Tata Indica. They are on the highway, will reach campus in five minutes.'

'I'll inform the gate,' I said.

'You will pay cash?'

'Yes. Why, you take credit cards?' I said.

'We do, for foreigners. But cash is best,' Vinod said.

I asked my maids to go to their quarters and not disturb me for the next four hours. I called the guard-post and instructed them to let the white Indica in. I also told them to inform me if anyone else came to meet me.

The bell rang all too soon. I opened the front door to find a creepy man. Two girls stood behind him. One wore a cheap nylon leopard-print top and jeans. The other wore a purple lace cardigan and brown pants. I could tell these girls didn't find western clothes comfortable. Perhaps it helped them fetch a better price.

The creepy man wore a shiny blue shirt and white trousers.

'These are fine?' he asked me, man to man.

I looked at the girls' faces. They had too much make-up on for early afternoon. However, I had little choice.

'They are okay,' I said.

'Payment?'

I had kept the money ready in my pocket. I handed a bundle of notes to him.

'I'll wait in the car,' he said.

'Outside the campus, please,' I said. The creepy man left. I nodded at the girls to follow me. Inside, we sat on the sofas.

'I'm Roshni. You are the client?' the girl in the leopard print said. She seemed more confident of the two.

'Yes,' I said.

'For both of us?' Roshni said.

'Yeah,' I said.

Roshni squeezed my shoulder.

'Strong man,' she said.

'What's her name?' I said.

'Pooja,' the girl in the hideous purple lace said.

'Not your real names, right?' I said.

Roshni and Pooja, or the girls who called themselves that, giggled.

'It's okay,' I said.

Roshni looked around. 'Where do we do it?'

'Upstairs, in the bedroom,' I said.

'Let's go then,' Roshni said, very focused on work.

'What's the hurry?' I said.

Pooja was the quieter of the two but wore a fixed smile as she waited for further instructions.

'Why wait?' Roshni said.

'I have paid for the entire afternoon. We'll go upstairs when it is time,' I said.

'What do we do until then?' Roshni said, a tad too aggressive.

'Sit,' I said.

'Can we watch TV?' Pooja asked meekly. She pointed to the screen. I gave them the remote. They put on a local cable channel that was playing Salman Khan's *Maine Pyaar Kiya*. We sat and watched the movie in silence. The heroine told the hero that in friendship there is 'no sorry, no thank you,' whatever that meant. After a while, the heroine burst into song, asking a pigeon to take a letter to the hero. Roshni started to hum along.

'No singing, please,' I said.

Roshni seemed offended. I didn't care. I hadn't hired her for her singing skills.

'Do we keep sitting here?' Roshni said at three-thirty.

'It's okay, *didi*,' Pooja said, who obviously loved Salman too much. I was surprised Pooja called her co-worker sister, considering what they could be doing in a while.

The movie ended at 4 p.m.

'Now what?' Roshni said.

'Switch the channel,' I suggested.

The landline rang at four-thirty. I ran to pick up the phone.

'Sir, Raju from security gate. A madam is here to see you,' he said.

'What's her name?' I said.

'She is not saying, sir. She has some packets in her hand.'

'Send her in two minutes,' I said. I calculated she would be here in five minutes.

'Okay, sir,' he said.

I rushed out and left the main gate and the front door wide open. I turned to the girls.

'Let's go up,' I said.

'What? You in the mood now?' Roshni giggled.

'Now!' I snapped my fingers. 'You too, Pooja, or whoever you are.'

The girls jumped to their feet, shocked by my tone. The three of us went up the stairs. We came to the bedroom, the bed.

'So, how does this work?' I said.

'What?' Roshni said. 'Is it your first time?'

'Talk less and do more,' I said. 'What do you do first?'

Roshni and Pooja shared a look, mentally laughing at me.

'Remove your clothes,' Roshni said.

I took off my shirt.

'You too,' I said to both of them. They hesitated for a second, as I had left the door slightly ajar.

'Nobody's home,' I said.

The girls took off their clothes. I felt too tense to notice any details. Roshni clearly had the heavier, bustier frame. Pooja's petite frame made her appear malnourished.

'Get into bed,' I ordered.

The two, surprised by my less than amorous tone, crept into bed like scared kittens.

'You want *us* to do it?' Roshni asked, trying to grasp the situation. 'Lesbian scene?'

'Wait,' I said. I ran to the bedroom window. I saw a white Ambassador car with a red light park outside. Aarti stepped out, and rang the bell once. When nobody answered, she came on to the lawn. She had a large scrapbook in her hand, along with a box from the Ramada bakery. I lost sight of her as she came into the house.

40

'Y ou are a strange customer,' Roshni commented.

'Shh!' I said and slid between the two naked women.

Roshni quickly began to kiss my neck as Pooja bent to take off my belt.

I started to count my breaths. On my fiftieth exhale I heard footsteps. By now the girls had taken off my belt most expertly and were trying to undo my jeans. On my sixtieth inhale came the knock on the door. On my sixty-fifth breath I heard three women scream at the same time.

'Happy birt … Oh my God!' Aarti's voice filled the room.

Roshni and Pooja gasped in fear and covered their faces with the bed-sheet. I sat on the bed, looking suitably surprised. Aarti froze. The hired girls, more prepared for such a situation, ran into the bathroom.

'Gopal!' Aarti said on a high note of disbelief.

'Aarti,' I said and stepped out of bed. As I re-buttoned my jeans and wore my shirt, Aarti ran out of the room.

I followed her down the stairs. She ran down fast, dropping the heavy gifts midway. I navigated past a fallen cake box and scrapbook to reach her. I grabbed her elbow as she almost reached the main door.

'Leave my hand,' Aarti said, her mouth hardly moving.

'I can explain, Aarti,' I said.

'I said don't touch me,' she said.

'It's not what you think it is,' I said.

'What is it then? I came to surprise you and this is how I found you. Who knows what … I haven't seen anything, *anything*, more sick in my life,' Aarti said and stopped. She shook her head. This was beyond words.

She burst into tears.

'MLA Shukla sent them, as a birthday gift,' I said.

She looked at me again, still shaking her head, as if she didn't believe what she had seen or heard.

'Don't get worked up. Rich people do this,' I said.

Slap!

She hit me hard across my face. More than the impact of the slap, the disappointed look in her eyes hurt me more.

'Aarti, what are you doing?' I said.

She didn't say anything, just slapped me again. My hand went to my cheek in reflex. In three seconds, she had left the house. In ten, I heard her car door slam shut. In fifteen, her car had left my porch.

I sank on the sofa, both my knees useless.

Pooja and Roshni, fully dressed, came down by and by. Pooja picked up the cake box and the scrapbook from the steps. She placed them on the table in front of me.

'You didn't do anything with us, so why did you call a third girl?' Roshni demanded to know.

'Just leave,' I told them, my voice low.

They called their creepy protector. Within minutes I was alone in my house.

I sat right there for two hours, till it became dark outside. The maids returned and switched on the lights. They saw me sitting and didn't disturb me.

The glitter on the scrapbook cover shone under the lights. I picked it up.

'A tale of a naughty boy and a not so naughty girl,' said the black cover, which was hand-painted in white. It had a smiley of a boy and a girl, both winking.

I opened the scrapbook.

'Once upon a time, a naughty boy stole a good girl's birthday cake,' it said on the first page. It had a doodle of the teacher scolding me and of herself, Aarti, in tears.

I turned the page.

'The naughty boy, however, became the good girl's friend. He came for every birthday party of hers after that,' said the text. The remaining album had pictures from all her seven birthday parties that I had attended, from her tenth to her sixteenth. I saw how she and I had grown up over the years. In every birthday party, she had at least one picture with just the two of us.

Apart from this, Aarti had also meticulously assembled silly memorabilia from school. She had the class VII timetable, on which she drew horns above the maths classes. She had tickets from the school fete we had in class IX. She had pasted the restaurant bill from the first time we had gone out in class X. She had torn a page from her own slam book, done in class VIII, in which she had put my name down as her best friend. She ended the scrapbook with the following words:

'Life has been a wonderful journey so far with you. Looking forward to a future with you – my soulmate. Happy birthday, Gopal!'

I had reached the end. On the back cover, she had calligraphed 'G & A' in large letters.

I wanted to call her, that was my first instinct. I wanted to tell her how amazing I found her present. She must have spent weeks on it …

I opened the cake box.

The chocolate cake had squished somewhat, but I could make out the letters:

'Stolen: My cake and then my heart,' it said in white, sugary icing, with 'Happy birthday, Gopal' inscribed beneath it.

I pushed the cake box away. The clock struck twelve.

'Your birthday is over, Gopal,' I said loudly to the only person in the room.

♦

Even though I had promised myself I wouldn't, I called Aarti the next day. However, she did not pick up.

I tried several times over the course of the week, but she wouldn't answer.

Once she picked up by accident.

'How are you?' I said.

'Please stop calling me,' she said.

'I am trying not to,' I said.

'Try harder,' she said and hung up.

I wasn't lying. I was trying my best to stop thinking of her. Anyway, I had a few things left to execute my plan.

I called Ashok, the *Dainik* editor.

'Mr Gopal Mishra?' he said.

'How's the paper doing?' I said.

'Good. I see you advertise a lot with us. So thank you very much.'

'I need to ask for a favour,' I said to the editor.

'What?' the editor said, wondering if I would ask to suppress a story.

'I want you to hire someone,' I said. 'He's good.'

'Who?'

'Raghav Kashyap.'

'The trainee we fired?' the editor said. 'Your MLA Shukla made us fire him.'

'Yeah, hire him back.'

'Why? And he started his own paper. He did that big Dimnapura plant story. Sorry, we had to carry it. Everyone did.'

'It's okay,' I said. 'Can you re-hire him? Don't mention my name.'

The editor thought it over. 'I can. But he is a firebrand. I don't want you to be upset again.'

'Keep him away from education. Rather, keep him away from scandals for a while.'

'I'll try,' the editor said. 'Will he join? He has his paper.'

'His paper is almost ruined. He has no job,' I said.

'Okay, I will call him,' the editor said.

'I owe you one. Book front page for GangaTech next Sunday,' I said.

'Thank you, I will let marketing know.'

◆

A week after my birthday Bedi came to my office with two other consultants. They had a proposal for me to open a Bachelor of Management Studies course. Dean Shrivastava also came in.

'MBA is in huge demand. However, that is after graduation. Why not offer something before?' Bedi said. The consultant showed me a presentation on their laptop. The slides included a cost-benefit analysis, comparing the fees we could charge, versus the faculty costs.

'Business Management Studies (BMS) is the best. You can charge as much as engineering, but you don't need facilities like labs,' one consultant said.

'Faculty is also easy. Take any MCom or CA types, plenty of them available,' said the other.

I drifted off. I didn't care about expansion anymore. I didn't see the point of the extra crore we could make every year. I didn't even want to be in office.

'Exciting, isn't it?' Bedi said.

'Huh? Yeah, can we do it some other time?' I said.

'Why?' Bedi said. Then he saw my morose face.

'Yes, we can come again,' he agreed. 'Let's meet next week. Or whenever you have time.'

Bedi and his groupies left the room.

'Director Gopal, are you not feeling well?' the dean said.

'I'm okay,' I said.

'Sorry to say, but you haven't looked fine all week. It's not my business, but I am older. Anything I can help with?'

'It's personal,' I said, my voice firm.

'You should get married, sir. The student was right,' he chuckled.

'Are we done?' I said.

That cut his smile short. In an instant, he stood up and left.

My cellphone beeped. I had an SMS from Sailesh, marketing head of *Dainik*:

Raghav accepted the offer. He joins tomorrow.

Great, thank you very much, I replied.

Hope our association becomes even stronger. Thank you for booking Sunday, texted Sailesh.

41

The arrival of a black Mercedes in the *Dainik* office caused a minor flutter among the guards. A big car ensures attention. I stepped out and put on my new sunglasses. I went to the receptionist in the lobby.

'I am here to meet Raghav Kashyap,' I said, and gave her my business card.

The receptionist couldn't locate him. Sailesh saw me from the floor above, and came running down the steps.

'Gopal bhai? You should have informed me. What are you waiting here for?'

'I want to meet Raghav,' I said.

'Oh, sure,' he said, 'please come with me.'

We walked up to Raghav's cubicle. An IT guy crouched under his desk, setting up his computer. Raghav had bent down as well to check the connections.

'You re-joined here?' I said.

Raghav turned around. 'Gopal?' he said and stood up.

'I had come to the marketing department and saw you.' I turned to Sailesh. 'Thank you, Sailesh.'

'Okay,' Sailesh said. 'See you, Gopal bhai.'

After he left, Raghav said, 'It's strange. The editor called me himself. I had no money anyway. Thought I will rejoin until I have enough to re-launch *Revolution 2020*.'

'Can we go for a cup of tea?' I said.

'Sure,' he said.

We walked up to the staff canteen on the second floor. Framed copies of old newspaper issues adorned the walls. Dozens of journalists sat with their dictaphones and notebooks, enjoying evening snacks. I could tell Raghav felt out of place.

'I'm used to a small office now, *Dainik* is huge,' he said. He bought two plates of samosas and tea. I offered to pay but he declined.

'Cog-in-the-wheel feeling, eh?' I said.

'Not only that. The stuff we did at *Revolution 2020*, I can never do that here,' he said.

The stuff you did at your paper, I wanted to tell him, led to premature bankruptcy. However, I hadn't come here to put him down.

'It's nice to have a job. Plus, you like journalism,' I said.

'That's why I took it. A six-month trial for now.'

'Only six months?'

'They want me to edit other people's stories. It is supposed to be more senior in title, but I like being a reporter. Let's see.'

'A job pays the bills. Of course, it helps to be employed if you want to get married,' I said.

Raghav laughed. We hadn't talked about personal stuff for years. However, he didn't doubt my goodwill. That's the thing with Raghav. He could unearth the biggest scams, but at another level, he trusted people so easily.

'Who's getting married?' Raghav said, still laughing.

'You and Aarti. Aren't you?' I said. I reminded myself I had to smile through this.

Raghav looked at me. I had never discussed Aarti with him. In fact, I hadn't discussed anything with him in years.

'I hope I can talk to you as a friend? We were once, right?' I said. I took a bite of the samosa and found it spicy as hell.

Raghav nodded on a sigh. 'Things aren't going so well between me and Aarti.'

'Really?' I faked surprise.

'I haven't spoken to her in weeks.'

'What happened?' I said.

Raghav squirted tomato sauce over his samosa.

'It's my fault. When the paper started, I didn't give her enough time. Soon, we drifted apart. The last couple of months she seemed so disconnected,' Raghav said.

'Did you guys talk about it?' I said.

'No, we planned to, but didn't,' he said.

'She loves you a lot,' I said.

'I don't know,' Raghav said. He twirled his samosa in the sauce without eating it.

'She does. I know her from childhood, Raghav. You mean everything to her.'

Raghav seemed surprised. 'Do I?'

'She wanted to marry you, isn't it?'

'At the wrong time. Look at me, I am nowhere with respect to my career,' Raghav said.

'Your career is different from others. You can't measure it in money. In terms of helping people, you are doing quite well.'

'I blew that too,' Raghav said.

'You are fine. You are a sub-editor at a big paper. And if you marry Aarti, you can go far.'

'What do you mean?'

'You know there's pressure on Aarti's family to enter politics?' I said.

Raghav kept quiet.

'You do, right?'

'I heard,' he muttered.

'So, Aarti's father can't and Aarti won't. Son-in-law, maybe?'

Raghav looked up, intrigued. 'How you think, man!'

I rolled my eyes. 'I'm not smart. So, I have to make up for it in other ways.'

'You are *not* smart?' he said.

'You do love her?' I asked.

'Things aren't okay between us,' he admitted.

'You can fix them I am sure. After all, your charm worked on her the first time,' I said.

Raghav gave a shy smile.

'Don't call her. Go meet her at the hotel. Take an entire day off for her. That's all she wants, your time and attention. She'll return your love ten times over,' I said, looking sideways.

Raghav kept quiet.

'Promise me you will go,' I said and extended my hand.

He shook my hand and nodded. I stood up to leave. I repeated Shukla-ji's line.

'Life may not offer you the same chance twice.'

Raghav walked me to my car. He barely noticed the car though.

'Why are you doing this for me?' he asked.

I got into the car. I rolled down the window. 'Aarti is a childhood friend. Besides ...'

'Besides what?' Raghav said.

'Everyone has to do their bit,' I said as the driver whisked me away.

◆

I didn't keep in touch with Raghav after that. He called me many times. I either didn't pick up or pretended to be busy. One of the times I did pick up, Raghav told me he and Aarti had started talking again. I told him I had inspectors in my office and hung up.

I had sworn on Baba's soul that I would never call Aarti. She didn't either, apart from a single missed call at 2 a.m. one morning. I called her back, since technically, I had not initiated the call. She did not pick it.

The missed call and call-back drama between men and women almost deserves its own user manual. I gathered she had made the call in a weak moment, and left her alone.

I invited the boring consultants back for the BMS programme talks. The plan made a lot of sense. We started the process to expand into business studies. We had a new set of government people who had to approve our plans, and thus a new set of palms to be greased. We knew the business would be profitable. Millions of kids would be tested, rejected and spat out of the education system every year. We had to keep our net handy to catch them.

I spent more time with the college faculty, and often invited them home in the evenings. They worked for me, so they laughed at my jokes and praised me every ten minutes. I couldn't call them friends, but at least they filled the empty space in the house.

Three months passed. We launched the BMS programme and, with the right marketing, filled up the seats in a matter of weeks. I rarely left the campus, and did so only to meet officials. Meanwhile, the case against Shukla-ji became more complex. He told me the trial could take years. He tried for bail, but the courts rejected it. Shukla-ji felt the CM had betrayed him, even as the party sent feelers that he could be released from jail provided he quit politics. I went to meet him every month, with a copy of the GangaTech Trust accounts.

One day, Raghav called me when I was at home. I didn't pick up. Raghav continued to call. I turned the phone silent and kept it aside.

He sent me a message: 'Where r u Gopal, trying 2 reach u.'

I didn't reply at first. I wondered if his repeated attempts meant trouble, like he had discovered another scam or something.

I texted: In meetings. Wassup?

His reply hit me like a speeding train.

Aarti n I getting engaged. Wanted to invite u 2 party nxt Saturday.

I couldn't stop looking at this message. I had wanted this to happen. Yet, it hurt like hell.

Unfortunately, I'm not in town. But congratulations!!!: I sent my response, wondering if I had put one exclamation mark too many.

Raghav called me again. I avoided his call. He tried two more times, when I finally picked up.

'How can you miss our engagement?' he said.

'Hey, am in a faculty meeting,' I said.

'Oh, sorry. Listen, you have to come,' Raghav said.

'I can't. I am leaving for Singapore to explore a joint venture,' I said.

'What, Gopal? And why don't you ever call back? Even Aarti says you are too busy whenever I ask about you.'

'I am really sorry. I am busy. We are doubling our student intake in the next two years,' I said.

'You will miss your best friend's engagement? Won't she be upset?'

'Apologise to her on my behalf,' I said.

Raghav let out a sigh. 'Okay, I will. But our wedding is in two months. On the first of March. Please be in town then.'

'Of course, I will,' I said and circled the date on the calendar.

'I'll let you attend to your staff. Take care, buddy,' Raghav said.

Instinctively, I composed a 'congrats!' message to Aarti and sent it. She did not reply.

I looked around my big house as empty as my soul.

42

On 1 March, I booked a room at the Taj Ganga. The fourth-floor room had a little balcony, with a view of the hotel pool and lawns. I had tossed the SIM card out of my phone two days ago. I had told my staff I had to go out of town. I stayed in my room the entire day. I came to the balcony at eight in the evening. In the faint light of dusk, I read the card again.

Mrs and Mr Anil Kashyap
Invite the pleasure of your company
For the wedding of their beloved son
Raghav
with
Aarti
(D/O Mrs and Mr Pratap Brij Pradhan, DM)

At 8 p.m.
On 1 March 2010.
Poolside Lawns,
Taj Ganga, Varanasi

I could see the wedding venue downstairs. The entire garden area was littered with flowers and lights. Guests had started to arrive. In one corner the DJ was setting up the dance floor and testing music tracks. Along one side of the lawn were the food counters. Kids were jumping about on the two ornate chairs meant for the bride and groom on the small stage. The actual wedding pandal, where the ceremony would be held, was covered with marigold flowers.

I stood there in silence, listening to the shehnai, faintly audible on the fourth floor.

The *baraat* arrived at 9 p.m. Raghav sat on a horse. The DJ increased the volume of the music. I watched from above as Raghav's relatives danced in front of the horse. Raghav wore a cream-coloured *bandhgala* suit. Even though I hate to admit it, he looked handsome even from this distance. I would have worn something more expensive, but still not looked so regal. I scolded myself for making comparisons again.

Aarti arrived at the venue at nine-thirty. She walked slowly to the stage. A gasp of wonder shot across the crowd as they saw the most beautiful bride they had ever seen in their life.

She looked like an angel, in an onion-colored lehnga with silver sequins. And even though I didn't have binoculars, I could tell she looked perfect. During the ceremony, cousins gathered around Raghav and Aarti. They lifted the couple, making it difficult for them to garland each other.

I couldn't bear it after the *jai-mala* ceremony. I had wanted to see Aarti as a bride, but I did not have to watch the whole wedding live.

I came back into the room, shut the door and drew the curtains. I switched on the TV at full volume to drown out the sounds coming from outside.

I replaced the SIM in my phone. Messages popped in one after another as the phone took its first breath in days.

I had forty messages from the faculty, ten of them from the dean himself. Most of them talked about various issues in the college. Raghav had sent me five messages, asking me if I had received the card. I couldn't tell how many missed calls he might have made. One message startled me the most. It came from Aarti. It said:

Come. But only if you want to.

I thought about replying, but remembered that she won't exactly be checking her phone on stage.

I called the dean.

'Where are you, Director Gopal?' the dean said in a high-pitched voice. 'We are so worried.'

'Dean Srivastava ... Dean Srivastava ...'

'Gopal!' he said, sensing the tension in my voice.

'Get me out of here,' I broke down completely.

'Where are you? Where are you?'

'Taj Ganga, 405 … I don't want to be here.'

'I am coming,' he promised.

In an hour I was seated beside the dean in his car and on my way back to campus.

'So, what were …' he began but fell quiet. He understood, after one look at my face, that I didn't want to talk.

'Dean Shrivastava, I want to work hard. Let's take GangaTech to new heights. I want us to be present in every field of education. Keep me busy. So busy that I don't have time to think.'

'You are already so busy, sir.' He looked troubled.

'More. Why aren't we in coaching classes?' I said. 'There's money there. I want a proposal for engineering and MBA coaching. Okay?' I said, my voice ringing.

'Are you okay, Director Gopal?' the dean said.

'Are you listening to me? I want the proposal,' I said, screaming loud enough to make the driver shift uncomfortably in his seat.

'Yes, Director,' the dean said.

He dropped me home. I went straight to the bar near the dining table. I opened a new bottle of Black Label whisky we'd bought for the inspectors. I poured it out in a glass to the brim. Neat. The maids filed in.

'Where were you, sahib?' they said.

'I had work,' I said. The whisky tasted bitter, but I swallowed it all.

'Dinner?'

I shook my head. The maids left the room. I went to the bookshelf and took out the scrapbook.

I poured myself another glass. I drank half of it in one gulp, but when my body rejected it, I had to spit it out.

I fell on the floor. I used the scrapbook as a pillow and went off to sleep.

Epilogue

I checked the time. The hospital clock showed 6.00 a.m.

'So getting drunk and crashing down is a habit,' I said.

Gopal gave me a sly smile.

'That's the only time it happened,' he said. 'Apart from tonight, of course.'

I saw Gopal's face. He seemed young enough to look like a student. Yet, his face had the hard coating of experience, of bitter lessons from life that made him appear older than his biological age.

'So, Aarti and Raghav got married a year ago?' I said.

'A year and twenty days,' he said.

'What has happened since?' I said.

'Shukla-ji is still in jail. I meet him every month. I am trying to buy back his share of the college with my earnings and make it my own college. He needs money for his other businesses. Let's see.'

'What about Raghav and Aarti?' I asked.

'I am not in touch. I stay in my college. Elections are in two months. He is the one.'

'Meaning?'

'Raghav's contesting. His picture is on election posters all over the city,' Gopal said.

'It could have been you. How do you feel about that?' I said.

Gopal shrugged. 'He'll be a better MLA than me. What would I have done? Made more money. With him, there is a chance he could change something.'

'That's generous of you,' I said.

Gopal sat up straight and restlessly removed the sheets off him. 'But I am still not a good person, right?' he said.

'I never said that,' I said.

'I told you, I am not worthy enough to be a hero in your story,' Gopal said.

I kept quiet.

'I could be the villain,' said Gopal, his eyes sparkling.

'I'll let the readers decide how they want to consider you. I simply write about people. I don't cast them as heroes or villains,' I said.

'Raghav is a good man. I am not half as good as him,' Gopal said.

'Stop judging yourself,' I said.

'Chetan-ji, put your hand on your heart, and tell me, am I a good man?'

I realised my approval meant a lot to him. Yet, I wanted to be genuine. I thought about it for a while.

'Forget it, sir. Don't answer it. Let's take a walk.'

He got off the bed. He seemed much better. We took a morning stroll in the hospital lawns.

'Never drink so much again, promise me,' I said.

'I won't,' he said.

'Promise me you will find somebody,' I said.

He shook his head. 'That I can't promise.'

'Do you miss her?' I said.

He kept quiet.

'Did you meet her after her marriage?'

He shook his head. I figured out now why he had hesitated to come to Ramada to drop me. I checked the time. I had a flight in two hours. I had to rush to the hotel, pack and head to the airport.

'I have to leave,' I said. He nodded. He came out to drop me to the car.

'The revolution will come,' Gopal said. 'We will have a better nation one day.'

'I know,' I said.

'You also write about it. Once GangaTech becomes big, I will try to fix the system. I am sick of giving envelopes to people.'

'We have to change things,' I said.

'Everyone must sacrifice for it,' Gopal said.

'Yes, I agree,' I said as the driver started the car.

'Bye, sir,' Gopal said as I left.

◆

I rushed back to my room and packed fast. I came downstairs in the hotel lobby to check out.

'Did you have a good stay, sir?' a pretty girl in a sari asked me.

'Yeah, memorable,' I said.

I saw her nametag. It said: 'Aarti Kashyap. Guest Relations Officer'.

She smiled. 'Happy to hear that, sir.'

My car drove out of the Cantonment area. I saw a huge political party hoarding at the traffic signal. I couldn't read from a distance, but I saw a young candidate's picture. I called Gopal.

'All okay, sir. Will you make it in time for your flight?'

'Yes ... Gopal?'

'What?' he said.

'You are a good person,' I said.